LOND

Boun

Garry and Roy Robson

London Large: Bound by Blood

ISBN 978-0-9934338-2-5 Paperback

ISBN 978-0-9934338-3-2 eBook-Kindle

Published by London Large Publishing

For more copies of this book, please email:
info@londonlarge.com

Cover Designed by Spiffing Covers: http://spiffingcovers.com/

LONDON LARGE

Bound by Blood

Prologue

1

May 2004

'Give me your hand boy, you don't want to get lost in the crowd,' said Harry. The crowd was surging around them and across them, behind them and before them, as they turned the corner into Zampa Road and pressed on towards the stadium. Through the turnstile - Harry slipped the operator five quid and lifted Little Ronnie over it - and onto the concourse. The crowd swarmed and heaved around them; the boy lost hold of his father's hand and panicked for a second, until his Uncle Ronnie, keeping close behind, scooped the boy up out of the crush onto his shoulders.

Now Little Ronnie could see everything: the slowly surging mass of people all around him, men and boys mostly, the food stalls, the programme sellers and, as they emerged from the top of a flight of stairs and into the stand, the great, sparkling expanse of grass spread out before him.

It was a bright, sunny day in late May and on this, the day before his seventh birthday, the boy was sure he had never seen anything more beautiful, more thrilling than what was spread out in front of him now. His entire body was humming with expectation, with excitement, and with powerful, faithful and unconsidered love for the two men who had brought him.

The players came on to the field; pandemonium erupted. The noise and the movement and the mania frightened him - this was his first time. Harry felt him tense up; he put his arm around his son's shoulder tightly and said, 'Don't worry boy, you'll be alright.'

2

His dad knew what he was talking about: as it turned out Little Ronnie *had* been alright. And then some - it had been the best day of his life. Their team had lost again - his dad and Uncle Ronnie did not seem all that surprised - but he was already coming to understand that it was *being there* that mattered, not the result. It was the thrill of being there.

His euphoria continued after the game, when the three of them went for his post-match birthday treat: all the pizza and ice cream he could get down. When he could take no more his dad and uncle moved him on to the pub, where he sat in the corner quietly while they sank a few pints and got merry and bright with their mates. Uncle Ronnie seemed especially popular: 'Your uncle don't come to a lot of games these days son, he's too busy making his millions in the City,' his dad told him, so people were happy to see him.

Little Ronnie fell asleep in the pub and had to be carried over his dad's shoulder when they got out of the cab outside their flat on the Silwood Estate; exhausted and happy, he was now dead to the world. His dad crept upstairs and eased the boy down onto his bed as gently as he could, still fully clothed, took his shoes off and turned to slip out of the room.

'But dad, what about my story?' said the boy.

Crafty little bastard, he's got me.

'It's late boy, you're tired. We'll do it in the morning.'

'But dad, you promised.'

'Did I?'

'Yeah, in the pub. *Where the Wild Things Are.* You promised.'

Harry fished the tattered volume from the shelf, settled down on the bed and began. This, if anything, perked the boy up. He sat up and nestled his head on his dad's upper arm as he read. When the story was finished, Harry kissed the boy gently on the forehead.

'Thanks dad, that was the best day I've ever had.'

'Glad you enjoyed it son. Good night, Wild Thing,' Harry said, moving again towards the door. As he hit the light and moved to leave the room Little Ronnie said, 'I love you dad.'

'I love you too boy. Always will,' said Harry.

Part 1

1

This was his time. At this moment in his life he could have anything he ever wanted; women, yachts, a mansion with a swimming pool in deepest Surrey. It was the women he wanted more than anything now - now he'd made it. After a short lifetime of dreaming and praying for success here he was, on the top floor of The Ritz, overlooking the London skyline. He felt like London was all his - like he really owned it. A world of endless possibilities lay before him.

'Sort another line out will you babes?' he said to his impossibly sleek, skinny and beautiful supermodel girlfriend. Jacynta Packington murmured yes and carried on getting set for another night of fun and games in the marbled bathroom. That was where Bazza liked to go large. They'd met a few months before, at a celebrity bash to celebrate another number one single. Their whirlwind romance was near perfect for the times, a celebrity journalist's wet dream, delivering a stormy on/off affair of two beautiful young stars at the top of their game. Since they'd met the tabloids had been filled with lurid tales of the affair, of the arguments and bust-ups and reconciliations, of the sex and the drugs, of their infidelities.

Kicking back, he recalled the previous week's centre spread in one of the red tops that gorge on celebrity relationships like vultures on the corpse of a slaughtered animal, and a wry smile spread across his face: 'Bazza Beds a Brace of Bouncing Beauties.' *Sex God*, he thought, *No. 1 Party Animal*. His world was moving faster than a tornado tearing up a row of houses, and it was a world full of low-hanging fruit. He hadn't even bothered to ask the names of the bouncing brace of beauties but had just picked them out of the scrum that had been lying in wait for him as he exited the back entrance of another gig in another provincial town, a town he'd forgotten about as soon as he'd left it.

He hadn't yet reached the point where all the media hype annoyed him. He craved the attention that he felt was his due, now that he was one of the world's most marketable superstars. Jacynta had read the article of course, like she'd read all the others since they'd hooked up. But she had a career to build and being associated with the new Prince of Pop was doing it no harm at all. So she kept quiet - she'd take what she could before the relationship blew up once and for all. Faithfulness was most definitely not on the agenda.

Bazza had never been the sharpest tool in the box, and had dropped out of school at 16 after failing his exams. But he was an angular, blonde and blue-eyed boy with a finely chiselled face, had a passable voice after auto-tuning and just the right amount of late-adolescent arrogance to make him irresistible to the kiddies. And his backstory was spot on: raised in an utter dump by a single mum after his father overdosed on barbiturates, in and out of trouble with the police as a boy, a proper little tearaway. Redeemed by his love of music. The British public ate it all up and begged for more, voting for him in their millions as he romped home as the winner of *Britain Blazes Bright*, the most watched talent show on TV, the show that had propelled him to global stardom.

Within the space of a year Bazza Wishbone had gone from wannabe nobody to one of the biggest pop stars on the planet. He didn't know how long it would last but one thing was for sure - while it lasted he was going to gorge on success like a hungry wolf. He was going to gorge until he could gorge no more.

'Come on then babes, I'm ready for you,' he heard Jacynta call from the bathroom. The marbled bathroom. He bounded in to find her dressed in high heels, a dirty look and not much else. She bent down to get at the marching powder set out by the sink; Bazza followed suit.

The charlie hit the spot, and as the drug surged through his body he stretched out on the cool floor in a state of euphoria and thought again of just how lucky he was. When Jacynta eased herself down to join him - lower, lower, as if in slow motion - he wondered if it was all a dream. Could he really be here, top of the charts, top floor of the Ritz, with one of the world's top supermodels getting on top of him? Her silky smooth blonde hair caressed his face; her lithely perfect body joined itself with his. His pulse raced, and as the blood pumped around his body he embraced her and proceeded to make the most of his good fortune. Yes, he could take whatever he wanted now - every minute of every day belonged to him, up here on top of the world.

Much later, when they had finished, he curled up on the floor and Jacynta brought him a pillow and cover from the bedroom. He was tired now. 'If this is a dream I hope I never wake up,' he thought, as he closed his eyes and let the sleep take him.

2

Outside the Ritz the killer stood behind a street light, head down low. It was cold and raining so he didn't look out of place wrapped up in his long trench coat, collar up, ensuring the hoodie he wore beneath his coat covered his face. He looked up at the top floor and considered his course of action. He knew without doubt his prey was in there. He wasn't sure of the room number, but he soon would be.

He'd been outside now for some time and had seen Bazza and Jacynta pull up in a limo, witnessed the army of photographers descend on them like a pack of braying hyenas, watched as the army of fans, all young girls, screamed with uncontrollable hysteria, with unquenchable desire. He wondered jealously what it was that fed such unthinking adoration. He watched as the celebrity boy-god of the moment, shielded by a phalanx of heavies, pushed his way through the crowd to the front of the hotel, stopped for a moment to wave and soak up the adoration and disappeared into a world of opulence the likes of which his adoring army would never see or know.

The killer decided to go for a walk, to let things settle down a bit. He set off up Piccadilly, took a stroll around Leicester Square and settled down in one of the pubs that adorned the side streets off Leicester Square, all the time keeping his head down low, hoodie on, shades pushed up on to the bridge of his nose. He was early so he ordered a pint of London Ale and supped slowly as he reflected on the task at hand.

He was a small fish, and felt the resentment that small fish feel when they spend most of their time swerving from the path of big fish. Tonight, however, would be different; tonight he was going to take down a big fish, and to hell with the consequences.

If Bazza wants to play in the big pond he better watch out for the sharks.

Ping! He read the text that came through on his mobile and replied. The meet was on. The landlord called last orders so he went to the bar for a second pint. Just enough to steel his nerves but not too much to make him sloppy. He sat over it until the girl he'd been waiting for entered the pub. Svitlana Kovalenko caught his eye and moved across the room; she looked tired and drawn but was pretty with light auburn hair and a winning smile. She sat down next to him.

'Hello,' she said in one of those east European accents that had become so much a feature of the metropolis in recent years.

'Have you got it?'

'Yes,' she replied.

Svitlana worked on the desk at the Ritz. Like all the central London hotels it could only function now with employees from the far-flung corners of the world. So many employees started and finished their stint in the great global village each month that it was almost impossible for anyone in authority to keep up with the constant flux.

Finding a chancer who was just passing through to describe the layout and confirm the name of Bazza's room had been easy. She had already provided the killer with a plan of the top floor suites. Two grand and a glass of wine was a small price to pay for the information he was about to receive. He had given her to believe he was a thief who'd like a chance to root about in some of the pricier rooms. What difference did it make to Svitlana? Where she came from, money talked. In any case she'd be heading out soon to take care of her ailing mother. She passed him an electronic key and a piece of paper with the name of a suite on it and walked her 'thief' through the plan. She would text when the coast was clear. In through the tradesman's entrance, through the kitchen and up the lift reserved for staff. Turn left, 3rd door on the right, a quiet entry: game on.

He knew Bazza had the girl in tow. He didn't have a plan for her. He'd cross that bridge when he came to it. Then the retreat, back down in the same lift, lower ground floor, stroll out through the car park and melt into the London night. Head down, hoodie up, shades on tight. He knew he'd be on every CCTV camera he passed, then on the TV, and all over the Internet, and in the grainy pictures in every paper. He also knew the images would be useless as long as he kept his face under wraps.

Svitlana herself had no idea who he was. He looked at her with a mixture of desire and contempt, contempt for the unsuspecting, the weak and naive. She was pretty, no doubt about that, and in different circumstances he'd be all over her whether she liked it or not. But as the pretty girl left to return to her late-night duties he had no regrets that the only thing he would be giving her tonight was an appointment with the grim reaper.

Time for the kill.

3

The pretty girl's text was a long time coming, so the killer had a string of coffees in a late-night place and then a slow meander through the West End streets, back past Leicester Square and then up Piccadilly. He was steeling himself, enjoying the building tension. The text arrived at 4am. At last! Back entrance. Tradesman's lift. The pretty girl waiting to show him to the top floor. So innocent, no clue that a sawn-off shotgun was hidden under the heavy coat.

'Wait here, hold the lift.'

The killer arrived at the room of his victim exactly according to plan.

He gave a gentle knock on the door. All was quiet. He opened it with his master key and quietly let himself in. Bazza was roused from his slumbers, sitting up and becoming aware of someone in the suite. Jacynta had left him in the bathroom and gone to bed, as usual. Had she ordered room service? Or was it a female staff member slipping in to get a piece of him? It wouldn't be the first time. He hadn't managed to get Jacynta into a threesome yet, but he lived in hope and there was a first time for everything.

He rubbed his eyes and sat upright. A man entered the bathroom quietly and stationed himself, silently, two feet away from the still-sitting Prince of Pop. Bazza's heart somersaulted and pounded hard against his ribcage, and his eyes almost jumped out of their sockets with shock. This was no groupie come for an early morning seeing-to. Bazza was looking down both barrels of a shotgun. Instinctively he put his hands in the air.

'You? What do you want? My wallet's in my trousers, over there, in the wardrobe. Loads of money. Take the lot.'

The killer smiled. 'I'm not here for money. I'm here for you.'

'What? ...'

The light came on in the bedroom and a moment later Jacynta entered the bathroom. She gulped in bewilderment; terror, sheer terror, took hold of her as she surveyed the scene. A heavily-clothed man pointing a shotgun at Bazza's head. She stood transfixed, unable to scream, unable to move. Her body felt like it was in a straitjacket. She could barely breathe.

'Please,' begged Bazza, 'you don't need to do this.'

It wasn't the pain that he feared. It wasn't his past life that flashed before his eyes. It was the future life he would never live that consumed his final thoughts. The adoration, the love, the money...the women. His mum had told him money and fame wouldn't make him happy, but he was too young to listen, too young to care. He was too full of life, too full of the moment; he just wanted more. It couldn't end now. Not here, like this.

He stared at the weapon that was about to end his time on earth, filled with horror, covered in his own urine, choked by desperate, animal fear. Through his parched, jammed mouth he tried to appeal to the intruder:

'Please. Please, I...'

The killer stepped forward and gave him one barrel. The blast and flash of the sawn-off snuffed out his final words. At such close range the pellets did not have time to disperse and collided with Bazza as a single mass, smashing into his face and blowing half his head clean off. Mangled, splintered bone, flesh and grey matter smashed into the wall and splattered across the bath as his corpse hit the marbled deck. The right side of his head remained intact, like one half of a broken crimson death mask. The air filled with the stench of cordite and fresh blood.

Not so beautiful now, are you, pretty boy?

The killer turned to face Jacynta and pointed the shotgun at her face. Her heart exploded; her mind reeled; her face was pale as wax. The killer smiled and his eyes lit up. The light from the bedroom gently outlined the contours of her body. On one thing he was in accord with Bazza - if there was such a thing as perfect female beauty, he was staring at it. His success in ending the life of Bazza, combined with the sight of the girl's naked body, filled him with an overwhelming sense of power. He had never felt so in control in his life. He could stroll into one of the world's most prestigious hotels, blow away a superstar and have his woman, if he wanted. He was the big fish now.

But his plan had always been to exit the room less than 15 seconds after the job was done, before the noise had filtered through to the sleepy residents and some of them became brave and inquisitive enough to come looking for its source. And anyway, he'd completed his mission. He had not come for her. He reached for the door handle, opened the door and left, quietly and without fuss.

Svitlana Kovalenko was still there, standing by the lift, in a state of frozen panic.

'What happened in there?' she managed to say. 'What was that…?'

Bang. The killer unleashed the second barrel on her, from 12 feet away. The pellets dispersed, broke through her ribcage and tore several holes in her heart. As she gasped for breath and fell to the floor he watched for a few seconds before opening the lift door, content that she could not survive her wounds.

It had all gone like clockwork: down the back way; lower ground floor; easy stroll through the car park; melt into the London dawn.

Bye bye pretty boy, see you in hell.

4

Earlier that day the world's worst patient had been relaxing at home.

'Turn that bollocks off will you Liv, it's doing my nut. They just go on and on, round and round and round.... celebrities, nonces at the BBC, EU going to bits, the migrant crisis, all day fucking long.'

Spurred to action, H jumped up, snatched the remote and started channel hopping. Nothing held his attention for more than two seconds until he came across a Kardashian pontificating at great length on nothing in particular. The programme held him mesmerised by a mixture of bafflement and contempt. Olivia noticed the look of complete puzzlement on his face, and smiled broadly in anticipation of the rant that she knew was now inevitable.

'What the fuck is this?'

'It's the Kardashians.'

'The what?'

'The Kardashians, they're a really famous American family.'

'What are they famous for?'

'Well, people follow them on TV, and social media.'

'But…but what…why?' H was beginning to seethe and knew he had to find some reserves of self-control; he began by resisting the temptation to launch the remote at the T.V.

'Liv, doll, how did it come to this? What the fuck went wrong?'

'H!' Olivia snapped, 'Blood pressure!'

They'd been here before: it was one of their little rituals. H knew he was on the wrong side of history. He sighed a deep sigh and flopped back onto the sofa.

'Let's watch a film...stick *Get Carter* on for me, will you?'

'Again?'

'Yes, again. This nonesense is giving me palpitations. You want me to rest, don't you?'

Olivia sighed, and reached once again for the Michael Caine box set. Harry Hawkins - an impatient patient at the best of times, and these were not the best of times - was now splayed out on the sofa like a cantankerous bull walrus, hooting and hollering for all he was worth. He'd been cooped up at home for months now. First the hospital, then the sanatorium, and now this: The sofa. The TV. The tablets. The 'resting'.

'London's Top Copper.' That's what they called him. At least they used to. But he hadn't done any coppering in nearly a year now, since his hell-for-leather rollercoaster ride through a gang war that almost brought London to its knees, and the pursuit of the ringleaders of an establishment paedophile conspiracy - a pursuit which led to his best friend going down for a thirty year stretch for murder and himself at death's door in the intensive care unit of Guy's hospital, with a nervous breakdown as his reward for surviving.

In the aftermath of all the blood and chaos H had been 'proper nutted off,' as his friend Confident John Viney had it, much to the merriment of his legions of enemies, villains and media commentators alike. Now he was just killing time - or was time killing him? - while he waited for his next psychiatric 'assessment.' This one would be the clincher; his shrink was on the clock, coming under pressure to make the call on when - or whether - the big man was stable enough to return to work. His body seemed sound enough now; countless hours of physiotherapy had seen to that. But where was his head at? H himself, befuddled and numbed by anti-depressants, bored out of his head, longing for action, didn't know. He was hoping the shrink would tell him.

The afternoon wore on. Carter/Caine did the business. H dozed through the boring bits. Olivia read her book. The dog yelped in his sleep. H snapped out of it and livened up for the big finale.

'Go on my son, sort this fucking lot out. Bunch of wrong 'uns. I...'

'H?' Olivia said.

'Yes babes?' said H, now immersed in the screen and looking at her from the corner of his eye.

'How many times have you seen this film, would you say?'

'A few.'

'A few hundred, you mean. You know it word for word...punch for punch.'

'What's your point, doll...?'

'Maybe you could do something different. Talk to me, read something, listen to the radio for a bit, take a little turn in the garden...maybe have another look at that pamphlet on meditation they gave you in the sanatorium.'

Fuck me, not all this again.

'Alright, I tell you what babes, let's go for a drive. Get your coat on. We'll go for a nice drive and find a boozer that does a decent…er…orange juice.'

'No H. Don't start. You know what the shrink said, no gallivanting about until you finish these tablets and she's had another look at you.'

H groaned. 'I've had enough of all this. I've got to have something to liven me up. I've been a good boy, haven't I? I've kept up with the tablets. No booze. Early to bed, early to rise, nothing silly. Just let me watch my films in peace, will you? I'm watching *Get Carter.* After that I'm going to watch *The Searchers.* And after that, unless you start behaving your fucking self, I'm going to watch *In Which We Serve.'*

Olivia shuddered, and wondered for a second what it must be like to be a villain and have Harry Hawkins on your case for real. But inwardly she was pleased, and almost thrilled, to see him being so stroppy and difficult. Her bear was rattling the bars of his cage. The old H-power was returning - he was, slowly but surely, becoming himself again.

5

H was watching Michael Caine force a bottle of whiskey down the throat of his adversary, urging Carter on in his final act of relentless vengeance, when there was a knock at the door.

'Get that will you Liv, this is the best bit.'

Olivia went to the door and was surprised to see Amisha Bhanushali and Graham Miller-Marchant smiling at her.

'Hello Liv. How's the patient?' asked Amisha.

'Oh, getting more cantankerous by the day. He discovered the Kardashians earlier, haven't seen him so angry at the modern world for months. He's almost back to his old self.'

Amisha and Graham laughed as they entered. They found H chomping at the bit at the sight of Cainey battering his victim to death with the butt of his rifle. He was gagging for more but was delighted when he saw them walk through the door. He hit the pause button.

'Hello guv.'

H embraced her, holding her tight for several seconds, and shook Graham's hand with gusto.

'You seem to have forgotten, I'm not your guvnor anymore Ames.'

'Yeah. But you will be soon, right? Final meeting with the shrink soon?'

H winced. He still didn't like talking about the fact he had to see a psychiatrist; he found it demeaning, to have people think he couldn't deal with life's ups and downs on his own. To H life was like a game of poker. Some cards you dealt, some got dealt to you. You hold, bluff, raise and when you're ready you go all in. You can win with a pair of twos or go bust with a full house, but however the cards fall you take the consequences and deal with it yourself. He changed the subject.

'How are things at the Yard? Any decent murder cases on the go?' he asked.

'Not really. Things have quietened down. The Russians and Albanians seem to have stopped slaughtering each other left, right and centre, for now at least. Word is they had a big meet and agreed some new ground rules. We haven't had anything high profile for months. Mostly back to the usual family murders and kids stabbing each other to death on council estates.'

'Calm before the storm,' muttered H, half to himself.

Olivia, not wanting H to start talking shop, announced that she was making tea and Amisha followed her into the kitchen. Since the events of nine months before - when dealing with the combination of a gang war and a paedophile conspiracy that had pushed H, Graham and Amisha to their limits - Amisha and Graham had taken Olivia fully into their trust. They, along with H's old friend Ronnie Ruddock and the Russian oligarch Kyril Kuznetsov, were the only people in the world who knew the truth about what had happened. They were now bound together in a circle of mutual trust - or mutual mistrust in Kuznetsov case - none of them could ever break.

When they'd first met, Oliva had been cautious of Amisha. With her gorgeous long black hair, her 'posh' accent and Cambridge education she'd felt a little intimidated, and considered H's new police partner as a rival for his affections. Now, however, they'd become very close. Whilst H recovered slowly under the watchful eye of Kasia Kotula, his shrink, Amisha had recovered her equilibrium under the watchful care of Olivia, who had marvelled at her new friend's strength, courage and character. Terrible things had happened to Amisha that the Metropolitan Police and the world at large would never know about. The two of them had spent day after day talking things through, for months. The trust between them was unbreakable. As they started to chat in the kitchen Olivia now had a secret of her own to reveal, and there was nobody else in the world who she would rather reveal it to first. Not even H.

'How have you been Ames, everything alright? How are things with you and Graham?'

Since her ordeal Amisha had split with her boyfriend and replaced him with Graham, who had become estranged from his wife several months before. It had been tentative at first; it seemed as if the relationship had been necessitated by the web of secrecy that held them all together. But now she'd come to care for him; for the first time in her life she was in love. There were times when Amisha opened up to Olivia about it all, but with the boys chatting away in the next room this wouldn't be one of them. She dodged the question and shifted the conversation back onto Olivia.

They did some small talk and Amisha took tea to H and Graham. When she returned to the kitchen Olivia dropped her bombshell.

'I've got one other piece of news,' she said.

'What?'

Olivia lowered her voice. She didn't want H overhearing. She wasn't sure how to tell him. Or how he'd take it.

'I'm pregnant… I've had the scans. It's a boy.'

Amisha's eyes opened wide and her mouth dropped in shock. She knew Olivia thought she'd missed her chance of having kids and that, inwardly, she would be delighted, though nervous, at the prospect of a near forty-year-old woman and a fifty-six-year-old dinosaur bringing up a kid in the modern world. She gave Olivia a huge hug.

'Oh my God! Congratulations... Another H roaming the streets... "Little H." The whole world had better get ready. How far gone are you?'

'Five months. I'll be starting to show soon.'

'Whaaat!? Five months? You've got to tell him, Liv. Soon.'

6

The call came into Scotland Yard's murder squad at 4:30am. Several months had elapsed since they'd had a case anywhere near as high-profile as this. The Chief Constable had been called and pressure for a fast and efficient investigation and a quick result was already coming down the chain to Chief Inspector Hilary Stone as she punched Graham Miller-Marchant's number into her phone. This one was going to take top priority.

Graham, who liked to programme different ring tones for different people, jumped out of bed as soon as he heard the call come in from Hilary and hit the accept button.

'Morning ma'am.'

'Hi Graham. Hold on to your seat - we've got a big one. I need someone with experience of handling major cases to get on it, asap. It'll be as much about handling the media and public expectations as a murder investigation.'

'I'm your man, ma'am. What's the case?'

'You know this pop star kid who's all over the place now…the one who won *Britain Blazes Bright* last year?'

'Bazza Wishbone? Of course, it'd be hard not to. What about him?'

'He's currently lying dead in his bathroom in the Ritz with half his head blown away. And there's a young staff member, a young girl, almost cut in half, in the hallway outside his suite. Shotgun attack, by the look of it. It's already trending on social media. I need you and Amisha over there pronto. Take control. Call me from the scene before talking to anyone. Assess the situation and put me in the picture, quick as you please.

'On it ma'am.'

'Make sure you are, Graham, make sure you are. We're going to need a result on this one - "sharpish", as H would say. We're only just clawing our reputation back after last year's shenanigans…we'll need to look good on this one.'

Graham ended the call and got straight onto Amisha. They'd been partnered up for several months now - on and off the job - and already had one of the best clear-up rates in division.

'Hi Graham,' said Amisha, 'to what do I owe the pleasure at this early hour?'

'Drop everything. New case. All hands on deck. The pop star, Bazza Wishbone, seems to have parted company with his head, or half of it, in his suite at the Ritz.'

Amisha had already seen so much death and destruction that nothing shocked her any more, but this was a genuine surprise and she swallowed hard at the news. She double-checked she'd understood correctly.

'Bazza Wishbone?'

'Yep. The very same. We've not had one this high profile since…'

He was going to say since the murder of socialite Tara Ruddock in St. James' Park, the year before, but the sentence petered out. It had been the most difficult case they had ever been involved in and had spawned an inquiry that was still ongoing. After multiple interviews and reviews the story he'd concocted with Amisha about how they got through it all had held up; it seemed the pressure was abating. But the personal wounds, especially those on Amisha, still cut deep and would take some time to heal. If heal they ever could. A moment of awkward silence followed before Amisha picked up the thread and asked Graham how long it would take him to get to the Ritz.

'I'll be there in thirty. Meet me there as soon as you can. We're going to come under a lot of pressure on this one Ames. Hilary is already growling. Get your game face on.'

London seemed calm and peaceful as Graham made his way through the early morning streets from his flat in

Clapham. Despite the impending pressure of the investigation he felt calm, self-assured, like it was something he could handle. The traffic lights, for once, were on his side and all turned green as he approached them, as if orchestrated by some divine London force that was watching over him. He arrived several minutes early to find Amisha outside, sitting in her car; she was lost, as usual, in cyberspace. Graham tapped on her window to re-focus her reality and gave a reassuring smile.

Out in the real world the mob was already forming. Despite express instructions from the Ritz's night duty manager, Olivier Delveaux, not to breathe a word to anyone about what had happened, several members of staff had been unable to contain themselves and had tweeted the news. Millions of people around the globe were already in the know - the inevitable social media shitstorm was beginning to blow.

As they forced their way through the crowd of hysterical, wailing fans and the first representatives of the world's media conglomerates Amisha filled Graham in on what she knew, or at least what she thought she knew.

'There's good news and bad news Graham. Which do you want first?'

'The bad.'

'According to social media reports Bazza's head is clean blown off his shoulders.'

'Guess that's pretty bad for him. What's the good?'

'The rumour mill says we have an eye witness. His girlfriend, the supermodel Jacynta Packington, was in the room when the murder took place.'

Graham was about to meet the woman he'd seen on a thousand and one screens, who many considered to be the most beautiful woman in Britain. His heart rate accelerated.

Wow, you don't get to meet Jacynta Packington every day. Or Bazza Wishbone, come to that...whatever's left of him.

7

Sergeant Bob Wisdom, an experienced plod with 20 years of service under his belt, had been first to the respond. Efficiency was his watchword and the crime scene was already well under control and secure when he ushered the two detectives into Bazza's suite.

Constable Peter Holden was standing guard in the room surveying the carcass, Amisha noticed as she walked in, with something that looked like amusement. She looked around the suite briefly and headed for the bathroom, where she saw that the Internet rumours had been exaggerated. Around fifty per cent of Bazza's head was still intact, just enough for her to recognise the young man she had seen on her various screens so many times in his short career.

Forensics were on the way; she made a quick initial assessment of the situation before they arrived. To make a mess like this the killer must have got up very close and personal with Bazza. The weapon was almost certainly a shotgun. The killer must have let rip from not much more than six inches away. Maybe even closer. No sign of forced entry. This was either someone Bazza had let in or who was in possession of a key. From the single pillow and sheet, it looked as if Bazza had been sleeping alone on the bathroom floor. Amisha went back into the bedroom; only one side of the bed in there looked like it had been slept in.

'Sergeant Wisdom, someone on Twitter is talking about an eye witness, Jacynta Packington. Rumour mill working overtime?' Graham said.

'No, that one's true. She's a few rooms down, being looked after by WPC Yvonne McAuley. She's in a bad way - we haven't had a peep out of her yet. I wanted to wait until you got here before deciding what to do with her.'

'Was she hurt or attacked Sergeant?' Graham noticed Amisha's face tighten and her voice go up a gear when she asked the question.

'Not sure. She seems to be in a state of shock. That, or she's off her head on something. Or both. Her and young Bazza had been at it on the marching powder before it all went pear-shaped, unless I'm very much mistaken. She doesn't look injured, no visible bruising or contusions, anything like that.'

Amisha snapped on a plastic glove and had a better look around. Except for the gore spread across the bath and floor, and a powdery smudge on the surface by the sink, the plush marbled interior was neat and tidy. A selection of creams and beauty products were deftly arranged in the cabinet. All the lids were on and there were no obvious signs that they had even been used. Amisha lifted the lid on the bin to reveal an assortment of tissues and cotton buds. Jacynta Packington was clearly someone who liked to keep things orderly, despite what looked from the outside like a chaotic lifestyle.

'Was the door closed when you arrived Sergeant?'

'Yes, Detective Sergeant.'

'There is no sign of a struggle, in either the bedroom or the bathroom,' said Amisha, 'and from what you say I doubt Jacynta Packington was attacked.' Graham noticed the sense of relief as the tension in her face eased - the dead she could deal with. Interviewing rape and torture victims, on the other hand, was not something she relished much these days.

Graham had been going through the clothes in the wardrobe and pulled out Bazza's wallet. He displayed the contents to Amisha as he summarised the situation: 'So we've got a huge wad of notes in the wallet, credit cards intact, an unforced entry, a witness unharmed. The killer came for Bazza. He was targeted and this was planned...Let's go have a look at the second body.'

They exited the room and moved down the corridor. Another police constable stood guard over the slaughtered remains of the girl.

'The manager says this is - was - Svitlana Kovalenko. Ukrainian. A reliable, steady worker by all accounts. Poor girl…a long way from home,' said Sergeant Wisdom.

The two detectives studied the girl's body; it was not in good shape.

'Definitely a shotgun,' Amisha said, 'killer was maybe 10-15 yards away. Came out of the room, was heading for the lift, saw her and just opened fire.' She looked inside the lift, which Sergeant Wisdom had ensured was now held, and saw blood splatter.

'Looks like she had just walked out of the lift. The door was open when the killer fired.'

The night manager reappeared. He'd been on a conference call with his superiors, busily going through options on how they could manage and contain the situation. They'd concluded, rightly, that it was not containable and the best they could hope for was a damage-limitation exercise. Delveaux was told to be as helpful as he could with the police, and to wait until the press officer arrived to try and control the message. Whatever that would be.

Graham laid down the law: 'We'll need lists of all staff and their rotas and to interview everyone who works here, whether they were on duty or not, and details of every guest. And CCTV from every camera you have.'

Olivier Delveaux said 'Of course,' gave a curt nod and wheeled briskly away to start setting things in motion.

'Right,' said Graham, turning to the Sergeant, 'let's go talk to our superstar eye witness.'

8

They found Jacynta sitting in one of the adjacent rooms. She was drinking a strong cup of builder's tea, probably loaded up with sugar. The classic copper's standby, in situations like this.

'Hello Ms Packington,' said Amisha. The girl looked empty, completely desolate. She gave no reply and stared into space. The cup in her hand shook as she tried to gulp down another mouthful.

'I'm Detective Sergeant Amisha Bhanushali, and this is Detective Inspector Graham Miller-Marchant. We're from New Scotland Yard.'

Jacynta sat mute, looking desperately alone but also strangely self-assured. Unlike Bazza she had not been raised by a single mother on a crappy council estate in the middle of nowhere. For her it had been all horsey fun and Swiss finishing schools; but her parents had been distant and cold and when they'd tried to get her married off to the 'right sort of chap' she rebelled - taking her drop-dead looks with her into the world of high fashion. Everyone could see she was going to be huge the first time she hit the catwalk. Not only was she beautiful, she had that special something that makes everyone pay attention. That, combined with her fastidious attention to detail, cunning use of contacts and sheer ambition had ensured her rise to the very top of the modelling world. Her rise had been almost as dramatic and exciting as Bazza's.

Bazza himself had been part distraction, part CV-builder; they were using one another, and she'd never expected it to last. Nothing lasted in her world, but Bazza had made her feel a little less lonely. And now he was gone. Experience had made her strong and self-sufficient, but at this moment she felt more sad, alone and scared than at any time since her first days at boarding school.

She looked now at the pleasant young policewoman with the winning smile who had just introduced herself and got a sense that this was someone she could trust; someone who knew how to be agreeable, but who also knew something about heavy gravity. She broke her silence.

'Hello, Detective Sergeant Bhanushali.'

'I understand how difficult this is, and is going to be, for you. I'm not just saying that - I speak from experience. I'm not going to ask you lots of questions about what happened right now. But I have to ask you one.'

Jacynta forced a smile. 'Shoot.'

'Do you have any idea who the killer was?'

'No, I didn't really see his face. He had it covered…sunglasses, a hoodie.'

'Okay. Is there anyone we can call, family members, a friend who can stay with you until things settle down?'

'There's my mother. But I rarely see her. I prefer to be alone. I'd like to just go home, if I may.'

Amisha saw through the shock and drug after-effects in the girl's flushed cheeks, to the deeper sadness in her eyes, not just at the death of her lover but into the sea of loneliness in which she swam.

'Well, the thing is you're witness to a murder Jacynta, so you'll have to come to the Yard. If you like the WPC here - Yvonne - can drive you home, and stay with you, and bring you to the Yard this afternoon. Three o'clock. Does that sound like a plan?'

'Yes. I'll be there at three. Thanks.'

9

Graham stepped back and studied his handiwork on the board: the case de-briefing was set for 11am, the press conference for 12 noon and Jacynta Packington was due to arrive at Scotland Yard at 3pm

'Why didn't you push her for some kind of statement?' Hilary said to Amisha just before the debriefing commenced. 'Everything was still fresh in her mind and it's the usual practice to press eye witnesses, to see if they can provide descriptions, give us little details. Precious time has been lost, Amisha.'

'She wasn't ready ma'am, and she was pretty spaced out. She and Mr Wishbone had clearly had a session on the cocaine before it all kicked off. On top of that, she was in shock. She was barely compos mentis. I thought we'd get more out of her after a rest.'

'I've read your notes. Hardly any words were exchanged between you. Could you not have pushed her a little?'

'I just didn't think that was the right way to go ma'am. I'm sure she'll co-operate fully when she gets here.'

'Hmm…OK, let's see how she performs later.'

The de-brief began. Hilary had already put together a team of 12 detectives, headed up by Graham. He called the meeting to order and described the events as far as they understood them. Photos were distributed and Graham talked the team through what they had so far, which was mostly speculation about a targeted hit and the subsequent murder of an innocent bystander. Given the publicity the initial forensics report had been fast-tracked and was due later that day; eye witness Jacynta Packington, who had been too shocked to talk earlier, was coming in at 3pm. This last piece of news triggered a ripple of anticipation in the room.

Graham appointed a sub team to start questioning the hotel staff and another to do likewise with the guests. The CCTV images had arrived and another team were appointed the task of going through them. He and Amisha would handle the interview with the eye witness and initial discussions with forensics. They would reconvene at 9am sharp next morning. It was going to be a long evening's work.

Graham agreed with Hilary that the two of them would handle the press conference. Neither of them was exactly straining at the leash to get this done; the wounds from the last high profile case the previous year were still fresh. Back then braying packs of hyena-reporters, bloggers and twitter nuts had dogged their every step, heaping upon the Metropolitan Police more scorn, ridicule and contempt than it had ever faced before. The old rules had been abandoned, any lingering respect for the police and their authority gone. It was a different ball game now, they'd learned. And Harry Hawkins had borne the brunt of it, dragged over the hot coals of public derision like a sacrificial goat. His ordeal was very much on Hilary's mind as they approached the newsroom.

Hilary and Graham strode determinedly along the corridor leading to the conference room, took deep breaths and burst through the door into the most cacophonous welter of screaming, gesticulating media types they'd ever seen. The blood of the pack was up, that was clear, and the previous year's nightmare began to look like a Kensington Palace tea party. Last time round it had been psychopathic gangsters and murdered aristocrats - and who really cared about *them*, when push came to shove? This time round it was Bazza Wishbone. Bazza Wishbone, of *Britain Blazes Bright*: someone who mattered to the Great British Public.

'Dear oh Lord, Graham, it's like a bloody zoo,' Hilary whispered as they took their seats.

'Please don't offend zoo animals like that ma'am, or I shall be obliged to report you to the diversity directorate upstairs.'

They both laughed.

That was their first mistake.

10

Graham had toughened up and come a long way since the year before, through bitter experience and H's guidance, and these days took a much more hard-headed and sceptical view than he'd once had of the priorities of contemporary policing in the metropolis.

Hilary tried to call the room to some sort of order. People sat down and the noise abated a little. Now it was possible to see what-was-what from the podium. The front rows were occupied with the usual representatives of the global big hitters -BBC, SKY, CNN, Al Jazeera and the rest - and the British newspapers. The accredited new-media types were also well represented, and in the fifth row, both Hilary and Graham noticed, with dismay, sat a glowering Joey Jupiter.

The slicked-back shiny hair; the Andy Warhol 'Chairman Mao' t-shirt; the massive comedy beard; the gigantic plastic phone glued, as ever, to his right hand. H's nemesis, his online tormentor in chief, king of internet mob rage. Graham recalled some of the big man's rantings on the topic of Jupiter, and his lyrical descriptions of the kinds of beating he would like to administer to him.

Poor H. Had to deal with all this and run a bastard of an investigation. My turn now.

As if on cue, Jupiter shot up out of his seat and made his voice heard above the rest.

'Yes, Mr Jupiter,' said Hilary, deciding to try and get the worst out of the way first.

'Can you help me with something, Chief Inspector Stone? I think we are all at a bit of a loss - we've had the head, by all accounts, blown off Bazza Wishbone, one of the most loved figures in the country. In the Ritz, of all places. The *Ritz*. This comes hot on the heels of last year's events, in which the city all but went into meltdown as armed gangsters went to war on the streets and respectable women were butchered in the centre of London. I'm sure we can all remember the panic and fear of those months, the feeling that your organisation had lost control, and that none of us was safe.'

The trap was sprung and Hilary fell right in. 'Indeed we can, Mr. Jupiter,' she said.

'Then can you explain to us why, less than a year later, with Bazza Wishbone's mortal remains still warm in the morgue, that yourself and Detective Inspector Miller-Marchant were laughing heartily as you took your seats, as if you didn't have a care in the world? Is this appropriate, Chief Inspector?'

The room exploded into a maelstrom of frenetic movement, catcalls, jeering and more shouted questions.

'And another thing: what are your chances of cracking this case in the absence of the great Detective Inspector Hawkins? Were his efforts not central to the restoration of order last time round? Can we expect him to return to duty soon? Or is he still in the sanatorium, chasing corn flakes around his bowl with a little plastic spoon?'

The room went into overdrive: it seemed to be spilling over with ravening lunatics.

'What the hell is happening, Graham? 'Hilary turned and asked. 'These people are accredited journalists?'

But Graham had heard enough, and was already in motion. Without thinking he rose from his chair. A large part of him wanted to jump the podium and give Jupiter a beating. But, although he now understood H a lot more than he did a year ago, he was not H. He collected his thoughts.

'We will resume when you've all calmed down,' he said, as he walked out of the room.

11

Jacynta arrived on the dot at 3pm. She was met by Amisha and ushered into an interview room, where Graham was already waiting. She'd kept it slick and professional, despite her inner turmoil. It wasn't in her nature to go into a public appearance unprepared.

She looked stunning in her chic, laid back street style. Her blond locks were held back by elegant tortoise shell sunglasses, highlighting her striking features and perfect complexion. Her hair fell effortlessly past her shoulders and onto a black peasant top cinched at the waist. Loose fitting casual grey trousers and a few items of understated gold completed the look. Regardless of the seriousness of the circumstances Graham's jaw nearly hit the floor when she entered the room. It was a reaction that didn't go unnoticed.

Graham got up and pulled out one of the three cracked grey plastic chairs which were impossible to ever get comfortable in.

'Er, hi,' he said. Amisha saw that she would have to take charge.

'Hi Jacynta, thanks for coming in. Feeling any better? Ready to help us now?'

Jacynta nodded.

'Good. OK…could you take us through the events of last night, early this morning? Take your time.'

Jacynta took a deep breath, composed herself and gave her account of how she'd been woken by a commotion and gone into the bathroom to see a figure standing over Bazza with a shotgun. How she'd stood frozen with fear and seen the killer blow her lover's head to smithereens. Once or twice she lost her way and tears were rolling down her cheeks by the time she completed the story. It had not been very detailed.

'And the killer; can you give us any kind of description?'

'No. he kept his head down. It was dark. He might as well have been a shadow. All I know is he was wearing a big coat, a hoodie, and jeans, sunglasses. But it was too dark for me to even say what colour. All I can say is he was about six feet tall.

'You're sure it was a man?'

'I assume...assumed so. Quite big and bulky. He moved like a man. I never heard him speak though. All I heard was Bazza, pleading for his life. That's what woke me up...it was terrible.'

Jacynta broke down, collapsing forward into herself and sobbing gently. Amisha could see she needed a minute or two. Graham wished he was somewhere else.

After a time Amisha put her hand on Jacynta's shoulder and asked if they could continue.

'I'm sorry Jacynta,' Amisha said, 'but we really do have to ask you these questions. What happened after Bazza was shot? Did the killer interact with you, threaten you in any way?'

'He stood for a few moments, looking at me and then he raised his shotgun. Despite the dark he kept his sunglasses on. I was frozen with fear...he looked at me for a few seconds, then left quietly. He was checking his watch as he left. A few seconds later I heard another gunshot. I was terrified, I just stayed where I was, until somebody came.'

'Somebody?'

'Yes, the hotel manager I think, and then a policeman. A normal policeman...in a uniform, I mean.'

Silence returned; Jacynta stared into space, motionless.

'Okay Jacynta, that's terrific. Thanks. You've been a big help so far. How about if we take a little break and then ask you a few more question, not about the murder, but background stuff. You know, what you were doing last night, who you two hung out with, Bazza's friends.'

Jacynta produced a mirthless laugh.

'What's funny?' asked Graham.

'Friends? His friends? You don't have friends in this world.'

12

Graham, who had come to terms with having a supermodel in his interview room, decided it was time to set a crisper tone, and took over the questioning after a short break.

'What about enemies then? You say he had no friends - I want to come back to that - but did he have enemies? Anyone ever threaten him, to your knowledge?'

'All the time,' Jacynta said wearily, 'all the time. Death threats, hate mail, a lot of evil stuff on Twitter - your people looked into a few of the worst examples. It's horrible…they never leave you alone.'

'You're talking about Bazza now, or yourself?'

'Both of us. People like us get it all the time…sick cowards, just spewing it out from behind their screens. Bazza got a lot more of it than I did though. Jealous boyfriends threatening him, random haters, that sort of thing.'

'Did anyone ever confront him physically, up close?'

'Not as far as I know.'

'OK, thanks. Can I take you back to the subject of Bazza's friends, or lack of them? What did you mean – we're given to believe by the media that he was very popular,' Graham said.

'Well, when you become famous you soon learn that there's a difference between popularity and friendship. These two things are not connected. At all. Bazza was super-popular - he had a way about him. He was charming, funny, exciting to be around…and very sexy. So people liked him. But as I say, you learn. You learn that there are basically two sorts of people – those who think they love you, or know you, but who don't understand the first thing about you really, and those who befriend you for what they can get out of you.'

Amisha, who had done her homework and already read through an acreage of old newspaper and celebrity magazine articles, now intervened and talked with Jacynta about the months of the on/off relationship with Bazza, building up a picture of their known associates.

They talked more about fame, what it was like to live your life in the public eye. Amisha asked if she or Bazza ever had any stalkers or fans that followed them or persistently tried to contact them. She was considering the possibility of a John Lennon style fan murder.

'Listen,' said Jacynta, 'everyone out there wants to be famous these days. Everyone's a wannabe. I suppose talent programmes like the one Bazza was on make people think they can all do it. I suppose that breeds a lot of jealousy and that being the case lots of people out there could want to kill him.'

Amisha noticed how Jacynta averted her eyes when asking questions about stalkers or fan harassment. She pushed the point, more directly.

'So there's nobody you know of who has been stalking you or Bazza?'

Jacynta's eyes remained averted as she mumbled in the negative. Amisha continued to question her about her career and the people around her and Bazza. They talked about people she knew in the business, Bazza's manager Nigel Blandish and the army of hangers on that surrounded him. They talked about the parties, the sex, the drugs. Jacynta was very open about the drugs.

Tell me about Tarquin de Montfort,' asked Amisha. She had done her homework. She had also watched H's interview technique many times. The sudden related but seemingly unrelated question sprang from out of nowhere. It took Jacynta by surprise. She swallowed hard.

Tarquin, son of an Earl, was one of those slippery hangers-on, who exist to oil the wheels of the celebrity life.

Not a household name by any means, but one known to those who regularly read the celebrity columns.

'We often go to his parties. He is just someone who's there, one of those people who is well known for being well known, if you catch my drift.'

The questioning was helping Jacynta to come out of shock, allowing her to start thinking through the consequences of her predicament. One of the reasons for her success was her speed of recovery after a knock back. As the interview ended Graham asked her if she could keep a low profile while the investigation was ongoing, keep away from the twitter monster and not comment to the press about the case, nor mention it on any other form of social media. She thought Graham was kind of cute but his request was naïve. She had zero intentions of keeping a low profile.

'That's not how this works. When you're on the fame treadmill you play it for everything you've got, darling.'

13

The forensic people had taken all the samples of blood, sweat and tears - and anything else that might give a trace of DNA - they could find, and were beavering away. It was 3.50pm when Amisha and Graham met Toby Mortimer in the New Scotland Yard canteen for an initial discussion.

Toby was a sixty a day man and had just been in the car park for a puff so was a few minutes late when he entered the canteen. Tall and wiry, with a hunched neck and sharp features, he manoeuvred himself inelegantly into a chair and sat down. He was of a nervous disposition and a permanently anxious smile exposed stained teeth that revealed his lifelong smoking habit.

'Hi Toby, have you got anything for us?' said Graham.

'Not really. It's early days, we have DNA samples but not enough time to confirm identities yet. I doubt we'll find anything which might allow us to identify the killer, it seems like he knew what he was doing.'

Toby angled his head and gave a nervous twitch. It was a twitch over which he had no control and always gave whenever he was too unsure of himself to present an alternative argument. Amisha had had several dealings with him in the past and spotted his discomfort, and knew he had a theory. She also knew he craved certainty before talking to detectives about murder scenes, and he didn't have any. She'd have to force him to speculate.

'Any thoughts on the dead girl, Toby?'

Anxiety flashed across his face, but after another twitch or two Toby started to talk.

'Well, it's just…'

'Just what?'

'Well, it's the angle of the blood splatter. Doesn't quite tally with your assessment of what happened. She wasn't in front of the lift or behind it. It seems to me she was standing next to it.'

'So' said Graham, 'she was coming out of the lift at the same moment the killer was walking towards it.'

'And, well…' continued Toby.

'Well…' said Amisha

'Well, it seems as if the area around the lift had been recently cleaned. And her finger prints were the only ones on the button that calls the lift.' Toby's twitching was speeding up. He had a theory but wasn't sure of the evidence.

'Go on…' Amisha and Graham said in unison.

'Well, in my opinion the evidence suggests, if you include where the body fell, the fingerprint and the blood splatter, the evidence suggests she was waiting by the lift.'

'Waiting? So, she was the killer's accomplice?' said Graham.

'Well, that's speculation, and speculation is for detectives. I only deal in facts.'

'But you think she was waiting by the lift and holding it for someone?' said Amisha.

Toby said nothing, but nodded his head - and twitched.

'Food for thought,' said Graham as he and Amisha made their way to the 4pm debrief, for which they were running slightly late.

When they arrived at the meeting the other detectives on the case were waiting. Graham gave an overview of the initial forensics as presented to them by Toby. The team were still gathering CCTV from the hotel and surrounding areas and had nothing to corroborate or refute Toby's theory. But it made sense. Bazza's booking had been made some weeks before and the electronic card key the killer had used had been programmed to open Bazza's suite door some three days earlier.

'Check the staff timetable, see if Svitlana Kovalenko was on duty at the time the key was activated,' Graham told Jill

Bannister, who was heading up the sub-team responsible for interviewing and checking on the hotel staff. 'And get me full details of the background check on her.'

Other than that there was not much to report, apart from the Jacynta interview, which Graham summarized, and a long list of interviews that needed to be conducted including those of Bazza's mother Maureen Docherty, his manager Nigel Blandish, and socialite and man about town Tarquin de Montfort - who probably supplied Bazza and Jacynta with their marching powder.

14

'Alright Liv,' H shouted up the stairs, 'D-day it is. I'm off. Wish me luck.'

'Good luck darling. Give her a bit of the old H charm. You'll be fine.'

H paused at the hallway mirror on his way out and had a look at himself.

Mr Potato Head. Standing in my spot, where I should be. Again. How does he do it?

He studied the bloated hulk, the ravaged crimson face, all shovelled by Olivia into a decent blue suit… and felt nothing. The figure in the mirror stared back, mute and stupid looking, and tried to stare him down. It had been like this for a long time now. He put it down to the pills. He'd ask again today if he could be taken off them.

Snapping out of it, the big man flung open the door and crunched purposefully in bright morning sunshine across the gravel of his front garden, strapped himself into his car and set a course for Kasia Kotula's 'rooms' in Pimlico. Traffic was not too bad. As he hit the Well Hall roundabout he sparked up the CD player and brought Sammy Davis into the proceedings. Never a bad idea; Sammy always livened him up, made him feel a bit better. Sometimes a lot better. Today his mood needed to be positive, and he was aiming for charm. For all the good it would do him - he was often disconcerted, during his sessions with Kasia, by the feeling that she could somehow see right inside him, past his front. And H had always been a front man.

He ran on, 'Mr Bojangles' keeping him buoyed-up as he negotiated the dog's dinner of the central Lewisham traffic system, and reflected on his time with Kasia. He'd fronted up at their first meeting and treated her to a large helping of patronising, know-it-all-bluster. Told her he understood that he was required to attend their meetings but that he was not the sort of a man who needed anyone's help to sort himself out, thank you very much darling. She'd looked at him, steely-eyed over the top of her no-nonsense glasses, and given it to him straight: 'Well, Detective Inspector Hawkins, what can I say? You are in therapy now. We can either do this the hard way, or we can do it the very hard way. Those are your options. You want to get your job back? Your life back? Or are you going to just stand about trying to frighten me with this Richard Burton impression?'

Tasty. Very tasty. In both senses. A force to be reckoned with.

H's first impression of her had solidified into genuine respect and admiration over the months. She knew what she was doing, and she'd winkled more sense out of the mess of his inner turmoil than anyone except Olivia. He was almost sad that today's might be the last of their weekly meetings. Almost. The fact was that he just wanted to get back to work…but had only a very fuzzy idea where he was 'up to,' to use Kasia's phrase. And Olivia's. And Amisha's, if it came to that.

Where are you up to, H?

Fucked if I know.

15

Kasia's rooms, all colour-supplement minimalist, were as austere as her look: sleek, tied-back black hair, steel rimmed glasses, black fitted roll neck sweater, grey pencil skirt and higher heels than H guessed were normal in the psychiatric profession. He had her down as being about 40, and he liked what he saw, as usual, as he settled into his chair opposite her.

'Good morning Detective Inspector,' she said, observing the formalities as ever. H figured this must be a Polish thing. Or a psychiatrist's thing. Or a Polish psychiatrist's thing. He glanced at her legs.

'Morning Kasia. How are you today?'

'Very well thank you. Eager to get started. We don't have as much time as I'd like and I want to review our work, from the time we began.'

H didn't much like the sound of this. He gave a small nod.

Kasia looked at her notes. She seemed to have some sort of chart set out on the top page. 'You were somewhat distressed and disoriented at our first meeting. And very angry. You told me that you considered therapy to be - I am quoting you here, Detective Inspector - "a lot of old bollocks". Is this still your view?'

H looked her in the eye, and gave a sigh. He worked on getting his head in the right place and focusing on his usual strategy - tell her just enough to keep her sweet, to make her think he was on board. But the anxiety he always felt when he was trying to perform this balancing act was already starting to creep into his guts.

What if she won't let me go back?

Keep her sweet...Say something, you fucking muppet.

'OK, let me put it a little differently,' Kasia said. 'How do feel now, today, compared to our early meetings?'

'Well, I…better. A lot better.'

'In what way?'

'Less angry…less panicky, I suppose…'

Silence.

'OK, do you recall what your main issues were at that time, what we talked about?'

'We talked about my collapse, my breakdown. My time in hospital. The whole thing with the paedophile ring, and my mate Ronnie taking care of the top man in it... Skyhill. I felt bad for Ronnie…I was knackered. You said I'd been traumatised, that the ghosts of past conflicts had overwhelmed me, but I just felt completely knackered. And angry.'

H's jaw was working, and his foot was pumping. He knew it, but these things were hard to control. He hoped Kasia would see it as a bit of nervousness, but the fact was he was feeling the pressure that always built up inside him at these meetings, as he tried to reveal little bits and conceal some of the big things at the same time.

'Angry about what, Detective Inspector? Specifically.'

'About what those bastards had done to the children...About them getting away with it for years because of who they were… About all the violence happening at the same time I was putting that case together - murderous gangsters going at it hammer and tongs, all over London, all the blood and guts everywhere... Angry that we were losing control... Angry at the amount of porridge they gave Ronnie…thirty years, for putting a horrible nonce out of his misery.'

H paused and took a breath. His emotions were starting to run away with him. This was the point of danger: Kasia ate this stuff up, but he ran the risk of saying too much as he was dishing it out. Of letting something slip. She still only knew the official version of the events of nine months before.

Kasia had her eyes, her piercing blue eyes, fixed on his; it was X-ray time.

'But your friend Ronnie committed a murder. A cold-blooded murder. He threw a man from the top of the tallest building in London. For this he received his just punishment. Do you not see this? You are a policeman, are you not?'

'That bastard had Ronnie's wife killed. He ruined the lives of countless children. He deserved to die.'

'Detective Inspector, you are not speaking like an officer of the law. Why do you want to return to your work…to support this kind of savage justice?'

This was too much. H's stomach was churning like a cement mixer. He needed a breather. Five minutes in, and he needed a breather.

'I…can we stop for a coffee? I'm gasping.'

H was beginning to lose control. She was getting to him, getting him to lower his guard. It was becoming impossible to keep it all straight; to keep on telling the sanitised version of the story - the one in which he was an upright defender of law and order and Ronnie, who loved him like a brother and had sacrificed himself for him, was the villain.

'OK, I'll bring coffee. But we have to talk about this, Detective Inspector. I have to understand where your anger is really coming from…and whether you are in a fit state to resume the proper duties of a policeman.'

'Okey dokey,' said H, 'got it. Right you are.'

Fuck it. She has absolutely got me by the bollocks here.

16

H sat on the toilet with his head in his hands and tried to order his thoughts. Why was he so angry? Why was he sitting here free to come and go as he pleased, while Ronnie was in Durham doing a thirty stretch? And his son was banged up on remand refusing to see him, looking at a long stretch himself under the watchful eye of Basim Dragusha, one of the deadliest villains H had ever come across. Too right he was angry.

H thought about his friend; his loyalty, his courage, his style. And his depths; he had never underestimated Ronnie's courage - he'd known him as a teenage street fighter who never took a step backwards, a fine and selfless soldier, an upstart nobody who'd barely been to school but who had built a serious business empire with his quick-witted mind and his own bare hands, and an utterly devoted family man – but he'd been astonished by what his friend had done for him. And the manner of its doing.

Nine months previously the two of them, heedless of danger, had stood up when no one else would and brought down a top-level paedophile ring. Things had gotten a little out of hand, it was true, when Ronnie's lust for revenge on the man who'd had his wife killed took control of him and he'd launched Lord Timothy Skyhill to meet his maker from the top of a very tall building. But they had done what needed to be done.

At the time H had been running on high-octane emotion, as they surged across the metropolis joining up the dots and dealing with the big picture as it emerged. H had assumed that Ronnie had been operating at the same level as himself: enraged, vengeful, careless of the consequences and not a little deranged. But his friend had been one step ahead all along - thinking, planning and scheming as they went. Keeping tight what for H had seemed like a mess.

Ronnie's business empire had been no stroke of luck. He was a tactician of the highest order. He had controlled and tidied up everything - from having a CCTV system knocked out to disposing of evidence and sorting out a credible alibi for his friend - without H even knowing it. By the time H had woken up in Guy's hospital, a couple of days after Skyhill's death, Ronnie had everything nailed down. He'd held his hands up, kept H out of the picture and copped for the lot.

Ronnie had sacrificed himself, and his liberty, for his friend.

'The coffee's ready, Detective Inspector,' he heard Kasia call.

The big man roused himself; he gave his face a sluice at the sink and swept back his hair, what was left of it, with a flourish. Mr Potato Head stared back at him from the mirror. H addressed him directly:

'Sort yourself out, you big fucking melt. You think this is hard? Ronnie would love to swap places with you.'

A big, deep breath.

Just keep her sweet.

He burst back into the room.

'Ah, Detective Inspector, there you are. I was beginning to worry that you'd "made yourself scarce".'

Kasia was playfully incorporating some of H's idioms into her speech, like Olivia, and Amisha - and plenty of others - before her.

Give her a bit of the old H charm. You'll be alright.

17

'Look, Inspector, we all get angry about lots of things. Your anger's not going to disappear, but I need to be sure it will not control you, cloud your judgement in an investigation. That you have it under control.' Kasia was going to push him hard, show him no mercy.

H knew this was the key moment: everything he'd done with Kasia had been leading up to this. He had to talk through his anger, once and for all, without going off the deep end. Convince her he had himself sorted out, that things wouldn't go wobbly if he was put under pressure. He had to go through a potted history of the previous year's events, show her enough to get her teeth into, but never reveal the truth. And he'd never been a good liar.

So he went through his time in the Falklands in more detail, and described the flashbacks that had started several years later. He was angry that his comrades had died and that he'd had to kill young men at the behest of politicians. He was angry that so many soldiers who'd fought alongside him had later taken their own lives - more now than had died in the conflict.

That was the Falklands out of the way. H was building up a head of steam now, and moved on to go through his anger at the high level nonce conspiracy, how they had managed to get away with it, how they had the reach and power to close investigations for decades, how they had tried to wreck his career and destroy him, which amounted to the same thing.

So far so good. All that's true.

'And what about Ronnie' Kasia asked, 'and everything that happened between you and him? What about those issues?'

H stopped to take a gulp of coffee. His hands were shaking and Kasia noticed the involuntary body movements.

He noticed her notice. The shaking wasn't from what he'd just said but in anticipation of the lies he was about to tell, and the emotions that would explode inside him when he told them. His future depended on them. He stalled for time.

'Sorry, I… that stuff's not easy to talk about.'

'Take your time Detective Inspector, whenever you're ready.'

H took the respite to get things straight in his head. He thought through what had actually happened, to ensure he could separate truth from lie.

This was it; he was going to have to talk Kasia through a version of last year's chaos, Skyhill's murder and what Ronnie had done. This was where most of the lies were. He put his head in his hands; his mind wandered back.

*

Ronnie, who H now understood was even of more of a forward-thinking genius than he had realised, had known they'd have to act quickly, before Skyhill knew they were onto him and surrounded himself with more bodyguards than an American President on a day trip to Iraq. Ronnie had also known they would never both get away with what they were doing and had planned H's alibi even as they sped to the scene of the showdown. He'd phoned Kyril Kuznetsov and called in one final request as part of the deal on keeping quiet about the oligarch's involvement with the nonces; that got every CCTV camera in the London Bridge area knocked out, and the car he and H had travelled up in spirited away.

After launching Skyhill off the top of the building he'd taken H back down into the chaos of the grand gala. People were running everywhere amid the fire alarms and acrid aftermath of smoke bombs, unsure of who was who. He'd taken off H's balaclava and trench coat, set them alight and started several other fires to throw the police off the scent.

Once a paratrooper, always a paratrooper. The whole room was going up in smoke when H, semi-conscious, came to and asked him what the fuck he was up to. 'Shut it H,' was Ronnie's reply, as he brought his hand gun down hard across H's head and knocked him unconscious again. Ronnie had made sure there were witnesses to the beating.

The next thing H was aware of - he'd lost a lot of blood from the wound in his thigh and had required an operation - was a few days later when he woke up in hospital. Olivia, Amisha and Graham were at his bedside and told him what Ronnie had told them.

They then spent several days convincing him to stick to Ronnie's story, which was very simple. Ronnie had rung H and told him he had acquired evidence confirming that Skyhill had ordered the hit on his wife. Realising that Ronnie was on his way to kill Skyhill, H had followed him to try and stop him. They fought, Ronnie shot H in the leg and knocked him unconscious. He'd set the place alight because he thought it would add to the confusion and help him escape. In truth he knew he never would and only put up a show of resistance, for the sake of looking authentic, before letting Old Bill nab him.

H admired the cunning of the story, but refused to go along with what was supposed to happen next.

'There's no way on God's green fucking earth I'm letting Ronnie do time for me.'

'It's what he wants, guv. It was either both of you or one of you,' Amisha had told him.

'No. It's not right. If Ronnie's going down, I'm going down with him.'

The argument went on for days. It was only after H went to see Ronnie, who was on remand in Brixton, that he'd reluctantly agreed.

Ronnie had given it to him straight. 'Listen, you cantankerous old bastard. Twenty odd years ago Tara told me what her old man was like, what he did to her as a kid, and swore me to secrecy as long as we both lived. If I'd stepped up when I should have and dealt with the old cunt none of this would ever have happened. I've lost the only woman I've ever loved and it's on me.'

'But ...'

'H, shut it. Please. Don't hold your hands up for this. I can take the porridge, now I've straightened everything out. I can sleep at night, live out my life behind bars. I'm not going to say it'll be easy, but I've found a sort of peace. But if it comes on top for you as well it would all have been in vain, I'll lay awake at night thinking about how I took my best mate down with me, because I didn't have the bottle to do what should have been done twenty years ago. We're mates, brothers, so do this for me. Please. I'm begging you H, stay free. Promise me.'

*

Kasia brought him back to the here and now.

'Ok to proceed Detective Inspector?'

Having thought through what had really happened, H now steeled himself for the big lie.

Keep it tight H, keep it tight.

18

'I'm angry that my best friend Ronnie was given such a long sentence. OK, I accept he broke the law and that he should have let justice take its course. But Skyhill would probably have got away with it. I guess I'm "conflicted".'

He almost choked on the word - he hated all this newspeak. But it went down well with Kasia, as he'd hoped it would, and she was beginning to purr. This was music to her ears.

'Well, we're all conflicted Detective Inspector. It's a matter of how we handle those conflicts.'

She pushed him a little further. 'If Skyhill was here now how do you think you would react.'

H wasn't conflicted at all. If Skyhill was here now he'd smash his fucking brains out on the floor, and ruin Kasia's sleek gunmetal-grey rug.

'I'd arrest him.'

'Really?'

'Absolutely. I wouldn't throw him out the window, if that's what you're getting at.'

They skirted around the subject a little more, Kasia continuing to probe. If she set off a murderous rant, there was no way he would be going back to work. He was struggling to hold it together. His sense that he had betrayed his friend was overwhelming him. Killing bad guys was one thing, he could live with that no problem, if they were bad enough and deserved it, but betrayal... That made his skin crawl, every night and much of every day, seven days a week.

'So you don't feel anger that your friend shot you in the leg and knocked you unconscious? You feel the system let him down and that you, personally, are responsible, as if you betrayed him somehow?'

Bingo. Kasia had flipped the switch that launched H's inner A-bomb. The chain reaction had started, the nuke inside was about to detonate and reveal an ever-expanding mushroom cloud of fury.

H knew she could bring him to this. But he'd come prepared and it was time to play his ace card. As the anger and the inner turmoil boiled over H channelled it in a different direction. They'd had several chats about his son's plight without focusing on it. He was holding a pair of deuces but it was time to go all in.

'Yes I'm angry. But…I'm mostly angry at myself for the way I've let my boy down. He's going to go to prison for a long time, they'll eat him alive in there. He's just a kid. How did I mess up so fucking badly? I think, Kasia, more than anything, that I'm angry at myself, the mistakes I've made, the things I seem to be powerless to put right. And my son absolutely refuses to see me.'

He looked Kasia in the face, and noted the look of approval in her eyes. This was clearly going to be a rich seam, and he went on to mine it further. He talked at length about Ronnie's childhood, his marriage to Julie, how it had all fallen apart. It was a sorry tale of failure and regret, and at the end of it he felt exhausted but strangely liberated. He'd talked about real pain, in a real way, without revealing the big lie he was afraid of exposing, and Kasia had lapped it up. She was now positively glowing.

'Well, inspector, that's quite some monologue. I think it took real courage and honesty to face so many truths about yourself, to confront such pain. Now I see where the heart of the matter is. I think we are really beginning to get somewhere.'

Beginning? Beginning? Fuck it, I thought I'd cracked it.

OK…stay on track. Give her what she wants.

'Yes, it felt good to get all that lot out. Maybe there's a bit of light at the end of the tunnel. I can see now how all this has been helping me,' H said, setting things up for the big question. 'Maybe getting back to work would help me pull myself together as well?'

'Well…I'd like to extend the therapy, book some more sessions. We've made a big breakthrough today, Detective Inspector.'

'Yes we have…and I think we can do a lot more. But don't you think I'd also benefit from running the two things together? Seeing you and going back to work? All this sitting about doing nothing is doing my mental health no favours at all.'

'You think you're ready?'

'I know I am. I need to be useful. Doing nothing is eating me alive.'

Kasia said nothing. She sat quietly, reviewing her notes, deep in thought. The room was almost as quiet as the grave. H could hear only his own breathing and the gentle ticking of a carriage clock. His fate was in her hands.

At last she raised her head. 'Here's what I propose, Detective Inspector,' she said. 'Light duties only - desk work. Absolutely no dealings with the public, or active case work. Research and support. For a six-month probationary period. On the condition that you continue to attend weekly meetings with me, for three months in the first instance.'

Desk duties? Desk duties?

H felt a momentary impulse to hoot and holler, but held himself in check. He was busting to get back on the streets. It was where he belonged, what he was born for. But something was better than nothing, and discretion was, sometimes, the better part of valour. This was step one - it would do for now.

'Very sensible Kasia, very sensible. Sounds like a plan.'

H said his goodbyes and bowled out of Kasia's rooms with more of a spring in his step than he'd had in a long, long while.

Yes! Fucking yes! The Guvnor is back!
Almost.

19

Jack Butcher, one of the last of the old school armed blaggers, was skating on thin ice. Life inside was changing, and changing fast. He was half way through a thirty stretch for armed robbery, an event during which he'd smashed a security guard to death with the butt of his shotgun. The heist had made big news and the lump of porridge he'd been dished out had been a topic of much discussion. The powers that be had made an example of him, given the manslaughter and the fact that he'd gotten away with over a million quid. Most of it he'd splashed on fast cars and a yacht before the long arm of the law reached out and felt his collar on the Costa del Sol.

During his time inside the number of firms vying for control of Durham, the high security prison he found himself in, had expanded with ever increasing speed as more people came into the country. Nobody considered him the top man anymore. In the early days he had been able to keep control of the nick, maintain his position as the daddy and keep a lid on things. But he'd long been under threat and the firms that controlled daily life inside were no longer run by old school villains from the Mersey or the Thames or the Tyne but those drawn from places Butcher and his ilk had barely even heard of. Russian mobsters, Albanian mafia, Islamists and members of many other organisations were now detained at Her Majesty's Pleasure.

The days were becoming ever more difficult. He still had his own cell and commanded enough respect to be feared by many of the prison population. But not all of it, not by a long way. The new kids on the block didn't want to stand in line and be handed their slice of the cake like well-behaved kids at a birthday party. They wanted the whole fucking cake, they wanted it now and they had no respect for authority.

Butcher was a big man, six foot three inches, thick set with the rippling muscles that working out in the prison gym virtually every day for fifteen years had put on him. If he'd looked any more like a bulldog he'd have had to go around barking and licking the pavement. His squashed-up face and splayed nose stood atop a thick set neck and broad, powerful shoulders. He was not a man to be trifled with. His nickname in his early years, when he was rising through the ranks, had been 'The Butcher,' and not just because he happened to share a name with a profession that was well versed in cutting up chunks of flesh. As an enforcer for one of the south London gangs that once controlled the London drug trade his reputation as a ruthless wrecker of limbs was second to none.

It was his habit, at breakfast time, to sit with his boys and go through the day's agenda. He watched as Terry Palmer, John Donovan and Billy Walsh hunkered down over their scrambled eggs. They'd been through a lot together, inside and out, what with one thing and another, and these were the only men he trusted in the entire nick. They'd all had their taste of *La Dolce Vita*, before the extradition treaty with Spain was signed. The fun and games were over now, but they did what they could.

'I don't feel all that clever today boys. I think I might have a touch of the old Delhi Belly. I'm gonna skip workout and rest up. I'll be in my cell. When you're finished in the gym come and get me up. We need to go and put it on this new Scouser who fancies himself. We'll need to mark his card and bring him on board.'

Half a dozen men from a competing firm walked past, holding their trays, and sat down at the table opposite Jack's table. The tension in the air was palpable - it could have been cut with a knife. The volume of the conversation went down a notch or two.

'It's gotta come on top sooner or later Jack. This mob are getting bolder by the day. I've got a feeling they're planning something. I can sense it.'

'Get a grip, son. They're a handful, no doubt about that, but they won't have a go at us. There's nothing in it for 'em. We keep to our bits and pieces; they keep to theirs. As long as no one oversteps the mark it'll be alright. We all know where we stand.'

'But this mad bastard that's running them now Jack. I've got a feeling he doesn't even fucking know where the mark is,' said Billy. 'I think he's just taking his time, sussing everything out.'

'Just keep 'em peeled Bill, yeah? Have your wits about you - this goes for all of you. Don't do nothing stupid. Keep the peace, unless they take a proper liberty.'

Billy sighed. It seemed to him like Butcher was running scared.

He was wrong. Butcher wasn't scared; but he was underestimating the threat. He still thought he'd be able to handle the situation when it came on top. But Butcher was playing by the old rules. He didn't quite get the extent to which these nutters were a different kettle of fish; they'd been forged in the meltdown of Yugoslavia and its aftermath, where mass murder and brutal ethnic cleansing had been the order of the day. Butcher simply did not understand the levels of unrestrained, utterly destructive violence that these men had witnessed, and been engaged in.

But the time was coming when he would.

20

'Eighteen, nineteen, twenty.'

Ronnie Hawkins counted as he lifted the bar above his chest on his third set of reps. He'd entered the prison nine months earlier as a scrawny and scared little boy. Now pumping 250lb press benches in multiple reps was just the start of his extensive workout. The muscles that made up his arms were on fire as he placed the weights back onto their rack, his chest heaving for oxygen. He sprang up from the exercise bench and moved purposefully to the next phase of his circuit.

Time for a little leg work.

In the short time he'd been inside a transformation had taken place in the young man. His chest was now a mass of heaving force and his stomach a rippling series of power packed muscles. But the change in his physical appearance was as nothing in comparison with the transformation inside his head. It registered in his face. This, too, had been transformed - from a mask of lost, wet-eyed self-pity into a face that few in the nick now had the bottle to look into for too long. It had the kind of animal intensity and seriousness, lack of humour and penetrating blued-eyed hostility that said trouble.

Serious trouble.

Given that his old man had put many of the villains in the place away it seemed it was only a matter of time before someone would wreak mortal vengeance on him. Despite being locked up with the nonces for his own safety, in the early days a few enterprising individuals had found a way to get at him and he'd received a good few slaps and a couple of proper kickings. But he had found a protector; or rather, a protector had found him. Basim Dragusha, high-ranking Albanian gang overlord, had come to his aid.

For Dragusha, beefing Ronnie up and turning him into a fighting machine had only been the start of the project. By now the kid had been turned, well and truly turned: from all that he'd been before into a ruthlessly loyal foot soldier of the closely-knit firm controlled by his master.

The screws turned blind eyes and the other inmates watched on in awe and with grudging respect as Dragusha applied the techniques that broke the boy down and rebuilt him in his own image. Dragusha, a cynical observer of the flaws in human nature, had learnt and used the techniques many times during the war in the Balkans.

These techniques, well known to the many Islamists amongst the prison fraternity who had been trained in grooming and turning lonely and disaffected young men into suicide bombers, were tried and tested across generations. They'd been around since medieval times, since when human nature had not changed one iota. With an isolated and frightened candidate, it wasn't that difficult to reshape and direct the human mind. Dragusha had spotted immediately that Ronnie Hawkins, son of the bastard who'd captured him and put him here, on remand, was ripe for the taking.

First came the control, telling him exactly what to do and when. That was the easy part, given Ronnie had no friends and needed the protection. Next they gained his trust, bringing him into the fold, appearing to let him into their confidence. At the same time Dragusha had given him plenty of Black Mamba or other synthetic weed, to destabilise him and keep him raw.

Control and an element of trust established, Dragusha had moved to phase three. The complete annihilation of what little self-esteem Ronnie still clung to. Dragusha had placed him with a trusted henchman, the sadistic Edon Dibra. They'd kept him in his cell for weeks on end, giving him endless sleepless nights, and plenty of bitch-slappings without really hurting him. Interrogations about nothing in particular, searching for all his weak points. Ceaseless lies about his cruel and dishonest father, a father with no loyalty towards his son, forever encouraging him to buy into self-pitying nonsense about how the world had let him down.

Dragusha regularly had books brought up to him from the prison library. He liked stories, fables, allegories. His favourite book was George Orwell's Animal Farm. As simple an allgory as it was he understood its essential truth, which was that if you tell a lie long enough eventually it becomes the truth. So the next phase was to disrupt his memories, break them down, give him some new ones. It was easy to convince Ronnie that Harry 'H' Hawkins had hated and abandoned him, and wished him harm.

After the breaking-down the building-up began.

'Human is like dog,' Dragusha had opined as he passed Ronnie various treats for good behaviour or thought patterns, whilst still punishing any last vestiges of the old Ronnie. There then followed many long, rakia-fuelled nights of preaching about brotherhood and loyalty, the beauty of vengeance, the glories of righteous violence in a just cause, repeating mantra-like sentences explaining why Ronnie must turn from the life that had failed him and show unswerving loyalty to his new group, the group that would provide him with a home - a family - and protect him. Dragusha's speeches seemed to mimic the rhythm of the human heart as he offered friendship for loyalty, and hope of a better life. Dragusha was no religious fanatic; it wasn't rewards of the afterlife he offered, but a chance to live this life well, to show courage and live like a wolf, as nature intended, free from the shackles of his sick family and the weak, broken society that had led him to this place.

No longer in a position to resist, Ronnie lapped it up.

When the brainwashing was complete Dragusha kept Ronnie in isolation, wound up and primed to go off, when desired, like a human bomb. His full initiation came one night in their candlelit cell, marked by a cutting-of-hands and blood-sharing ritual. 'You one of us now,' Dragusha had told him, 'You need new name. From now you called Ujku - means 'The Wolf'. Say your name.'

'Ujku.'

'Again, louder!'

'Ujku!'

'Again, again, again.'

'Ujku!, Ujku!, Ujku!'

Dragusha smiled. 'Never forget what your Rudyard Kipling say,' he told the exhilarated young man. 'The wolf is the strength of the pack, and the pack is the strength of the wolf.'

'Never forget.'

*

So here Ronnie was, working the gym like a professional athlete, fit, strong, powerful. He felt at home with his new people, convinced they had his best interests at heart, no longer aware he was being played like the pawn he was, in Dragusha's ever changing games of chess. As Dibra entered the gym Ronnie, who had now just reached his 100th press-up, sprang up, flexed his muscles and howled like the wolf he had become. A disturbing, manic craziness shone through his eyes. The young man once known as Little Ronnie Hawkins was in a place that few modern men understood - Dragusha had made Ronnie strong and unselfish, a potent combination - and utterly loyal to the pack and its leader.

'Ujku, Basim wants to talk to you in cell,' Dibra said.

21

Amisha and Graham were on the A2. It was eighty miles or so to Margate, a seaside town in the county of Kent. Like it's unofficial sisters, Brighton and Southend, it had been infamous in the 1960's for gang violence between the mods and rockers. But unlike Brighton, and even Southend, it hadn't managed to move on and repackage itself for the 21st century. These days it was populated - clung to limpet-like, really - by the unemployed, stranded asylum seekers and struggling retirees. The towns strung out along this bit of coast had some of the highest unemployment rates in the country. In the summertime day trippers from London still came down in reasonable numbers on sunny days to enjoy the sandy beach, but few went as far as booking a week's holiday. Margate was, to use the official euphemism, 'blighted'. To most people it was just another dead-end coastal town.

Miller-Marchant kept a steady pace as he looked across at Amisha. She was staring into space, rather than into her screens, something that had become a little more common since her ordeal of the previous year.

There were times when she wanted to talk about it. And times when she didn't. Graham had learned to read the signals and this was one of those days when she didn't. He left her alone with the dark thoughts that tormented her, and his mind drifted back to the event that changed everything: the shootout at Grays.

*

'Work it out. You'll think of something,' H had said to him after the carnage, and before tearing off with Ronnie Ruddock to the centre of London to take care of Lord

Timothy Skyhill. As the sirens drew closer he looked around at the scene of devastation that his few minutes in H's small private army had wrought. Dead bodies lay scattered around the isolated warehouse, Amisha, horribly abused and bloodied but somehow dignified and unbowed, had retrieved her clothes and put them back on. The sadistic coward who'd hurt her lay whimpering on the floor, blood still oozing from the shattered face H had left him with.

The approaching plod would have heard reports of gunfire, so they'd secure the perimeter and wait for the armed response unit from the Met to arrive and set up. Graham and Amisha had just enough time for a last-minute conference, to work out what the hell they were going to do.

Graham had spoken to Amisha quickly and bluntly, despite her trauma. He'd wandered into all of this pretty much by chance and didn't have all the facts. He needed to bring himself up to speed, fast.

'Amisha, I've been following H for the last couple of days. I'm not sure exactly what's happened down here. I don't know how you got here, or who's been holding you, or why, or where H and Ronnie are going now. I know it's all tied up with Tara's murder and I expect the guilty party will soon be meeting his maker. I can see what's happened to you, but please…what's the big picture? Who are these people? How did you get here?

Amisha filled him in. Her investigations into the dark web. The high-level paedophile ring controlled by Skyhill. His decision that Tara, who knew too much, had to be removed from the equation. The role played by the oligarch Kuznetsov. H's blind fury, and Ronnie's.

Graham was in deep turmoil, his heart hammering at his chest, his whole body trembling. What to do, what to do? He'd always been great at data analysis and could wow a room of his superiors with slick PowerPoint presentations about crime rate reduction in deprived areas. But he'd never expected to find himself in a situation like this. This was way off-slide.

He had two choices and not enough time to think through the implications of either: truth or lie.

Truth - he would tell it like it is. He followed H and Ronnie on gut instinct as he believed they were on to something. He arrived, shot one of the firm at the warehouse in self-defence, H and Ronnie took care of the rest. They found and liberated Amisha. Outcome of Truth: he becomes the hero, gets a commendation and a promotion. The obvious choice. 'Malcolm', the little pervert who'd tortured Amisha, gets a good long stretch. H and Ronnie get banged up for life, probably without even holding it against him; they had done what they'd had to do.

Lie - much more complicated. For starters he'd need to explain away Amisha's presence. She'd have to have travelled here with him, after a tip off...He looked out the window. It was pitch black apart from the lights of the police cars set up around the perimeter of the warehouse. Very soon armed men would be swarming all over them. The pressure was forcing Graham to think quickly, with the noise outside intensifying, and the adrenalin released during the conflict still coursing through his body.

In the end he'd boiled everything down to its essence: protect H or give him up. Either way it was the biggest call he'd ever had to make, and one way or another it would change his life. Even a few short weeks before he would have given H up. But things had changed. For the first time in his life he had killed someone; he'd stepped into H's shoes and learned how hard it was to wear them. His fear of and contempt for the big man had turned to something like respect. But protecting H was the harder choice, full of dangers for his career, his future, maybe even his freedom, if everything went tits-up.

Amisha and Graham talked it through one last time.

‘I say we go with the lie. We came here together after a tip off,’ Graham said. ‘Everyone was dead on our arrival. Gang war. I shot the last survivor because he was holding you hostage. That way I’ll be able to get you out of here without you having to speak to anyone - it’ll explain why you’re in shock. But it means what happened here stays with us…for ever.’

‘It’s either that or H goes down for life. We don’t know what he’ll do before this night is out and if he gets caught he’ll probably hold his hands up and tell the truth. But for now we go with the lie. If it all falls apart, we’ll get a bit of grief and then start looking for something else to do with our lives. But if H gets away with it… I can live with what I’ve done tonight.’

‘But what about” Malcolm” there. How do we explain him away?’ Amisha asked.

Graham looked across at the whimpering pervert on the deck. The revolver H had given to Amisha to finish off her tormentor lay on the bed from which she’d been liberated. It was almost as if H had left it on purpose. Graham picked up the pistol and checked the chamber. One bullet left. Time stood still. Graham held the gun to the man’s head and pulled the trigger.

Graham and Amisha locked eyes. No words were exchanged. They would now be bound, along with H and Ronnie, in a web of lies and secrecy. Graham would have spells of regret for months. At times, he couldn’t believe he’d done it. But he had.

*

Graham was on auto pilot as he followed the commands of the satnav off the motorway and into Margate. It was 11am on a pleasant day in early September so Graham took a short diversion; he thought Amisha might like a view of the ocean. He slowed the car to make sure she could take in the scene. The rancid grey sea was calm and placid.

'Welcome to Margate,' he said jauntily, 'home of the late, great Bazza Wishbone.'

22

They surveyed the town as they drove on. It was clear it had had a few bits and pieces of government cash from various regeneration funds thrown at it, and some attempt had been made to tart up the seafront. But most of the holiday makers had gone and the town was reverting to the desolate and forlorn atmosphere that haunts the British seaside town when the holidaymakers disappear and the core population re-appear from the shadows.

'Turn left. Then you have reached your destination,' the satnav said.

Graham pulled up outside the local authority block that had been home to Bazza. Both he and Amisha had seen much worse social housing; it wasn't hopelessly grim, nor the kind of place you'd automatically link with social deprivation or gangland violence. It wasn't even particularly unpleasant. It was just bland and grey, as if the god of architecture had waved a bored hand and created an insignificant nothing in the middle of nowhere.

Graham and Amisha walked up the stairwell to the second floor and knocked on number 42. A few seconds later it was opened by Maureen Docherty, the mother of four children - or three, now that Bazza had gone - all from different fathers. She remained a good-looking woman in her early forties, her figure still almost intact. She had wispy, long ginger hair that fell softly down to the small of her back.

It had been over a day since the death of her son and she was stunned and distraught. A sleepless night of tears and lamentations and vodka had left her eyes raw and bloodshot. Graham and Amisha flashed their warrant cards at her. Amisha held her stare and felt the pain behind the reddened eyes. 'Detective Inspector Miller-Marchant and Detective

Sergeant Amisha Bhanushali,' she said, as reassuringly as she could in the circumstances.

Maureen showed them into her flat and they took a seat on the fifteen-year-old leather sofa that dominated the small living room. The flat was in need of some decoration. Damp wallpaper was peeling from the wall behind the large TV screen and the sofa was split in at least three places. Life on benefits paid for food, cigarettes and a little something to drink, if you were crafty, but new furniture was not an option. Three pictures of archangels looking down from heaven decorated the wall, beneath a painting of the crucifixion.

Amisha had been involved in several murder investigations, but meeting the parents of a murdered child was the part she could see she would never get used to. Murder always seemed so random, so sudden, so unnecessary, so impossible to explain. Amisha gave her condolences, inadequate as they were bound to be, and said they needed to ask Maureen some questions about her son and his life, but also that if she wasn't ready they would come back another day.

'No, you're alright - let's get it over with,' Maureen said.

Maureen's parents had come over to England in the 1970s from County Donegal, and her father had worked on the motorways, laying tarmac as one of 'McAlpine's Fusiliers.' They had lived in several places before settling in Maidstone, the town Maureen had grown up in. Her father had died several years before, taken by liver cancer. Her mother, who was still alive, lived in a nursing home in Maidstone and was suffering from advanced Alzheimer's.

Maureen had four children. Barry - she never referred to him as 'Bazza' - was the first. His dad died of a barbiturate overdose when Barry was two years old. She'd found the boy hard to control as he was growing up, especially when the other kids had started to come along. As a young teenager he'd been in some bother with the police; the usual little bits and pieces, a little thieving and messing about with other people's cars. But he'd always been good to her, and he was a charmer so people liked him. He was popular and locally people were genuinely pleased that he had succeeded.

Maureen herself had been only 17 when he was born. The father of her second child, Joey, was also dead, mown down by a drunken driver in 1988. The fathers of her two daughters were both out there somewhere, although she had not seen nor heard from either of them for years. Gina, the elder of the two, was 15 and rarely went to school. Her interests lay elsewhere. Social services were all over the situation and were starting to make ominous noises about a 'major intervention' in the family; fact was, Maureen had lost control of the child and had no idea how to get it back. Nancy, the youngest, was a sweet 7-year-old who mostly lived in her own world, playing with dolls and dressing up in her mother's clothes. Maureen's current boyfriend, Tom, was an unemployed labourer who didn't much like labouring. After Maureen had given them her brief biography Tom, who had been lurking in the kitchen unsure of his place in the interview and, if it came to that, in Maureen's life, came into the room.

'Hi. I'm Tom. Can I get either of you guys a tea or coffee?'

They both asked for tea and, after Tom had left, continued their questioning.

'How long have you been with Tom?'

'Six months or so. He comes around a few days a week. He's been good with the kids. They like him.'

'Can we look around,' asked Graham, 'have a look at Barry's old room?'

'Yes, of course,' said Maureen. 'After Barry moved out I put his personal stuff in the garage and Joey took over his room so the girls could have one of their own, so there's not much of his stuff about upstairs. The kids are all in their rooms.'

'OK to talk to them?' asked Graham. Maureen nodded yes, like a condemned woman resigned to her fate with little concern about what happened next. Amisha decided not to question her further. She had suffered enough.

Graham made his way up the stairs. The bannisters, in solidarity with the rest of the house, could have stood a lick of paint. At the top, three children sat in their rooms with their thoughts and their loss.

23

Graham knocked gently on the first door he came to. Nothing. He knocked again, more briskly, and then opened it slowly. It was dark inside; the curtains were drawn and the only source of light came from the screen of a laptop, glowing beneath a giant poster of a heavily bearded man who Graham took him to be a celebrity gamer or suchlike. From the floor the mute, slumped, motionless figure behind the screen ripped out a fart as Graham eased himself further into the room, and the stink of it merged with others making up the distinctive fug - of recently smoked weed and dirty socks, scorched underwear and damp towels strewn across the floor. Graham's senses informed him immediately that he was in the lair of the typical British teenage boy.

This would be Joey's room then.

'Hi Joey,' said Graham. The boy did not look up from the screen. After a few moments of silence, he farted again. Graham saw that this was not going to be a walk in the park. He stepped forward a pace, extending a hand. 'Hi Joey. How are you? My name's Graham.'

Still nothing.

'Listen Joey, I'm a policeman. I'm investigating your brother's murder. Can I ask you a few questions?' The boy hunkered down further behind his laptop, increased the volume of the game he was playing, and farted.

Graham's mind went to a book he'd recently read. A WWII memoir. It contained a passage about the severe discipline meted out to privates on parade. No form of expression - not so much as a smirk or grimace, let alone an utterance - was allowed in response to the remorseless barking of the Sergeant Major. But a man could fart, and sometimes fart in commentary on a situation. So the soldiers developed a repertoire of farts, of different kinds, for different occasions and purposes. There was an unwritten rule that this was acceptable; and men with no other options or resources of communication could fart to their heart's content.

It dawned on Graham, looking at the heaped and totally withdrawn figure of the boy before him, that something of the sort might be occurring now. But he had neither the time nor the inclination to hang around in this wretched room, choke on the fug, and try to decode what the boy was saying.

He's either almost catatonic with shock or grief, or just exhibiting the normal behaviour of the weed-smoking teenage internet addict. Or some combination of both... I'm flogging a dead horse here.

He asked himself, as he so often did these days, what H would do. This conundrum was much easier to solve. He crouched down in front of the 17-year-old, got into his face, and said 'Listen to me, soppy bollocks. I haven't got time for all this now. But next time I come down here you're going to talk to me, man to man, and tell me what I want to know. Got me?'

Joey said nothing, but met Graham's eye for the first time. Graham straightened up and fished around in his jacket pocket. He pulled out a card and gave it to the boy. 'In the meantime, if you decide to liven yourself up and get in my good books, give me a bell. The ball's in your court.'

He straightened himself up and moved towards the door.

Right, time to have a crack at the sister.

24

'Hi, you must be Gina.'

The door was half open. Gina sat at the dresser. The room looked like the inside of a French whore's boudoir, and unlike her brother's was very well lit. It was filled with the smell of cheap perfumes and the dresser was stocked with enough makeup to decorate all the dancing girls in 'A Chorus Line.' Clothes littered the floor and what seemed like dozens of miscellaneous high-heeled shoes were piled on top of one another.

Well, well, well…Margate's answer to Imelda Marcos.

Graham opened the door a little wider but stayed on the threshold. A young beauty turned away from her make up mirror to face him. She had large green eyes lavishly decorated with black mascara and long, spidery false lashes. The eyebrows had received a similar amount of attention and the lips were smothered with a healthy portion of bright red lipstick. It should all have looked garish but Graham found it almost shockingly attractive. He was momentarily taken aback by her attractiveness and maturity.

No way is she only 15.

Some might have wondered about the appropriateness of her tarting herself up the day after her brother's death. Graham thought it might be her way of coping. She smiled at him.

'Hello,' she said.

'Hello Gina. I'm Graham Miller-Marchant. I'm a policeman, from New Scotland Yard. Can I talk to you about Bazza?' She looked him in the eye, then at his crotch, then back up again, and ran her tongue across her upper lip.

Well, she's more communicative than her brother, at any rate.

'It's a free country,' she said. Graham pursued the conventional line of questioning, asking her about Bazza's friends, his habits, whether he might have had enemies, his life with the family, his troubles with the police. Gina gave cursory answers, indicating after ten minutes or so that she'd had enough.

'Anyway,' she said with a bored sigh, 'if you ask me you should go and talk to all his girlfriends. A man with that many must have upset someone.'

Jesus, this one's a handful.

Yes, she was certainly more forthcoming than her brother; the withdrawn, somewhat pathetic heap in the adjoining room looked about twelve years old in comparison. Not only did this girl look experienced beyond her years - she acted and thought it as well. Graham was being severely provoked; he did his best, with limited success, to keep his eyes off her low cut blouse, her mostly bare legs, her mouth, her eyes. He tried focusing his gaze on a spot in the centre of her forehead.

'Did you know many of them,' he asked, 'Bazza's girlfriends?'

'Not really. The ones he had before he went to London were never around for long. He got through them pretty quick. If it was female, wasn't nailed down, and had two legs, Bazza would fuck it.'

From the mouths of babes.

'He must have put a few of their boyfriends' noses out of joint then?'

'I'd be surprised if he didn't. Especially once he got on *Britain Blazes Bright.* Girls were throwing themselves at him. Literally.'

Graham's ears perked up: this was starting to get interesting. 'Are you sure you can't remember any names? Of his girlfriends, or any boyfriends?'

'Not really...though if someone was really, really nice to me it might jog my memory,' she said, leaning back on her stool and opening her legs as far as the tightened fabric of her mini skirt would allow.

Graham averted his gaze and closed the door gently. 'This is extremely inappropriate, *extremely inappropriate*,' he thought to himself as he headed back down the stairs with a hard on.

25

H burst through the front door and into the living room wearing the biggest smile Olivia had seen on him in years. She looked him in the eye, with a broadening smile taking over her own face, and nodded at him inquisitively, as if to say 'yes?' H returned the nod with gusto, as if to say 'fucking yes!' Olivia stood up. H barrelled towards her and gave her his strongest, most loving bear hug. They stood together for a full minute, silent, holding one another, swaying slightly.

H broke away first.

'Let's celebrate! I could strangle a scotch.'

'Scotch? Slow down H. You're not allowed to drink scotch…Are you going to tell me what happened?'

'She's sending me back to work. Good old Kasia. God bless the Poles! Next week. Light duties only, she says, for six months.'

'Light duties? What does that mean exactly?' asked Olivia.

'Oh, you know, sitting at a desk, fucking about with a computer. Information gathering, backup for investigations, that sort of thing. For six months, she says. A "probationary period".'

Olivia breathed a sigh of relief - he wouldn't be out on the street until he'd found his feet, eased himself back in, built himself up again. This was wonderful news, just about the best she could have hoped for.

'In her fucking dreams!' H roared. 'I'll just keep my head down for a bit, get my feet under the table, straighten my people out…'

'H! Slow down. Get yourself in hand. We need to talk about this properly…Let's go to the kitchen and have a cup of tea.'

'OK doll, strong…' Olivia finished the sentence 'two sugars. I know H, I know.'

*

Olivia knew her way around a shrink; she'd had plenty of grief in her life, and she was a firm believer in the value of therapy. She told H she wanted it straight, none of his fun and games. She, like Kasia Kotula, needed to know how seriously he had taken it all, and wanted to assess the impact it had made on him.

'So what did you talk about…what made Kasia decide your therapy's over?'

'It's not over…she's making me sign up for another three months' worth of meetings. That's her condition.'

'So she doesn't think you're completely ready yet. OK. But what swung it?'

'I talked to her about Little Ronnie…how I feel about all that. Instead of trying to box clever with her I just let it out…how bad I feel about letting him down, how I can't protect him. What a shit father I am, basically, and how it makes me feel so bad. The guilt. Funny enough I felt better afterwards.'

'So you've finally had a bit of proper therapy. Well done H, I'm proud of you. That must have been hard. Is that how you're going to play it from now on, instead of giving it Johnny Big Bollocks and trying to pull the wool over her eyes?'

'Let's see Liv, Rome wasn't built in a day.'

'No, it certainly wasn't. Not with you on the firm. What about the tablets?'

'She's taking me off them…tapering off with a smaller dose for a couple of weeks. Then that'll be it. And she said no booze. That's a condition as well.'

'So if you're a good boy, and you sit behind your desk nicely, and you don't drink, and you attend your meetings with Kasia, and you don't go on any more bloodletting sprees with vengeful maniacs, in six months you will be rewarded with getting back to work properly, dealing directly, on a day to day basis, with the scum of the earth. Have I got that right?'

'Yep,' said H, his ear-to-ear grin returning. 'Spot on, as ever.'

'Good, so now we know where we are. Well done H.'

'Thanks babes. I tell you what though…'

'What?'

'I…'

'What? Spit it out H.'

'This thing with Ronnie. Little Ronnie. I can't stand it. He's my little boy and I can't help him. I don't know what to do…it's breaking my heart.'

26

Ronnie gave a sincere smile as he hugged his leader with deep affection. As the men embraced Dragusha felt proud of his project, of a job well done, and was surprised to find the hug triggered a feeling of fondness for the young man.

'Basim, you wanted to see me?'

'Yes, Ujku, we need to discuss, sit down. Outside this prison we have many activities. Activities all over world. As you know, our activities are rarely about murder or violence but mostly about smooth functioning of repeat activities. But, sometimes, we need to do some violence. You understand?'

'Yes,' said Ronnie.

'The situation in prison is not as it should. Other groups are preparing to attack us, to kill me, you, our brothers. You know I have spies in many areas here. They tell me plans are advance to move against us.'

'Who would dare? Who would take on Dragusha?'

This news of a threat to his new-found family filled him with righteous anger. He understood intuitively, before it was said, what his mentor was about to ask of him.

'Tell me, Basim. Tell me what I need to do.'

Dragusha had thought deeply about his plans, and how to make the most of his puppet. He already controlled large areas of the prison and could get anything he wanted. But what he had always wanted most was that thing which corrupts the good and attracts the evil, and the more of it you have the more of it you need. Power had always been his drug of choice. Power over Ronnie, power over the prison and power over the man who had put him here. He'd been planning this moment for months. There really was no downside. If Ronnie failed the word would be out that he could manipulate anyone, including the son of "London's

Top Copper", and said copper would be devastated at both the fact and manner of his son's death. A dead or badly wounded Ronnie was a good outcome.

If Ronnie succeeded the outcome was in its way just as good. Dragusha would tighten his control of the prison and strike fear into the hearts of all. He'd keep Ronnie under wraps and save him for another day but make sure his father found out exactly what had happened - exactly what his son had become. Yes, a living, triumphant Ronnie would work as well. He knew Ronnie would have his work cut out, that he had maybe a 25% chance of pulling it off… but now was the time.

His menacing eyes held Ronnie in their grip and a villainous smile spread across his face. It was time to put a pawn in harm's way. His command was short and clear.

'Bring me head of Jack Butcher.'

27

The Butcher lay in his cell, like he had done many hundreds of times before. He was not as relaxed and self-assured as he was in years gone by but remained confident no one in the prison would come after him. He was awake, he was a little tired and he was complacent.

Ronnie walked in, his heart now beating in an uncontrollable rhythm, faster than it had done at his morning's workout, in anticipation of what was about to happen. He'd never been in a situation like this. In one respect, at a deep level, he was discovering that he was like his father. Fear did not grip or paralyse him at the moment of trial. Unconscious and uncontrollable body reactions spurred him on, heightened his awareness and helped zone his concentration in to the task ahead.

The Butcher may have been tired, but shot up from his bed like a rocket as the adrenalin kicked in at the sight of the young man entering his cell with a knife in his right hand. He couldn't believe it was happening, that the young Hawkins kid had summoned up the guts to walk into his cell and have it with him toe to toe.

You have got to be having a fucking laugh.

The life and death struggle began. Ronnie, fuelled by the zealotry of the newly converted, attacked without fear of consequence. He went all in straight away, launching himself at the Butcher and trying to bring the knife up into his throat. The Butcher was older and slower, but a hundred street fights gave him the edge. He was upright and on his feet already; he blocked the blow, knocked the knife from Ronnie's hand and smashed his iron fist into the boy's midriff, forcing out every last drop of air he had in him. Ronnie had never felt anything like it and was bent double by the force of the blow. The Butcher grabbed him by the shoulders, smashed his face into the wall and threw him across the cell. Ronnie lay dazed and confused as a boot smashed down into his face, breaking his nose and forcing a river of blood to stream from his nostrils.

The Butcher had the flavour now; the smell of blood was in in the air and he was in the mood to give the kid a proper mullering.

'You dozy little cunt, you think you can stroll in here and give it to me? Who do you think you're fucking dealing with, some little two-bob prick? You're a bigger wanker than your old man. Get ready to die Hawkins.'

Ronnie staggered to his feet, eyes bulging with hatred and rage. The Butcher lurched towards him and swung. The young man ducked and delivered a blow to the guts that completely knocked the bollocks out of his adversary. Ronnie straightened up and stood tall. He could smell the fear now, and it excited him.

The Butcher didn't go down - he made sure not to go down - but he was hurt, and hurt bad. The pain ruined his judgement and he threw a clumsy, wide haymaker. Again Ronnie ducked, and delivered the mother and father of all upper cuts. The punch, honed by nine months of training and containing the venomous rage of half a lifetime, smashed into Jack Butcher's jaw and broke it into pieces.

Clunk. The sound of the Butcher's teeth crashing into each other was sickening, as the force of the blow reverberated throughout his skull. In all his years as an enforcer he'd never been hit so hard. He was stunned, his legs were buckling. He struggled to stay on his feet. *Don't go down…don't go…*

The huge man began to descend; slowly, inexorably, like a tower block collapsing in a controlled explosion. Ronnie helped him on his way, connecting with another thunderous blow to the jaw.

The Butcher lay beaten, bested.

But Ronnie hadn't finished. Dragusha had asked for this man's head. He found the knife, knelt down and raised it to the Butcher's throat. Was there any doubt, a moment's hesitation, a little of the old Ronnie still flickering in the embers of his vanquished personality? If so a fly on the wall would have been hard pressed to notice it before the killing commenced.

Ronnie stabbed the knife hard into the windpipe. The Butcher thrashed around uncontrollably and tried to beg for mercy, but could only gurgle blood through the widening aperture in his throat. Ronnie redoubled his efforts; he knelt harder on his victim's chest and forced the small knife further round. It got held up somewhat at the rear, finding the spinal column hard going, but after a struggle lasting several minutes it was over. Ronnie held the severed head in his hand and lifted it up above him in an act of triumphant supremacy. His demented face was covered in crimson. The wolf had taken his prey.

No thought of the magnitude of what he had done nor the consequences of his actions filled his mind. He was beyond that now. His thoughts turned only to his need for acknowledgement, to be praised by the man who had made him what he now was.

For the wolf is the strength of the pack, and the pack is the strength of the wolf.

28

Dragusha was in conference with his inner circle when Ronnie bounced into the cell with a circular package wrapped in a blood-soaked blanket, as excited as a little boy who has just put his football kit on in preparation for a kickabout with his dad down the local park. But to the assembled villains encircling their leader he looked more like an Albanian mountain warrior of old; beautiful, wild and savage, offering his victory to his chieftain as he held the trophy above his head.

Dragusha had half expected news of Ronnie's demise and had been planning a ruthless follow up operation with his henchmen. But with the dripping head of his main competitor now in the mix the next steps would be much easier. Any remaining resistance from Jack Butcher's firm would melt immediately. They would accept his terms, or get the same treatment.

Dragusha stared hard at Ronnie, his shark-like eyes penetrating, searching for weak points, anything that suggested Ronnie was not completely immersed in his new identity, anything that suggested he was faking it. He liked what he saw and smiled, like an artist satisfied with his final product. The training was complete, more than complete. Ronnie had exceeded expectations. Dragusha was never one to miss an opportunity; it was time for him now to reflect Ronnie's glory upon himself, and revel in it. Dragusha was a leader to the core, and understood exactly when and where a decent rhetorical flourish was required.

'Brothers, today Ujku has shown great strength and courage. He has entered the domain of our enemies and returned with great prize. He has shown great bravery. His courage and skill no one can doubt.'

Taking the package from Ronnie, Dragusha unwrapped it and held up the head, stared into its dead eyes and spat into the lifeless face. The brothers cheered. There was no doubt Ronnie had done the business. Yet Dragusha was doing more than hyping up the leadership of his firm - he found himself carried away and believing in his own oratory, not only proud that he had created such a seriously useful follower, but genuinely proud of Ronnie himself. He was growing to like the boy more and more. The feelings surprised him, although they would never interfere with a decision on how to use him.

Outside the cell, in the prison at large, Dragusha's minions were already busy, putting the word out that anyone who talked about what had happened in Jack Butcher's cell faced a death sentence. Dragusha didn't want the authorities taking what was now his prize possession from him. There were plenty of more moves to play out. The game had just begun.

He continued with his oratorical tour de force. 'If any of you still doubt, doubt no more. For us he was prepared to die. Ujku now our comrade, he deserve respect and protection. He is one of us. He is our brother.'

The pack cheered louder, seeming to merge into a single entity, carried away by the power of Dragusha's personality, bound together by the blood of the slaughtered enemy.

An image formed in Dragusha's mind. An image of an enemy who this would hurt more than the most fiendish torture, a punishment worse than death itself. There was one person to whom the rule of silence would not apply - he would make sure that one person would learn what had happened today.

The deeds of Ujku would bury themselves deep into the consciousness of Detective Inspector Harry Hawkins - and he would never, ever be free of them.

Part 2

29

Birmingham. Britain's second city, though Manchester disputes the claim. Brum. They called it the 'workshop of the world' once, back when old Britannia ruled the waves. Now it's a sprawling, super-diverse conurbation with two big but underachieving football clubs and a very complex road system. All in all, a place that provides plenty of cover for enterprise and innovation - and skulduggery and monkey business.

The driver of the empty articulated lorry navigating Birmingham's sleepy 1am streets knew this well. The vehicle was clean and not of interest to the police; he had disabled the lorry's satellite navigation and tracker systems and switched off and removed the battery from his phone. He flicked on the wiper blades to clear the late-night drizzle as he manoeuvred the vehicle around the concrete quagmire of spaghetti junction and onto the M6, the big old boy that connects Brum, via the M1, to London and the rest of the country. He shifted gears and moved his speed up to sixty-five miles an hour, five short of the speed limit, and settled unobtrusively into the inside lane. He checked his watch. Bang on time. At this rate he should arrive at his destination before the appointed hour. Better always to err on the side of caution in this line of work.

The lorry was designed to carry intermodal freight containers, which are delivered in standard sizes to container ports all over the world and loaded onto lorries or trains for the final leg of their journey. In fact, since they were first designed in America in the 1950s nearly all the world's goods have been delivered in them. They are the lifeblood of global trade, with millions of them zipping around mostly unseen from A to B to Z, every day of the year, containing almost everything that can be moved; except livestock.

Unloaded, the lorry's engine sounded smooth and easy. The driver checked his rear mirror and flashed his headlights. Nothing but darkness behind and in front of him. Perfect, he thought, as he reached for his flask of coffee. After two and a half hours on uneventful roads the driver reached Sheerness, a small town with a big port, close enough to London to matter. He pulled up in a lorry park overlooking the docks and sat and watched the ships come in.

The one he was interested in docked at 4am, loaded two containers portside and slinked back towards the North Sea.

The driver jumped, with some trepidation, out of his cab and walked across the lorry park, crept to the night-watchman's cabin and slipped the old boy inside an envelope containing two grand. The recipient smiled as he counted the contents, switched off the CCTV, popped the gate to the dock open and went for a little evening constitutional, pulling up his collar against the rain. The driver returned to his lorry, entered the docks and parked in one of the bays beneath the awesome cranes that dominated the seascape. He activated and climbed the metal frame of one of them and expertly loaded the two containers onto the waiting lorry.

The containers were both 2 TEUs, the standard unit of capacity of the worlds shipping containers. In imperial measures that was, more or less, forty feet long, eight feet wide and eight feet six inches high. They had a weight capacity of up to 58,000lbs, but these two were way, way below this; each contained goods weighing only about 3, 300lbs.

30

The lorry trundled out of Sheerness, through the Isle of Sheppey, re-joined the British Mainland and followed the winding A249 to the M2, one of the two motorways that connect London to Kent. The driver shifted gear as he joined the motorway, heading west through Kent towards the M25 London orbital motorway. With a little luck, he thought, he'd make it back to the Birmingham processing centre before the morning traffic kicked in.

A clear dawn was breaking over the English Channel and would soon be finding its way across the Kent downs. The driver could see the shimmer of the rising sun reflecting in his rear-view mirror, just poking its head above the horizon, when he felt a shudder in the engine. It coughed, then jolted, then metal bits rattled and ground together in a manner they were not designed to do. It sounded like two skeletons fornicating on a corrugated iron roof. This was not part of the plan.

This not good.

The driver left the motorway, pulled up on the hard shoulder and took a swig of his coffee. He was now in a state of nervous anxiety. He sprang the bonnet and went to take a look, as if somehow the act of looking was all that was needed to fix an engine that had given up the ghost. He might as well have been looking at plans to build a nuclear reactor, or reading the thoughts of Chairman Mao in Mandarin. He knew how to drive the things but had next to no knowledge of the inner workings of the internal combustion engine.

'Fuck,' he said to himself.

He put the battery back in his phone and called the man in charge of operations.

Fatos Gazjet answered, in expectation of good news.

'Hello. Progress is good?'

'No. Lorry is broken down on M2, few miles west of junction 5.'

'Ok. Stay calm. Check merchandise is OK. I send mechanic.' The driver ended the call, switched off his phone, placed it in his top pocket, and got set to check the merchandise.

The two containers had been customised for their purpose and had specially fitted peep holes. He went into the cab, took out a small step ladder and climbed onto the back of the lorry. He placed the small steps by the containers, climbed to the highest container and opened the peep hole. Everything seemed fine. As he was tracing his steps back down the ladder he saw, out of the corner of his eye, a high performance Land Rover slow down and pull onto the hard shoulder. He craned his neck and fought to contain his horror when he realised it was a police vehicle on motorway patrol.

He jumped from the back of the lorry to welcome the officers. They'd not long started their shift when they'd spotted the lorry and a man climbing up to inspect some containers. Unusual, they thought, to be clambering about on containers on the hard shoulder of a motorway.

PC George Owen - a seasoned old school career PC with twenty-five years' worth of attritional conflict with lorry drivers under his belt - liked to pick his battles. He was for staying in the vehicle until the rumbling and popping in his stomach died down; he was feeling dyspeptic and grisly after one sausage too many during his early, pre-shift breakfast. But riding shotgun with him was Kyle Johnson, fresh out of Hendon Police College, keen as mustard and an absolute dab hand with the vehicle's on-board information and communications platform. He sparked up the automatic number plate recognition gizmo automatically, without thinking, and said 'Come on George, let's have a look at this one...we can have a little poke about while we wait to see if the vehicle is of interest to us. Do you good to stretch your old legs.'

The older man groaned an older man's groan and threw his door open.

The lorry driver came towards them, all smiles and bonhomie as he fronted up.

'Hello, good morning. How you are today officers?'

'We're fine. Having some sort of trouble?' said PC Johnson.

'No, is all OK. Mechanic on way.'

'Everything tickety-boo with your load?'

'Huh?'

'You were up checking your load. Anything wrong?'

'Oh no. Always like to check. Make sure secure,' said the driver.

'Can we see your papers please sir, check what load you're carrying?'

The driver walked to his cab on watery legs. His heart was accelerating and his breathing became short and shallow as he suppressed the shakes. But he worked for an efficient organisation and the papers were in good order. The goods, so it appeared, belonged to a senior civil servant and his family of expats returning home after a five-year stint in Saudi Arabia.

'Here George,' said the young gun, 'looks like one of these babies contains a red Mercedes Sport; isn't that top of your wish list for when you make commissioner? Shall we open her up and have a gander?'

The lorry driver had stayed in the cab; he took a gun out from under his seat. He was just a driver, not a major figure, not even a soldier anymore. But he knew, on pain of death, that the merchandise had to be protected. He would do whatever it took: his own life depended on it.

The older policeman laughed heartily. 'No, you're alright son. Not now. I'll wait until I can buy my own.'

The driver tucked the gun away just before PC Johnson returned to the cab window to give back the papers. 'Have a good day sir,' he said, 'stay safe.' He strolled back to his vehicle and fiddled about with something on the front console the lorry driver couldn't see... and the Land Rover pulled away.

The driver sat until the police were out of sight and until his heart had returned to a normal beat, which took significantly longer. He then returned to the back of the lorry and checked the peep hole of the second container. He stood transfixed for several moments, while his stomach fell through his legs, hardly believing what his eyes told him. The containers were airtight but this one, or so he thought, had been adjusted to allow a good flow of oxygen. Had they been directed to the wrong container? He had no idea.

He closed the peep hole, went to the nearside of the lorry and threw his guts up onto the hard shoulder. After he'd emptied his stomach of all its contents he fell to his knees and kissed the ground, looked up at the skies and prayed for the souls of the ten people in the intermodal container on the back of his articulated lorry, the ten dead souls who had been guaranteed a life of hope, the ten poor wretches who had each scraped together their worldly possessions to raise the several thousand pounds required to build a new life in the promised land.

'May God have mercy,' he said.

31

By early morning there was not a cloud in the sky and the blue horizon looked warm and welcoming. H decided to get a cab on his first day back and nab another car from the Met's carpool - him and Olivia would need two cars again now he was back at work. He jumped out of his taxi and asked the cabbie what the damage was. He was asked for sixty pounds, but gave the driver a nifty and some advice about not overcharging his customers.

He wanted to walk the last part of his journey to soak up the atmosphere; past St James's Park tube station, right down Tothill St. and then another right down Broadway. His heart raced with a mixture of excitement and apprehension when the New Scotland Yard building came into full view.

H recognized and winked at one of the officers of the armed protection group that surround the building before navigating the dull concrete barriers, flashing his pass at the security guards and bounding up the stairs to the fourth floor, home of the murder squad. His murder squad. He thrust open the doors and careered into the open plan office. He felt like he'd come home.

It was impossible not to notice him as he swaggered through his workplace on his way to Hilary Stone's office and his 10am appointment. Eyes looked up and heads turned, drawn inexorably to the force of nature that had re-emerged like a hungry bear breaking out of hibernation, in need of sustenance, in search of prey. Kasia had told him to stay calm on his return to work, keep a low profile, but his nature was his nature. He was only ten seconds in the room and already as inconspicuous as a tarantula on the back of your hand. The office burst into a spontaneous round of applause. The prodigal son had returned.

H smiled and waved as he made his way across the office and gave a confident rat-a-tat-tat on Hilary Stone's office door.

'Come in.'

H was all smiles and first-day-at-school best behaviour – hair swept back, shoes shiny, tie done up nice and straight - as he entered the office.

'Hello ma'am.'

'Ah, Detective Inspector Hawkins, there you are! Lovely to see you.'

She paused for a beat, smiling demurely and letting him wait, before breaking out in a huge grin and changing tone completely: 'Bloody hell H, welcome back! How the hell have you been?'

H was buzzing. All those months slumped on the couch in front of the TV having his intelligence insulted seemed to already belong to the past. He was sitting on several months' worth of frustration and pent-up energy. He skipped the small talk and got straight to it.

'On top of the world ma'am, thank you very much. Delighted to be back. What have you got for me?'

'Patience Inspector, remember you've only been signed off for light duties. We're not letting you loose on your adoring public just yet,' she joked.

Blimey, she's found a sense of humour.

'I thought we'd start you off doing some background checks on Bazza Wishbone's friends and associates. It's all about Bazza at the moment - top priority. We can't be having global celebrities slaughtered at the Ritz, can we? Anyway, Graham's got a theory about a jealous boyfriend or some sort of resentful loner. Go through what we've got so far - if anything presses your buttons let Graham know and he and Amisha will do the interviews. How does that sound?'

H had no problem working for Graham, as long as it was a short term arrangement. He was gagging to get back on the street, as itchy as a horny rapper eyeing up the female extras at his video shoot, but knew he had to play the game. Bide his time.

'Ok ma'am, perfect. I'll have a word with Graham and get right on it.'

H was already moving towards the door when Hilary added a note of caution.

'H, I am genuinely pleased to have you back. Remember, Rome wasn't built in a day. Easy does it.'

'Yes ma'am, understood.'

Rome may not have been built in a day but if it was started on a Monday and H was running the show in his current mood it would have been done and dusted by Tuesday afternoon. As he exited the office Amisha and Graham were waiting outside to greet him. Hugs and kisses all round.

'I can't believe you're back guv. I'm so, so pleased to see you here,' said Amisha.

'Alright Ames, slow down with the "guv" stuff, will you?' H said with a sly grin, 'I'm only here doing the donkey work for Graham. Let's not get too carried away.'

Graham felt a surge of embarrassment; having the great man work for him didn't feel right. H noticed his body language reveal his unease but was in no mood to add to Graham's discomfort.

'Come on Graham, guv, show me the files and we'll crack on.'

32

H worked his way into his desk - it seemed to have shrunk a bit since the last time he'd performed the operation - and sparked up his computer. Graham pointed him to an electronic folder on his desktop - a big collection of documents and other bits and pieces relating to the team's enquiries so far. It seemed to contain the coroner's report, interviews with Ritz guests and employees, Jacynta Packington, Bazza Wishbone's family, friends and other Margate types, a few scraps of CCTV footage and some stuff taken from social media that Graham and Amisha had decided was of interest.

Fuck this for a game of soldiers.

H swung his chair around and surveyed the office, looking for a likely candidate for the position of H's little helper. It didn't look like there were going to be too many options.

Best avoid the ladies, they tend to take a dim view of being pestered by the likes of me these days.

A little manbot has got to be the favourite.

There were a lot of new faces about, and they seemed to be getting younger. All beavering away, tippety-tap, faces spellbound in the glow of their screens. H wondered how they stood it, day after day. And then got their faces straight into their giant plastic phones as soon as their shift was over. It was all beyond him.

He kept on scanning, reading faces, and...bingo! - a figure hunched over a desk on the other side of the room: glistening high-volume coiffure, hipster beard, serious dark-rimmed glasses, shiny blue suit, thin as a rake, not a day over 25.

He'll do. He'll do nicely.

'Alright my son? Detective Inspector Harry Hawkins said, wheeling across the room and extending his hand, 'I don't believe I've had the pleasure. Been with us long?'

'Six months now sir,' said Detective Constable Andrew Glass, his voice quaking a little.

'Good man. All settled in now then?'

'Yes guv, I…'

'Right you are then Andrew. Listen, do me a favour son - I need this lot on paper. I can't sit here trying to make sense of it all on a screen, it'll make my eyes bleed. It's all in the folder marked "H1" on this pendrive. Get that printed out for me will you? Quick as you like.'

'But sir, the use of pendrives has been banned for security reasons. You'll need to find a different…'

'Don't worry about all that bollocks, if anyone gives you grief just point them in my direction.'

He handed over the pendrive and wheeled towards the coffee corner like a four-year-old boy on his birthday, buzzing along on his new tricycle.

*

Forty-five minutes later a bulging package landed on H's desk. He looked up from the football news, took off his jacket, rolled up his sleeves and started with the coroner's report. Toby Mortimer and his team had done their usual meticulous job; it was all minute detail, dry as a bone. Not the sexiest document H had ever read; all this forensic detail bored him. Over the years H had done it all, seen it all, bought the t-shirt, and bought another one when the first one wore out. Nothing could surprise him anymore.

But he was struck by the image of half a face seemingly clinging onto what was left of an exploded skull. It wasn't the worst thing he'd ever seen, not by a long chalk, but it was one of the most grimly macabre. He tried to get inside the mind, the motivations, the senses, the body of the killer. Giving a helpless, kneeling victim one barrel of a sawn-off, straight into the nut, from only inches away…this has got to be some sort of psychopath, someone with a background in very serious violence, who can dish it out with casual ease. And he'd wanted to look into the eyes of Wishbone - H was not about to call him 'Bazza,' like everyone else - at close quarters as he pulled the trigger. A ruthless psychopath - and, H noted, a very controlled one.

One barrel. He only gave the poor bastard one barrel. Why?

H looked again at the photos of Svitlana Kovalenko, on the threshold of the lift, and felt the usual tug at the heart he always did at the sight of a murdered woman. Her face was still in one piece. No exploding heads this time around; the killer had given her the other barrel straight in the guts. H ran through the sequence of events in his mind.

One barrel each. No reloading. Everything planned, no fucking about. In and out in not much more than a minute.

He looked through the interview transcripts including Jacynta Packington's. Amisha and Graham had started to put together a picture of the social circle she'd shared with Wishbone. It included a good number of the movers and shakers of the London celebrity scene, H was coming to learn, as well as various hangers-on and moochers-about. Of interest, he thought, were Romeo Ferrara the footballer, who had a bit of form as a sex-pest; Wishbone's manager Blandish, an egotistic, ruthless bastard if ever there was one; and Tarquin de Montfort - did people have names like that? - who for H was a ridiculous figure from another world.

It was not a world he'd ever enjoyed visiting. But he was going to have to have a good look at it soon.

33

H had saved the most irritating section in the folder for last. Page after page of Twitter printouts - of *tweets.*

He had always lived in the flesh and blood world. The world of eye-to-eye contact, where you could size someone up and get an angle on them by using your judgement and intuition and where you could deal with them, if they needed dealing with, in the here and now. He could hardly believe what Amisha had told him, when she first came on board, about tweeting, and how important it was now.

But he'd soon got the message when Joey Jupiter went after him, using Twitter and other online media to ridicule him and turn him into a public laughing stock. Jupiter, as far as H was concerned, was a new kind of person who had emerged from the social media revolution; shallow and self-righteous yet somehow taken seriously, given so many people followed his tweets and read what he put on his blog. Jupiter had come after him during the investigation into the bloodbath in St James' Park and H saw then that whatever else it could be used for, social media had created a new type of mob rule, in which spineless little mongrels could get mouthy and threatening from behind their little plastic toys without any comeback.

He took a deep breath and waded in. Amisha had highlighted all the sections she thought were worth a look, but H started at the beginning and tried to work through everything methodically. He was astonished, before he got to the end of the first page, at the barrage of abuse, hate and death threats that had been sent Wishbone's way. To start with H felt himself to be in the presence of warped but mostly childish minds, but felt himself descending, by degrees, into a hellish sewer of jealousy and rage.

'Light duties,' Kasia said. 'Light duties.' *This is a fucking nightmare.*

'Andrew!' H roared, swivelling in his chair, 'Over here son, if you don't mind.'

*

H got back from the pub - orange juice only, but a very large helping of Shepherd's Pie eased the pain - and resumed his work. He'd had Detective Constable Glass highlight only those tweets in which someone had made an actual death threat to Wishbone, and mark up those who'd made more than one. This boiled it down to a list of 148 individuals.

He began to go through them, starting with those who had tweeted *#Bazzamustdie*. These would-be hard nuts and psychopaths were going to blow him up, cut his pretty little face to pieces, bomb his mum's flat, do him with acid… on it went, page after page. H could see no rhyme, reason or pattern to any of it but did see, in the end, an image in his mind of a cabal of cackling 15-year-old boys with a big bag of weed and an evening to kill. He couldn't take it seriously. And some of it was funny; H had always loved a bit of gallows humour. He was especially taken by some of the names they used.

He bundled the papers up, swung by the refreshments corner, made a strong tea and a coffee and wandered over to Detective Constable Glass' desk.

'Any chance I can pick your brains for a minute or two please Andrew?' he said, remembering something Kasia had said about 'courtesy' and 'tone'.

Andrew was secretly thrilled he'd been singled out by the big man. He'd heard so much about him and wanted to get closer, see him in action.

'Absolutely, guv. How can I help?'

'It's these Twitter death threats you marked up for me. I don't know how all this works…would you say all this is "normal'?

'Afraid so guv - celebrities and people in the public eye get this all the time now. Standard.'

'I know, I had a basin full myself last year. Or so Amisha tells me. But the death threats? Any idea how many of them ever amount to anything?'

'Very few, I should say guv. Very few. It's mostly kids and harmless oddballs.'

H found himself wishing, not for the first time, that personal computing and smartphones had never been invented.

'I did notice one thing though, guv, after I just looked at the tweets. I was just going to come over and mention it to you.'

'I'm all ears, Andrew.'

'Well, I noticed that a couple of the handles on the list - you know, the usernames - were taken from former members of *Big Erection*.'

H's face was a picture of blankness; it was as blank as the day is long.

'You know guv, *Big Erection*. The band Bazza Wishbone was with before he made it on *Britain Blazes Bright* and Nigel Blandish snapped him up.'

'Big Erection? Big Erection? Are you taking the piss Andrew?'

'No guv, that's what they called themselves. Seriously. But think about it…what if these two characters are the real Markey Yardlong and Deano Rising? Are the guys from Big Erection? That would be of interest, wouldn't it, given what happened?'

'What happened?' said H.

'Well, the big bust-up, the big betrayal. The Big Erection guys were all over the media, bitching and moaning about Bazza. A year or two ago.'

'Yes, that is of interest Andrew. Do you know how to connect these Twitter accounts to real people?'

'Of course.'

'Good man,' said H. 'Make it so. Please.'

34

Andrew had hit pay dirt on the Big Erection boys, and traced the two offending Twitter accounts in question to Mark Little and Dean Stephens, both 21 years old, both of Margate. H - who must have been one of the very few people in Britain not to have known it already - listened intently as Andrew told him the sorry tale.

It was almost too much of a cliché to be true. The five Margate schoolboys, in and out of trouble with the law and heading for nowhere, are inspired by a dedicated music teacher to start singing. They are redeemed and kept off the streets by their love of song and the attention of the ladies. They get better and better at their five-part harmonies, though none of them can really sing as such, and put together their standard hardboiled-street-player personae. They get their sob-stories straight – the broken families, the truanting from school and lives of petty crime, the drugs and booze, the lack of opportunities for people like them. The lack of hope.

But hope they find: Barry O'Doherty becomes Bazza Wishbone; Mark Little becomes Markey Yardlong; Dean Stephens becomes Deano Rising; Lee Hugman becomes Joey Hungman; and Jay McCleary becomes Johnson Hard.

They head up to the metropolis and the open audition for *Britain Blazes Bright.* They make it onto the stage; they spread their legs and fold their arms and glower at the audience. They pop their bodies and sing their little hearts out. But the panel don't like them; they've seen it all before. Big Erection are dismissed from the stage to howls of outrage from the audience, but backstage an emissary from Nigel Blandish collars Bazza and tells him the great man would like a word, in private.

And so the real drama begins: the evil London svengali drives a wedge between the lifelong friends, splits them up and takes the one he wants. *This one's got something, I'll have him.* The other four slouch back, tails between their legs, to Margate, with broken and venomous hearts. They were almost there…they could almost smell it. But Blandish has pulled the rug from under their feet and fucked them. And Bazza has betrayed them.

*

The media reaction in the aftermath of the Big Erection thing was huge, Andrew told H.

'For a month or so you could hardly move without seeing the boys' faces. "They wuz robbed", was the general sentiment. But then the story faded, as they do, and a few months later Blandish unveiled Bazza and announced that he would be his next big project. The rest is history.'

'So all these death threats, all that palaver, when did that start in earnest?' H asked.

'Looking at them now it seems they began pretty much straight away, but the more successful Bazza became the more they seemed to have ramped it up. Little and Stephens - or I should say Yardlong and Rising.'

'OK, got it. Good work Andrew. So now we know where we are,' said H.

He scanned, yet again, the digest of the two boys' best work that Andrew had put together. His eyes came to rest on one of the least hysterical and most recent efforts, posted by Mark Little three days before Wishbone was murdered:

'Hope you're enjoying the high life, traitor. Make the most of it. Your pretty face is going to hell.'

35

Kasia Kotula kicked off her shoes and collapsed onto her sofa with a glass of white wine and her laptop. It had been a long day, and she was not yet finished. She still had to wrap up her case notes on Detective Inspector Harry Hawkins.

They'd been on quite a journey together, and she would miss him. She'd found him to be an attractive and courageous man. She respected his unyielding, if unwieldy moral compass, and was impressed with the way in which he'd managed to work on year after year under enormous pressure without buckling. Above all he was strong and dignified, and Kasia valued strength and dignity above all in a man.

She sparked up the laptop and opened the Hawkins file. But before getting down to work she went online and brought up Joey Jupiter's blog. She'd been doing this for weeks now, since it had come up in one of her sessions with the big man, and monitored it for any mention of 'London's Top Copper!'

CELEBRATION DAY

> Sound the fanfare! Hang out the bunting! Raise Tower Bridge and let the flotillas pass! Tremendous news has reached us: this week sees the return of the mighty H. Yes, it's true - 'London's Top Copper' is to be restored to his adoring public. We can all now rest easy in our beds once again, secure in the knowledge that our hero is out there, sleuthing for all he is worth and keeping the streets of the capital safe for us all.

It has been decided that the 'big man', having undergone intensive therapy and psychological testing for the best part of a year, has now recovered his equilibrium and is ready to return to the fray. It is this blog's most fervent hope that he will be put straight onto the Bazza Wishbone case. Who better to untangle the warped world in which Bazza lived, with its endless parade of predators and possible suspects: the wheeler-dealers, the celebrity darlings, the crazed adoring fans, the drug dealers, the manipulative media honchos, the spurned lovers, the embittered former friends, the tattooed superstar footballers, the jealous boyfriends…

This is clearly a job for the Met's top man. A man who can cut through the confusion and bring to the problem at hand the full array of his extraordinary qualities: his famous 'copper's instincts'; his years of experience; his deep knowledge of human nature; his fearlessness; his unparalleled knowledge of the great metropolis; his criminal friends, his parenting skills; his fuzzy, booze-pickled mind; his addiction to extreme violence; his finely-honed ability to leave chaos, destruction and unanswered questions in his wake.

Cometh the hour, cometh the man.

36

The driver sat slumped in his cab. For how long he didn't know. The shock took some time to work its way through his system. His mind filled with images of dead bodies, things he had witnessed during the breakup of Yugoslavia in the 1990s, when men of evil had gained the upper hand and men like him had followed them, and done what they were told. The way that men like him always do.

He had thought all that was behind him.

I am working man now. I drive truck. I take my money, I send it home. I keep low profile…

He fought with the knot of dread in his stomach and raised his head, to see what he could see.

The motorway was now thick with traffic. The day was in full swing and the sun's rays bathed the driver's cab with a golden sunlight which filled his eyes and made him blink; but he remained motionless, frozen with dread. There was a rapping on the door, passenger side. Adrenalin surged through his body; he reached unthinkingly for his gun and got down low in his seat, ready to fire. The door opened sharply. It was the mechanic.

'Bonnet is open,' said the driver.

The mechanic checked the engine and proffered his judgement:

'We will need tow. Engine is fucked.'

The driver was in deep and had no idea what to do. This was way above his pay grade; he was no more than the shit on the shoe of the big guys, and this was a matter for the chief executive. But he had no idea who the chief executive of the organization he worked for was. All he knew is that whoever they were they would not look kindly on him. Despite his sympathy for the ten dead souls at the rear of his vehicle his mind was moving quickly from shock to consideration of his personal situation, to his own self-preservation. He was up shit creek without a paddle. If he played this wrong, he would be joining his cargo in the afterlife in the very near future. No more money for his wife and three kids back home. No more him.

He couldn't put it off any longer. He only had one contact. He took out his mobile and called Fatos Gazjet again.

'We have problem.'

'What kind of problem. Mechanic will soon arrive.'

'Mechanic is here. We need tow.'

Fatos was not a natural leader and flew immediately from agitation to anger. He'd been doing his best to keep the firm ticking over while Dragusha was on remand, denied bail and awaiting trial at Her Majesty's pleasure. Fatos was a half-decent number two, largely because of his close, war-forged connection to Dragusha, who the younger guys still regarded with awe. But having the crown on his head, even temporarily, pulled his spirits down like a lead weight. He wasn't up to it.

The bosses had considered replacing Fatos, but were wary of putting someone in place capable of challenging Dragusha as top dog. That might end badly, and destabilise things. So as long as Fatos and Dragusha were in constant contact and all the major decisions went through Dragusha they thought the operation would be stable. Business was business.

Fatos roared like a bull and vented his frustration. Then he calmed down a little, and tried to think through what Basim would do.

The ship had been on time; everything had been going to plan. Supplies inside the containers would have only just run out. He didn't have a vehicle capable of towing the lorry so he would have to hire one, even if it meant paying through the nose. He could find someone to drive it. If he could get a tow there today the lorry could make the processing centre by early evening things were not actually that bad.

Maybe he'd over-reacted.

On the other end of the line the driver steeled himself. He wasn't good at giving bad news, and Fatos's initial response had already left him shaking. He wanted the earth to open up and swallow him. He gulped as his mouth went dry.

'There's more,' he said.

'What more?'

'Is problem with one container… all merchandise is dead.'

37

Fatos sat in his caravan, hammering a bottle of rakia and clutching at the palpitations in his chest. Dragusha had been informed of the situation - all he could do now was wait for orders. The cars hissed past his window as he flung it open, desperate for air. He surveyed the scene; a slum of a place known as The Island in the middle of a one-way system in Bermondsey, deepest south east London. A triangular shaped travellers site that went unnoticed or ignored by the traffic that roared past it. The firm was doing well, making plenty of money. The feud with the Russians had died down after some high-level negotiations he knew little about. There had been some talk of moving to more illustrious surroundings. But Dragusha had nixed it; there was nowhere better, as a base of illegal operations, than a site in the middle of London where your average copper feared to tread.

Fatos had managed to bring in several shipments of migrants in Dragusha's absence and the process had been functioning perfectly. It was a business that reached far and wide across the whole of Europe and beyond. It had been set up, like all highly successful underworld activities, to be smooth and readily repeatable. It was at the top end of the people smuggling business - several thousand pounds sterling per head. To date it had worked well, as efficient as putting packs of coffee together on a well-oiled conveyor belt, and all Fatos had to do was make sure it didn't get jammed. There were kosher papers for the immigrants, authentic shipping documents, processing centres where the new arrivals were briefed and provided with details of where and how to find casual work, translators to help gain access to officialdom. It was easy money.

Fatos paced up and down the caravan, took another long hit of the rakia and sat down again. He picked up a copy of

The Sun and skim-read an article about the background of Bazza Wishbone, the recently deceased celebrity, and how his girlfriend had been coping with the loss. Above the article there was a picture of her looking beautiful but sad and distant, he thought.

Everyone has their troubles…even beautiful model.

He tossed the newspaper aside, drained the bottle and moved to the kitchen area of the hovel he called home. He opened a cupboard and took out another bottle.

Fact was he'd been under more pressure than usual lately. A group of young hotheads from the old country, newly arrived and eager to get a taste of the London action, had been testing his authority and patience severely. Zef Fejzullah, Idriz Rehexpi and Leka Agolli were a real handful and he was struggling to keep them under control. He knew they'd been doing private drug deals and making their own connections, in contravention of all the organisation's rules. They were treating the chain of command as if it didn't exist. He was expected to deal with local difficulties and if he reported upwards that he couldn't keep the lid on a few young tearaways he'd become a laughing stock.

Zef, a potent and lethal combination of impulsiveness, wildness and a confidence that seemed to far exceed his nineteen years, walked into the caravan without knocking, showing no respect whatsoever. Such behaviour, Fatos knew for certain, would never happen if Dragusha were around. He could see the look of disdain in Zef's eyes. But before Zef could speak Fatos' response was framed by the pressure he was feeling about the broken down lorry.

'Fuck off now. Next time, if you enter without knocking I blow your fucking brains out.' Zef laughed as he turned and left the caravan.

Fatos' phone rang; his palms were sweating so much it almost fell out of his hands.

'Update me on the issue,' said Dragusha. 'Be precise, be careful with your words.'

Fatos knew better than anyone that the big man expected honesty and directness from his subordinates. No beating about the bush; just facts.

'Lorry driver is still broken down on M2. He is on hard shoulder. Am arranging a tow. It seems air pockets were sealed on one container. Not sure how or why. All merchandise kaput. We have problem of disposal.'

Dragusha did not bat an eyelid; he was all business, as cold as the north side of a gravestone in January. The deaths of ten innocents meant no more to him than the loss of any other kind of merchandise, and less than some. His immediate thought, and responsibility, concerned the protection of the income stream.

This was a delicate matter. Getting rid of the of the bodies in a densely populated region like the south east of England would not be simple. And the survivors - or potential witnesses - in the second container could never be trusted to keep quiet about what and who they had seen. They would have to go. And he had the firm's brand to think about. He would need to prevent the rumour mill starting up, so secrecy and swiftness were paramount.

He asked a few more questions about the exact location of the lorry, when the tow truck would arrive, who the driver was, who would drive the tow truck. Armed with further knowledge of the situation he gave his instructions.

'Fatos, listen to me carefully now my friend. Pick five trusted men. Tell them you have mission of which they must never talk. Remind them of their oaths.'

Dragusha continued with his instructions. He briefly considered suffocating the living ten and having the containers returned to sea and thrown overboard, but this would take time to arrange and increase the risk of discovery before the disposal of the merchandise. So he advised the ten be kept alive, for now, and gave the dimensions of the grave that was to be dug, and the method of execution of the living cargo and the lorry driver - straight out of the Balkan Wars playbook. He then turned his attention to how to get the containers back out to sea and dropped after the executions were completed. They didn't cost that much in the great scheme of things and DNA had a nasty habit of sticking around. Dragusha was calm and matter of fact as he issued his instructions, like a company chairman at an annual board meeting announcing strategy for the coming year.

Fatos' palms were sweating again. He didn't want to go this route. Not again. 'Are you...'

The question was halted before it was complete.

'I gave you instructions Fatos. They are very clear. Follow them,' said Dragusha.

He ended the call and turned to the trusted lieutenant sitting beside him, who'd been listening in.

'Ujku, things are not going well for our brothers outside. We must help them,' he said, as he punched one more number into his burner.

38

The grey Mondeo - nothing fancy, Dragusha always said, only use cars nobody will notice or remember - and a tow truck were making their way down the M2 towards a broken down articulated lorry carrying a load of ten dead people and ten living people. In the tow truck were two hardened grizzlers Fatos had known forever - blood brothers from the old days. He trusted them completely. Fatos himself was behind the wheel of the Mondeo, accompanied by Zef, Idriz and Leka. He'd selected them partly because they were true inner circle, nephews and cousins of the bosses back home, and partly because he thought the experience would sober them up, make them understand this was a serious business; they were here to work, not party their way across London. They needed to be blooded, matured. So here they were, laughing and joking on their way to do something they thought would be a notch on their belts, delighted to have been chosen for the mission, on which they had been fully briefed.

Dragusha had told Fatos to make a judgement call about the best people to take, and the number two had powered through the rakia and made it.

'Up ahead,' said Zef, as he spotted the lorry, stranded like a beached whale on the hard shoulder. Fatos indicated and pulled up behind the lorry. The tow truck drove on by and pulled up in front.

The driver was nervous. He had an awful sinking feeling as they all pulled up, and wished the ground would just open up and swallow him. He was way, way out of his depth. He wasn't, and could never be, part of the inner sanctum. A driver was just a driver. Would they trust him to keep quiet about this? Violence wasn't in him the way it would be in the men who he saw get out of the vehicles, all smiles and greetings and backslapping like he was a long lost friend.

The younger guys lounged against the Mondeo, smoking and laughing, or rather baying, as the elder men secured the tow truck to the lorry while thousands of cars sped by, their drivers taking little notice of the cluster of men and vehicles on the hard shoulder, oblivious to the fact that they were yards away from a death convoy.

'Does mechanic we sent know of merchandise?' asked Fatos.

'No, I say nothing,' replied the driver.

'Good, good man. You have done well my brother,' said Fatos, putting him at his ease, relieved that there was one less problem to worry about.

Fatos paid off the mechanic and sent him on his way. After the tow truck was secured he left Zef to drive the Mondeo and clambered into the lorry's passenger seat. The driver's hands shook; it took all he had to stop his voice from quivering like a nervous schoolboy's.

'Where we are going?' he asked.

'Not sure,' said Fatos, 'need to think.'

39

Fatos sat in the cab of the lorry, almost motionless. Behind him, he knew, were ten dead souls and ten more people now clinging to life by the slenderest of threads, if they but knew it. He considered his options. England was officially the most densely populated major country in Europe, with around four hundred and twenty people per square kilometre. Where, these days, on this little island, could you dig a mass grave and dispose of corpses in the middle of the day? The highlands of Scotland, maybe, where population density fell to around ten people per square kilometre. The chances of tucking twenty cadavers away in the highlands were pretty good. But the highlands of Scotland were a long way off, and Fatos was in a state of high anxiety as he scrawled through the sketchy maps of Kent on his phone.

'Get proper map,' Dragusha had told him, 'This very important - get proper Ordnance Survey map.'

Fatos had said he would but time, and limited patience, had been against him.

Where the fuck I get proper map now? Phone is good. I use phone.

Kent is the most south easterly county in England, next to London, bounded on the north by the River Thames and the east by the English Channel. The maps seemed to reveal, as far as Fatos could tell, a varied landscape with low-lying clay marshlands and high ridges dominated by an upper layer of chalk. Both types of landscape might make good graves, in the right circumstances, but one thing mitigated heavily against them - they were completely exposed - and if there was one thing in this world Fatos didn't want right now it was to be exposed.

He thought about the river or the sea, just dump them and get out fast. But the bodies would certainly be discovered and Dragusha's instructions were very clear:

Silencers on pistols. Deep grave. No fires. Bury bodies at night. Limestone on top.

What fuck am I going to do?

Fatos studied the phone intently, looking for the answer to his logistical nightmare. His mind went back to previous missions similar to this, in the old country with Dragusha, to the days when slaughtering and disposing of dead bodies was their daily meat and drink. A forest, he thought.

Forests good…yes, forests good.

He swiped and scrolled on and soon discovered that Kent still had, despite its highly cultivated landscape, forest coverage of around 10 per cent. One of the largest areas was Bedgebury Forest, on the borders of the county. He entered the destination into his phone. The driver watched his hand shaking as he pressed the 'request directions' button.

While the request made its way to the nearest phone mast and thence onto a satellite somewhere in space Fatos untrousered his bottle of rakia and hammered the contents, like a thirsty marathon runner reaching a water station at the twenty-mile mark. By the time he'd finished gulping and gargling the answer to his question had pinged back. It was now early evening; the sun had moved across the skies and started its westerly descent. Its rays made their way into the cab and reflected back from his screen, the information he craved obscured by light. He readjusted his body to block out the rays. The answer was one hour and fifteen minutes.

The forest looked like there was plenty of access to what he hoped would be plenty of obscure areas. He needed to arrive much later, under cover of darkness, but he couldn't hang about on the hard shoulder much longer. The driver had told him the police had already been sniffing about.

He summoned Zef to his window and spat out his orders with as much bravado as he could muster, pretending he had control of the situation, that he had a plan.

'Go to this area, check out landscape, find best place where no people, but lorry can access.'

Fatos was a bad bluffer. The driver sensed his fear. The uncertainty, the edginess, was feeding his own, magnifying it. Zef also sensed it and thought that maybe he should be the one running the show.

'He fucking useless, this old man. He has no fucking clue,' said Zef to his young friends, as he pulled from the hard shoulder onto the motorway with a near total disregard for the flow of traffic, quickly shifting through the gears and blasting onto the fast lane like he was still back in his caravan playing Grand Theft Auto.

*

Bedgebury Forest is managed by the Forestry Commission. In common with most of England's Forests it was a tightly managed place, used extensively for walking, running and horse riding. Fatos didn't know this. He didn't think to check.

Forest is good.

Zef's assessment was pretty close to the mark.

'Where we go now?' asked the driver of the tow truck.

'Drive up and down motorway, until darkness comes. Keep to speed limit,' said Fatos. As the two men being pulled by the truck started their journey it was unclear which of them was the more anxious and out of his depth. Fatos searched his weary mind for a clue as to what Dragusha would do now, and remembered a fragment from one of his mentor's man-management talks: 'Always keep enemies and victims close until time comes. Keep them calm.'

He turned to the lorry driver: 'Relax, my brother; we solve problem soon.'

40

H was moving fast. He pulled out all the stops and had the Big Erection boys picked up and brought in by the evening of his first day back, and stayed around until they arrived. He sat back in his chair, behind the one-way glass of the interview room, and studied the face and body language of Mark Little. The boy squirmed and wriggled in his chair, his jaw working overtime, in absolute panic, high anxiety all over his face, like a twelve-year-old of H's generation waiting outside the headmaster's office for his first full-scale bollocking. The tattoos on his hands and neck made him look less like a hardened foot soldier of the Russian mafia than a little boy who'd got his mum to buy him a packet of temporary stick-ons in the corner shop.

Amisha and Graham entered the room and sat down together on the other side of the table. Little was joined by his brief.

'Put it on them straight away,' H had told them, 'full on. No fucking about. Put them under pressure and see how they react…no need to take all day about it. I'll be watching.'

Graham did the usual with the voice recording device and kicked things off: 'Right then, Mark - or is it Markey?'

'Mark,' said Little, weakly.

'Thanks for coming in. We've not arrested you, or placed you under caution, or anything else. You're here at our request to help us with our enquiries, correct?'

'Yes.'

'OK. Thing is, Mark, we've been having a look at some of the tweets you sent Bazza Wishbone. You and Deano. Some of them don't make pretty reading.' Graham thumbed through his sheaf. '"You're a fucking dead man, you traitorous scumbag", "Get ready to go to hell, Judas, it won't be long now", "Wait until the acid rain of vengeance hits your face, pretty boy"'

'I could go on,' said Graham. 'There's an interesting mix of modes and registers here Mark - I can see not all your time in school was wasted. But what are we to make of them?'

'I…we're just angry. We were venting. Bazza and Blandish stitched us up and now we've got nothing. We had to do something. We were almost there and now we've got nothing at all.'

'You've been in a bit of trouble with the police in Margate, I see,' said Amisha. 'Is that right? Common assault, drunk and disorderly, criminal damage, fair bit of drug stuff.'

'No, not drugs, legal highs. Black Mamba, stuff like that. I…'

'OK, let's just stick with the common assault then. A violent man, are you Mark?'

'Not really. I've just got into a couple of things when I've been out of my head.'

'Were you out of your head the night you went after Bazza, Mark?'

'I never went after Bazza…you don't think…for God's sake…'

Amisha and Graham let him stew for a bit. He piped up again of his own accord.

'Look at my record, it's just silly little bits and pieces. No violence, I've never been into violence. I've just lost it a couple of times since *Britain Blazes Bright* because I'm so pissed off. I…'

H tapped on the glass. Amisha went into see him and was advised to finish the interview and bring Dean Stephens in. This she did; Stephens lasted only slightly longer than Little before H started tapping.

*

H kicked off the review of the day's work, over dinner in the Bunch of Grapes.

'These little tosspots are all mouth. Worse than that, they're all mouth from behind their silly little keyboards. They couldn't fight their way out of a paper bag, leave alone put it on someone with a sawn-off shotgun. Or even have it done on their behalf. We need to focus on someone with a bit more about them than these. I reckon we've already got a few better candidates.'

Amisha realised she hadn't seen him this switched on in an age; she loved him in this mode. 'What are your recommendations then guv?' she asked.

'Well from what I've seen so far this footballer's definitely worth a look - something not quite right about him. Blandish looks a ruthless bastard who won't stop at much to get what he wants. And as for our mate Tarquin…he makes my teeth hurt. Absolute wrong 'un. I suggest we have a good, hard look at the three of them. For starters. Until something better comes along.'

Graham liked the direction things were heading in: 'Where do you think we should start, H?'

'Romeo first, I think. Lacks character, like most of these footballers now. Judging by the way he rolls around on the grass like he's been shot if someone so much as gives him an evil look. Yep, Romeo first, if he's got something to hide, his arsehole will flabber. Trust me, his arsehole will flabber.'

41

It was midnight by the time the three vehicles converged on the appointed place: a quiet, isolated road at the edge of the forest. Fatos felt like he was being watched by a greater force as he penetrated the woods in search of his pit of death. Tales from the old country, of supernatural creatures who haunt the woods at night, filled his imagination. The further in they went, the darker it got. The darker it got the more the hoots and hollers from the trees echoed and magnified thoughts of ghostly powers with knowledge of the crime he was about to commit. The light from his torch cast deathly shadows. He felt sick.

The forest floor was soft underfoot, muddy with the rains of the previous week.

'Here,' said Zef, when they came across an opening, 'plenty room.'

Fatos didn't know if this was a good spot. He just wanted it over. He took a glug of rakia and agreed on the setting.

'Open top container, put up ladder and get merchandise out,' he said after returning to the lorry. He found it impossible to refer to the ten about to die as people - merchandise kept it impersonal, he couldn't afford to think too much about their humanity. He'd heard once that even many SS men had to be tanked up on pills and booze when it came to hands-on mass grave work. He raised the bottle to his lips but his supply of Dutch courage was gone - he'd downed the lot. He wasn't exactly off his head - the job in hand was a sobering proposition - but he was drunk. No doubt about that.

Exhausted, disorientated and stinking of their own bodily waste the live merchandise exited the container one by one and congregated at the rear of the lorry, as instructed by their captors. One of the captives, a weary looking middle-aged man who had made the trek from central Asia, had a decent grasp of the world's lingua-franca and was the first to speak.

'Where are we? Why have we been kept in the truck so long?'

There was no reply. Fatos passed out the spades and pointed in the chosen direction. 'March,' he said.

The ten stood silent, disbelieving, unable to take the situation in, refusing to accept the implications of what they had been instructed to do. Disbelief quickly gave way to fear, followed closely by utter despair. They had not arrived at the promised land of milk and honey and opportunity, they had spent their life's savings on their own funerals. The captive who had spoken threw down his spade.

Fatos had anticipated resistance and knew he would have to make an example before the unwilling gang of grave diggers would fall into line. He slowly screwed the silencer onto his pistol, raised it and gave the mouthy guy one in the head. He fell to the ground. The lorry drivers guts' churned. The grave diggers slumped towards their fate. Zef smiled.

Fatos didn't know how long it would take to dig a hole deep and wide enough to take twenty people. Dragusha had given him the details for size and depth, but time was a different matter altogether. Initially it was chaotic as the diggers got in each other's way, unsure as to where to put the soil. Progress was slow and Fatos's rakia-fuelled anxiety intensified. He'd been here before, he recalled again, back in the days when mass graves were a common feature of the landscape. But then he was just a foot soldier, taking orders, doing what he was told. He was good at doing what he was told.

He never expected to be supervising the digging of another mass grave, not here, not in England. He didn't want to do it. He wanted out. This was too much. He could still get out. Get in the car, drive away. Leave these people to the authorities and what was left of their lives. But then his organization would be blown and his own life would be over. Maybe that would be better, he thought to himself as he watched the digging dead. Suddenly a woman screamed, threw down her spade and made a break for it. Zef reacted instinctively; he drew an unsilenced gun, took aim and gave her three in the back as she fled.

'No!' screamed Fatos, 'use silencer…we must use silencer.' Too late. The woman was now a lifeless, formless heap, her blood flowing into the ground. Even if you're in the forest, in a country with 430 people per square kilometre, someone is going to hear three gunshots in the middle of the night.

Pandemonium erupted. Fatos dropped his empty bottle, which he'd been holding onto as some kind of comfort blanket, and started firing wildly. One, two, three…the bodies went down. The fear and the bloodlust and the violence escalated as the remaining sentries followed their leader. The air filled with the stench of cordite and blood, and the hopeless cries of the doomed. It was a scene straight out of Dante's Inferno, and less than a minute after the first shot the diggers lay on the ground, their bodies shattered and mangled by the hail of jacketed hollow-point bullets. Dragusha's men always shot to kill: high impact, maximum destruction.

Fatos shook himself back into his senses: 'OK. Shots made big noise. We must be fast.'

They jumped to it. The six men dragged, rolled and pushed the ten bodies into their resting place and gathered the additional ten from the second container. It was back breaking work. Two men per body, orchestrated by Fatos, who was now wide-eyed, slathering at the mouth and screaming at them to hurry, terrified that a police car would be turning up at any moment to investigate the gunshots. Scenario after scenario played through his mind. None of them were good. He picked up one of the spades, ordered his men to do likewise and began covering the bodies. The eyes of the ghosts of the forest were on him. They knew what he'd done. They'd always know.

Dragusha had told him to dig the grave at least six feet deep. They were at maybe half that. The final layer of top soil was put back and Fatos hopped around the mass grave, pogoing manically, trying to flatten it out. He'd completely lost it; the panic, and the enormity of what he'd done, overwhelmed him. He had even forgotten one of Dragusha's core commands: 'Kill driver first.' And now the driver had disappeared.

Fatos only realised this as an articulated lorry, a tow truck and a grey Mondeo pulled out of a silent forest on the edge of the Garden of England.

42

The skies had stayed clear for a second day and the sun was glimmering off the sparkling glass tower that was New Scotland Yard as Romeo Ferrera swaggered towards the interview room, his brief traipsing along behind him like he owned the place. Amisha and Graham had yet to arrive, so H had a few minutes to study him from behind the glass. He did not like what he saw. It wasn't the fact that men like this earned in a week what H did in two years. Not at all. It was the arrogance and the sense of entitlement.

Like the majority of men of his background, H had loved football most of his life. He'd grown up watching and admiring players of the old school, men who were no different from those who paid to watch them. His favourites had always been the no-nonsense hard men, the unpassable defenders and midfield enforcers from Norman Hunter through to Stuart Pearce. The hundred-per-cent men, who took no prisoners and asked no mercy for themselves, back in the days before the beautiful game had been turned into a non-contact sport.

From behind the glass H made an assessment of the superstar now before him. He noted his luxuriant, slicked back dark hair, his five grand suit, his open-collared silk shirt, his hand-made Italian shoes, his gigantically chunky gold wristwatch. Ferrera sprawled back in his chair, legs akimbo, and busied himself with his big plastic phone, swiping from picture to picture to fragment of two-line text and back to picture, restless and impatient. His body language said, loudly and clearly, that he resented being here, having his time wasted; that he was above all this.

*

'We understand that you attended several parties, parties thrown by Tarquin De Montfort, over the last couple of years at which Bazza Wishbone was often present,' Amisha said. 'How well did you know him? Would you say you were friends?'

'Not friends, exactly, more like party buddies. I never saw him anywhere apart from the parties. I liked him, he was fun. But friends...no.'

'What about Jacynta Packington? Were you - are you - friendly with her?'

Ferrera shifted from side to side in his chair a little and scratched his nose, H noted, as he prepared to answer the question.

Here we go.

'Yes, I'm friendly with Jacqui...we have - had - a lot of fun. Her, Bazza and the others. So I've been friendly with her, yes.'

'Not as friendly as you'd like to be though, eh, Mr Ferrera?' said Graham, introducing a crisper tone.

'I don't understand what you're implying, I...'

'Listen, let's stop messing about, shall we Mr Ferrera?' said Graham. 'We've spoken to the people in your circle and more than one of them has told us that you had a thing for Jacynta and more than that, that you've been a bit of a nuisance. A bit of a stalker. Of Jacynta. And others before her. Are you a bit of a sex-pest, Mr Ferrara?'

Ferrera's brief shock his head; Romeo said nothing.

Amisha picked up the slack: 'Mr. Ferrera, we've spoken to our colleagues at Vine Street. They've told us all about your fun and games, stalking these models and making threats. And that you've been told by them and your club, behind the scenes, to rein yourself in. You seem to be an obsessive sort when it comes to the ladies, no?'

The brief shock his head. Romeo said nothing.

'So you've been sniffing around Jacynta Packington, being a bit of a pest,' said Graham.

'No, I…'

'Jealous of Bazza Wishbone, were you?' said Amisha. This was bad cop/bad cop. 'Jealous of the fact that he got to Jacynta before you? Or was it after you? Did you ever threaten him Mr. Fererra, at one of de Montfort's parties? We have eyewitnesses who suggest you might have, who saw you arguing.'

Ferrera said nothing, again on the advice of his brief. But his face was drawn; the smug look was long gone. His right leg was twitching like a tree in an electrical storm, his teeth were clenched, and his hand was all over his face, scratching his nose, tugging at his ear.

I knew it, he's shitting himself…put it on him Graham, put it the fuck on him.

'Mr Ferrera, can you account for your whereabouts on the morning of Bazza's murder, between 4 and 6 am?' said Graham.

'No, I was at home. Alone,' said Ferrera, from a parched mouth.

H had seen enough.

He tapped on the glass.

43

The leadership team on the Wishbone case, which had unofficially coalesced into H, Amisha, Graham and Andrew Glass, were in debrief, mulling things over. Graham asked H to share his impressions of the Romeo interview.

'He's as slippery as a bar of soap, no doubt about that, and he's definitely got something to hide. That much is obvious. He gets fixated on women, has the look of a nonce about him. I should think he's capable of doing some serious harm, one on one, when he gets the flavour.'

'But is he in the frame?'

'Nah…I doubt he's got the bollocks for it; a planned, cold-blooded slaughter that could easily have gone tits-up. Might have enough about him to pay someone else to do it though, if he had a full-blown thing for Jacynta. Worth following up on him, get closer to his inner circle, find out if he was dipping his wick before Wishbone came on the scene. Overall, an outside possibility, I'd say.'

'Thank you, Detective Inspector Hawkins,' said Graham, scanning the agenda on his tablet.

H took advantage of the pause: 'Andrew, how are you getting on with those background checks I asked for on Blandish and de Montfort? Headlines only please.'

Andrew cleared his throat. He'd had some success in digging around in the murky world of celebrity finance, and the forces that lurked unseen behind the gloss. He glanced at Graham, nominally in charge, to see if this was his moment.

'This lifetime please, Andrew,' said H.

In the few days he'd been on the case H had, more or less, taken it over. He was forever directing members of the team on where to concentrate their efforts as well as advising Graham and Amisha on the direction of travel. Graham knew it would come to this, but was surprised at just how on the ball H was after his long period of absence, as if he was making up for lost time. His focus and energy had been incredible. Graham didn't mind or feel threatened. He understood H so much better these days. He knew he wasn't acting out of ego, nor a desire for advancement. H was impatient, impatient to get to the nub of the matter. H hated bad men, and he was a seeker after truth.

Andrew gave his initial report on Blandish. They'd need court orders and a full team to investigate his finances properly but it was clear he was one of the wealthiest people in the entertainment industry, and had near full control over his many signings. Andrew gave a list of the artists he had fallen out with. None of them ever seemed to have much money after their brief spell in the limelight, and anyone who had taken Blandish anywhere near a court had wound up well and truly bankrupt.

Having given the background Andrew paused to milk his moment before delivering the most pertinent of his findings.

'It appears that Bazza had started secret negotiations with a new team of lawyers to decouple himself from the contract he had with Blandish, and that Blandish was not exactly over the moon about it when he heard. Not much gets past him. The contract as it stands gives Blandish complete control over both the finances and every track Bazza ever recorded, or ever would record. It's textbook stuff - a total stitch-up.'

Andrew was building up a head of steam, getting ready to go into more detail. H slowed him down.

'Good work Andrew. Highlights on Tarquin please.'

'Well, it seems that Mr de Montfort had been trying to get close to Bazza. Was fighting his corner. And it seems there may have been a bit of friction between him and Blandish, to put it mildly. It might be that de Montfort was trying to pull him into his own sphere, get him away from the dark side. Bazza had been attending de Montfort's "parties" for some time, I'm told.'

‘Great work Andrew,’ said H, making the young man feel like a little boy who had just got a gold star from the headmaster, ‘send out the details to the team and get more on de Montfort’s financial situation and connections - see if he has dealings with anyone naughty - especially on the drug front. Try and find out where he sources the marching powder and other bits and pieces for his parties.’

H leaned back in his chair, stretched out, linked his arms behind his head and addressed the meeting:

‘Right - what we have here, boys and girls, is a situation as old as time: one carcass, two vultures. This Tarquin looks to me like a great big dollop of absolutely fuck-all, but you never know with these people. Blandish is obviously the utter, ruthless bastard they say he is. We’ve got a right pair of beauties here. Let’s get in amongst them, see how they like it up ‘em.’

44

No one knew for sure how much Nigel Blandish was worth, but it had to be plenty. His office - 'headquarters' would be a better word, Amisha thought - occupied an entire townhouse in Wimpole Street in Marylebone. Blandish Global Media, tucked in unobtrusively among the high end medical practices and professional associations. It was just along the road from number 64, where Paul McCartney had lived for a spell, back in the sixties, and where he was said to have written 'Yesterday.' That, Blandish tended to say in interviews, was why he'd bought the property.

Amisha and Graham arrived early. They knew the great man was as busy as he was arrogant and wanted to maximise their time with him. They knew what these guys were like.

Blandish's office - they were ushered in after a short wait - was filled with certificates of platinum and gold records from the old days and pictures of him with celebrities, pop stars, other 'opinion leaders' and even a smattering of world leaders. He had contacts in all the right places. Awards and more pictures filled the space on his substantial Chesterfield desk. A large picture of Bazza, looking mean, moody and magnificent in tight jeans and leather jacket, took pride of place behind his chair, dead centre of the main wall. It was the place Blandish always reserved for whomever was his king of pop of the moment, the current numero uno in the ever shifting fortunes of the celebrity hierarchy. Where Bazza was concerned, business had been booming since his death, and Blandish was having a hard time keeping up with the number of units of the boy's product he was shifting.

'Ah, Detective Inspector Miller-Marchant, Detective Sergeant Bhanushali, please come in,' he said as he welcomed them into the room, phone glued to his ear. He finished his conversation and beckoned them towards the two leather-upholstered chairs on the opposite side of the desk.

He looked just like he did in the pictures - the self-made bruiser entrepreneur: dress shirt with wide open collar, short, thick set and almost hairless on top. Exuding some sort of primitive energy and chomping on a fine cigar. You couldn't have made him up. Amisha and Graham said their hellos.

'God what a terrible, terrible business,' said Blandish, 'any leads yet?'

'Nothing substantial,' said Graham.

'We need to know more about Bazza's background,' Amisha said. 'What he was like, who he mixed with.'

Blandish told them about when they had first met, Bazza's initial audition for *Britain Blazes Bright*. It was clear, he said, that the band he was with were never going anywhere. They simply didn't have it. But he had seen in Bazza not just a burning ambition to be someone, a desperation to overcome his background and his limitations, to shine brightly, but also a certain presence that he could spot from several miles away in a thick fog.

'I'm rarely wrong, even if I do say so myself,' continued Blandish. 'It takes only moments; I can always spot the ones who can be primed for success. I can smell them. That's why I am where I am.'

'But he was vulnerable, easy for you to take control of?' said Amisha, going in hard, to see how Blandish reacted. H had advised them to be confrontational.

'Oh, Detective Sergeant, please spare me your pointless Bazza sympathies. This is a tough game and nobody is forced to play it.'

'Have you met his family?' asked Graham.

'Yes, once or twice. You always meet the family. Do a photoshoot - it's good publicity. But other than that I can't say I really know them.'

'I wondered,' continued Graham, 'with all the success Bazza had, why they are living on the poverty line. Especially as Bazza took every opportunity available to wax lyrical about how much his mother meant to him, how she tried so hard as a single mother and all that.'

Graham noticed the flash of anger in Blandish's eyes but the plastic smile never fell from his face, as if it had been fixed in place surgically, the lower half of his face immobilised like the unchanging expression of a mannequin.

'Detective Inspector, I'm not responsible for how Bazza Wishbone chose to spend his money.'

'How much has he made, roughly, would you say, alive and dead?'

Amisha noticed Blandish was rattled by the line of questioning. He was getting angrier.

'I do not reveal my clients' earnings, whether they are alive or not, and anyway what's it to do with the case? I have another meeting in ten minutes; is there anything else you want to ask me?'

'Did he make any enemies on his way up, would you say? Anyone you think might have had it in for him?' asked Amisha.

'Not really. No one in particular. There will always be jealousy in this world, at every level of success, but I wouldn't say I've seen anything out of the ordinary.'

'What was your take on his cocaine habit, the papers were saying it was getting out of control, becoming self-destructive?'

'What about it?'

'Who supplied him?'

'Look. Its part and parcel of the world we live in. Personally, I never touch it. But in Bazza's world its everywhere. If he decides to use it then it's nothing to do with me.'

'Don't you think you had some kind of duty towards him, to ensure he didn't go off the rails?'

Blandish thought he had no such duty. He made people famous. He promoted them. Helped them live their dream. If they couldn't handle it that was down to them. He was too busy finding the next superstar to worry about the effect of fame on his protégés. And cocaine habits made news headlines, which was OK as far as he was concerned. But he didn't want to appear as disinterested as he was.

'Look. You do your best by these guys. You promote them, you give them contracts and lawyers and make sure they get their share of the cake. But I cannot control personal behaviour.'

'But Bazza wasn't getting his share of the cake though, was he?'

'As I said, I have another appointment now. My PA will show you out.'

Amisha was going nowhere: 'When was the last time you saw him?'

'About a week before he was killed. I met him in Belgravia to talk about his next single before he went onto a party.' Beneath the smile Blandish could barely conceal his indifference.

'Whose party?'

'One of Tarquin de Montfort's bashes.'

'His name has come up a lot in our investigations. How well did Bazza know him? Were they close?'

'I'm not sure. Tarquin's just one of those people who are always there. I don't even know where he came from, or where he gets his money, but he's always throwing grand parties. He spends his life sucking up to celebrities, trying to get close to them. I've heard he can become vindictive to those who don't want to know him.'

'Was Bazza one of those?' asked Graham.

Blandish's phone pinged. In his world, he was king and the two police officers from New Scotland Yard were no longer relevant to him as he chatted excitedly, finger raised to indicate to his visitors that they were on hold, to Jolly Jackson, his chief accountant.

'Downloads are through the roof,' he heard 'sales of Bazza's singles have quadrupled this week. He's still trending on Twitter. It's unbelievable, I've never seen anything like it.'

Blandish swivelled in his chair, as if Amisha and Graham were not in the room, and gazed at the picture of the young god above his desk with deep satisfaction. Looked like the picture was going to be in place for a few months yet. Death, it seemed, was good for business.

45

It had not been easy to arrange an audience with the somewhat languid Mr Tarquin de Montfort, even for police officers investigating a murder. He'd tried to cry off the meeting already, feigning illness - or so Graham and Amisha had thought - brought on by the stress of Bazza's murder. Now he had overcome his distress, and had made himself available.

The two detectives passed through the front door of his lavish eight-bedroom house in Belgravia, and entered the imposing grand hallway that served several reception rooms - sixteen foot ceilings, ornate fireplaces, windows you could get a car through. Young Andrew's background work, Graham had read with interest, had revealed that Chinese speculators, Russian oligarchs and Gulf state royalty had pushed the price of the houses in this neck of the woods up to the 40 million mark. And beyond.

The hallway was decked out in classic Greek friezes - on the frisky side, these - on the ceilings and walls. The hallway flowed into the wide staircase that led to the bedrooms. The basement had been converted into a sort of subterranean grotto with pool, jacuzzi, steam room, lots of dimly lit alcoves. This they all saw on the tour of the ground and lower floors given them by de Montfort's 'assistant', who introduced himself as Gaston, while his employer 'freshened up.' The tour did not extend to the upper rooms.

They had been waiting now for over fifteen minutes and Graham was beginning to chafe. Their elusive interviewee was, apparently, not somebody who could be hurried. Amisha looked about the hallway. Paintings of ancestors stared down at them, all expertly hung and ordered in chronological sequence. The portraits were of army men or extremely sober lords and ladies of the realm, stretching back to the seventeenth century. She wondered what they would have made of their distant successor, his celebrity-obsessed lifestyle and the monkey business around the house he oversaw.

Amisha wasn't quite sure what to make of him either, but she got some help when he eventually came springing down the stairs with a flourish in a glowing full-length gold brocade dressing gown. The man himself was full of breathless charm.

'Oh my darlings, I'm so dreadfully sorry to keep you waiting. Gaston, tea if you please. In the drawing room.' He ushered them towards the room with a flourish, sweeping his arms all the way.

Graham felt as if they'd rocked up to a West End musical production of Brideshead Revisited. Amisha struggled with an impulse to laugh out loud, and had other thoughts.

Thank God H is back at the Yard, tucked in safely behind his desk.

But the show was only just beginning. Once Amisha and Graham were seated de Montfort shrugged off his voluminous outer garment to reveal his inner dandy. He was straight out of central casting: double-breasted dark blue pinstripe suit with a pink shirt and an even pinker tie; handkerchief to match in the breast pocket; Italian shoes worth a Detective Inspector's monthly wages; two pairs of glasses, one fashionably dangling from his jacket pocket one perched halfway down his nose. He was long, lean and aquiline, his glistening shoulder length straw-coloured hair swept back. When it came to stereotypical self-presentation, this beauty put even Blandish in the shade.

He sat down, or rather perched himself on the edge of his chair, leaning into his guests. His eyes were visible above the frame of his glasses, and he emoted through them heavily as he spoke. His voice was plummy, resonant and drawling - a far cry from Blandish's clipped tone and estuary vowels: 'My darlings…such horror. Bazza was the sweetest of boys, the very sweetest. What kind of world are we living in?' He sat back in his chair with some drama. 'The quacks tell me I must rest, but I do so want to be useful. How can I help?'

46

Graham's irritation was growing; he wished H was with them. He would know how to deal with this…apparition. De Montfort drew a breath - he was getting ready to start up again. Graham cut in: 'How well did you know Bazza Wishbone?'

'Well, not very well darling. I meet so many people - rich and famous people, you understand. My role is to throw them all together and see what happens.'

'That'll be where your parties come in, yes? Tell me about those. Who comes to them?'

'Well, anybody who's anybody, darling,' said de Montfort, squinting over the rim of his glasses and implying that the likelihood of Graham and his ilk ever getting an invitation was way south of zero.

'The Saturday before last. Who was here?'

'Hmm, Bazza of course, Let me see…' De Montfort reeled off a few names, mostly the obvious ones Amisha and Graham had heard of.

'Who did Bazza keep company with?' asked Graham, 'Who was he talking to?'

'I can't say I noticed darling. He was just there, being his lovely magnetic self. All the ladies made a beeline for him. And a good number of the fellows too, of course. It was a lovely big huddle, basically, with dear Bazza at the centre.'

Amisha sensed it was time to change tack: 'What about the party essentials, Mr de Montfort? The powder and pills? We understand that they all come as part of the service. What were Bazza and his huddle partaking of?'

The question caught de Montfort off guard; he was not a happy drama bunny.

'Detective Sergeant, I do not deal in drugs and, furthermore…'

'It would be of interest to us to know who supplies you with these materials,' said Graham

'Well, *really*. I…'

Graham was tempted to go nuclear, H style, but decided this was not the time; so he bit his tongue, and listened.

'Inspector... whatever your name is, it was my understanding that you wanted to talk to me about a beautiful young man who has been so tragically murdered. So that I might help you to find the monster that did it.' De Montfort's voice was quaking now, and little tears were beginning to pool up in his eyes.

'If I'd known it was to start with you wrongly accusing me of things of which I am wholly innocent I would not have agreed to see you.'

Graham wasn't interested in bringing de Montfort to justice. He wanted to dig deeper, follow the money trail from this glittering fop's fantasy world to where the monsters were - the people who, if you crossed them, could blow half your head clean off in a plush hotel room in the middle of London and think nothing of it.

They seemed to have arrived at a lull.

'Alright, your Lordship,' said Graham, 'the situation is as follows. I'd like you to provide me with a full list of the people who attended the party. Please don't delay or it's possible you could be brought in and charged with obstructing the course of justice. And then we'll have our next conversation in Brixton nick, and I'm sure you wouldn't want that - they don't do a breakfast of champagne and strawberries. Is that ok?'

De Montfort pouted; yes.

'Good.' Graham nodded to Amisha that it was time to go.

47

One glass of white wine. I'm sure I can have one glass of white wine.

H was in the living room, feeling good. Relishing his involvement in the Wishbone case and listening to Frank - "Fly Me To The Moon". Olivia was in the kitchen knocking up dinner and arguing with herself about whether or not to have a glass. She was stressed as hell.

They say now you can have a glass from time to time, the doctors - that it's even good for you.

Helps the circulation, relaxes you, does the baby no harm at all.

Amisha would be around later, to back her up. It was time to tell H about her condition, about the existence and impending birth of his son, his new son. She'd left it late, to start with because she wanted, at her age, to be sure the pregnancy had a chance of going all the way. And partly because…

She'd been with H now for almost seven years. He'd hauled himself on crutches into her physiotherapy practice one wet Tuesday Greenwich morning. He had a torn calf muscle, an injury he'd picked up in reckless pursuit of a villain half his age - 'some soppy little mong', as he'd had it - just off the Old Kent Road. He was not a happy bunny, and try as she might she could not engage him in the kind of casual conversation she usually struck up with the patients on her table. He'd been gruff, and short with her, and he stank of booze.

But she was intrigued by him, and found herself thinking about him from time to time in the week before his next appointment. She was struck by the solidity, the heaviness, the world-weariness in him; but there was still a little glint in his eye, a little something that hadn't been worn away. And he was handsome. My oh my, he was handsome, at least to her. Just her type. Olivia liked them rugged and manly - not that she'd ever put herself about much.

She'd been single and lonely for four years when H came into her life. Her marriage to Mark Walsh, a PE teacher at the big comprehensive school in Eltham, had bottomed out after she'd lost the baby she was carrying. The pain of it had infected every aspect of their lives for a couple of years, gnawing away at them, pulling them apart rather than bringing them closer together. One day Mark never came home from work. He was gone, and was never seen or heard from again. No note, or text, or email - nothing. She did not file a missing person's report. Last she'd heard he was in New Zealand.

Olivia channelled her pain into her work. She quit her job at Lewisham hospital and struck out on her own. After three gruelling years of building her own physiotherapy practice things had levelled and she'd been able to expand to the point where she'd established a solid and popular business, with a staff of four, including herself. She continued to work long, long hours - not so much because she needed to but because of what it did for her.

She'd always loved physiotherapy - working with people, getting to know them a little, alleviating their distress, helping them. But her commitment to work was also a coping strategy, an attempt to keep the loneliness at bay. The void in her personal life was eating away at her, and she was now in her thirties. But most of the men she met seemed so boyish and self-centred. She was an old-fashioned girl at heart and she wanted an old-fashioned man like in the old Western movies, and she wanted a family.

And she had neither, nor prospect of them.

In the week before her second meeting with H she'd been preparing for it, almost without realising. Had her hair and nails done, paid a bit more attention than usual to her skin and make up. She'd even been out and bought a few bits and pieces - a little something for her spring wardrobe, she told herself.

She had butterflies in her stomach as she prepared for his visit, and was concerned about giving too much away, of losing her professionality.

She needn't have worried.

H shambled in through the door, bang on time, struggling again with his crutches, and this time further hampered by the fact that he was trying to keep a small bunch of roses in one piece.

'These are for you,' he said, pouring on the charm, his eyes sparkling. 'Sorry about last week, love. Not acceptable, I know. I'd had a few. Bad day at work, and this leg is absolutely doing my nut.'

'Well, we'd better have a look at it then hadn't we, Detective Inspector Hawkins?'

'H. Call me H. My friends do. My enemies as well, come to that. And I've got plenty of those. Anyway, it's H. For Harry.'

'H it is then, H. If you'd just like to take your trousers off and pop yourself up onto the table.'

48

Olivia's favourite record these days was Abba's "The Day Before You Came". It captured perfectly the feeling she'd had in the weeks and months before she met H, of being comfortable and safe, and living within her routines, but also of being numb and lacking something. It always moved her, sometimes to tears, and she was listening to it now, in the kitchen, with a glass of white wine.

The doorbell rang. 'I'll get it,' H shouted. Olivia heard high-spirited talk and laughter in the corridor, and then Amisha talking. 'That de Montfort's a funny piece of work, what you'd call a right slippery fucker.' H laughed with gusto and told Amisha he'd catch up on the interview tomorrow.

The pair of them came into the kitchen, beaming. Olivia greeted them. Smiles all round.

'Glass of wine?' asked Olivia.

'Oh yes, large one if you please, my lovely,' said H.

'Not you, Tiger. I was talking to the engineer, not the oily rag. Your orange juice is in the fridge.'

More smiles. This was a happy occasion.

Wasn't it?

The ladies sent H packing, back to the living room where a live rendition of Frank's 'That's Life' was filling the air. H made doubly sure no-one was watching and gave a little jig across the floor to the living room sofa.

'So Liv, how are you feeling? All set?'

'Just about. I'll have this bit of Dutch Courage and we'll talk to him. I wish I'd told him sooner Ames…what's he going to say? He's always said he doesn't want any more kids, that he's been worse than useless with the ones he's already got. And he's 56 now Ames, 56.'

Amisha said nothing. She took a deep breath, moved towards Olivia, stroked her shoulder, took the wine glass from her hand and looked her in the eye.

'There's no way round this Liv - you're just going to have to crash through it.'

'That's what H always says.'

'Then he'll appreciate your approach. Just do it - go to him now. I'll be here.'

*

Amisha listened from the kitchen. For a long time there was not much to hear. And then…the sound of one of them - or was it both of them? - crying, gently. And then silence. Amisha opened a bottle and gave them another ten minutes before creeping along the corridor and tapping on the living room door.

'Come in,' Olivia said.

Olivia and H were together on the sofa, holding one another, not moving. Frank was singing "I Concentrate On You". Amisha felt like she should be somewhere else and turned to tiptoe out of the room. As she reached the door she heard movement from the sofa, and H saying 'Oi, Ames. Don't go away, come back in.'

She turned and looked into his face. The area around his eyes was red raw, and his bulk was still heaving gently.

'Can I ask you something Ames?' he said.

'Sure.'

'How do you feel about being Little Harry's Godmother?'

49

Dragusha told his henchmen to keep away. It was to be him and Ronnie only. There had been a few murmurings as to the wisdom of his course of action but Dragusha's men knew better than to question their leader - even more so now that he was always accompanied by his wolf boy enforcer. Nobody wanted to go up against him.

So it was just the two of them who strode, bold as brass, into the part of the recreation area known to be the domain of the firm of the late lamented Jack Butcher. Ronnie first, Dragusha second. Six core members of the ailing Butcher firm, centered on Tony Palmer, John Donovan and Billy Walsh, had been in conference around the snooker table for some time, discussing a possible response to the brutal slaughter of their top man; but in truth they were like chickens clucking around the farmyard after having their heads cut off - they were no longer a match for a lot of these newer firms, and they knew it.

They were jittery even before they saw the duo stroll in. Full of purpose, looking tasty. But once Dragusha and the wolf boy started swaggering towards them their jitters turned to real fear, as they waited for a small army of tooled up nutters to surge in behind them.

They say you can smell fear, taste it; right now, the boys around the snooker table were gagging on it.

So this was it then - the endgame. With Butcher gone, his head still in the wind somewhere, Dragusha's inevitable next step was to take out his pawns. They stood ready, with their muscles taut, their mouths dry and their hands firmly gripped around snooker cues and whatever else lay to hand.

The seconds passed, but time stood still.

The six stood, rooted to the spot, holding their breath, unable to move or to comprehend why Dragusha would turn up unannounced with only Ronnie Hawkins for protection. They knew Little Ronnie must be a real handful now, assuming the rumours were true, but Dragusha was nobody's fool. Thirty more seconds ticked by, like the dying moments of a football match with your team one nil up.

Tony Palmer edged cautiously towards the door, working his way around and behind the two intruders, and poked his head outside. The landing was deserted. Not a soul in sight.

Was this a ruse? Did they want to negotiate?

Billy Walsh piped up first: 'What do you want?'

'We're going to rip your useless fucking cocks off and stuff them down your throats. Except for you, Walsh - yours is going into a parcel for your fucking whore of a mother.'

Ronnie Hawkins' words were met with stunned silence.

The fear and tension reached its boiling point, and the rage and hatred began to explode like smoke pouring out of a steam engine. The room burst into life. John Donovan was first to react, raising a snooker cue and swinging it, fast and hard, across the bridge of the younger man's nose, snapping it like a twig and flooding the lower half of his victim's face and chest with claret. Buoyed by this success, Walsh's boys attacked en masse, in an adrenaline-fuelled frenzy.

The fists and feet and snooker cues and balls and chair legs cascaded down onto the heads and into the faces of the interlopers. Dragusha held Ronnie close to him, holding him like a shield, making sure Ronnie took the lion's share of the pasting. The six were like a pack of wild dogs who had somehow managed to take down a lion; no longer restrained by fear but animated by the scent of blood, they forced their victims down onto the ground, jumped on them and kicked the living daylights out of them.

None of them stopped to consider the purpose of Dragusha's visit.

*

The pasting continued for over a minute before the screws arrived. By the time they'd brought the situation under control Dragusha lay on the floor, with Little Ronnie on top of him. Ronnie had taken ninety per cent of the blows and was just on the cusp of consciousness.

'Good timing,' Dragusha said to one of the screws as he lifted Little Ronnie up like a baby, cradling him in his arms and, surrounded by a posse of men in uniform, headed for the hospital wing. He and Ronnie were placed in adjacent beds. Dragusha was sore but at ease, quietly pleased with his afternoon's work; Ronnie was in agony. Every part of his body was bruised and battered. Dragusha turned to his protégé and smiled, content that the beating had gone well and the playing out of his theory that humans, if treated correctly, could be as unconditionally loyal as dogs. 'Good work Ujku, my brother,' he said, as the doctors started to assess the type and extent of the wounds the two men had suffered.

As Ronnie's grip on the conscious world faded he grinned with satisfaction at the endorsement of his master, the one man in this world for whom he would now do anything.

50

H bounced into Kasia's rooms. He'd been looking forward to seeing her. She seemed her usual self, sleekly sensuous in a restrained sort of way, serious yet welcoming.

'Good morning Detective Inspector, how nice to see you. How are you today?'

'Terrific,' said H, 'never better.'

Being back at work, digging into the Wishbone case and the news of impending fatherhood had transformed him. The news was a shock at first - raising a kid at his age would be no walk in the park - but he was warming to the idea more and more. He had visions of taking his son for kickabouts in the park, holidays in the sun, football matches. The fact that it meant he'd be doing child rearing activities for the rest of his life hadn't fully hit him; he was still in the afterglow of the news from Olivia. But for now he was in the moment, living in the here and now.

'So, Detective Inspector, how has your first week back at work been?'

'Blinding. I'm working on the Bazza Wishbone murder. Simple stuff, reading up on the background notes, making a few phone calls. Just background stuff, nothing too strenuous. Slowly slowly catchee monkey, just like you said.'

'Did I say that?'

H laughed. 'Well, maybe not those exact words, but you get my drift.'

'Yes, I get your drift.'

H thought he'd sit tight, answer a few questions, give her what she wanted to hear about his mental stability and then break the big news.

'How have you been sleeping since coming off your medication?'

'Like a babe in the woods. Early to bed, early to rise and all that.'

'And your drinking?'

'Not one drop has passed these lips, as God is my judge.'

This was just a figure of speech, thrown in by H to highlight his good mood, but Kasia took it literally.

'No need to call for the judgement of God, Detective Inspector. But I'm very pleased to see you in such a positive state of mind.'

They spoke a bit more about the issues they had touched on at their last meeting. H kept it together as once again they discussed his feelings about Ronnie Ruddock spending the rest of his life in jail, his attitude towards Skyhill, whether given equally stressful circumstances he'd be able to manage a situation professionally. H once again spoon-fed her the stuff she liked.

This is going well, let's talk about getting me back on the street.

'So, when do you think I'll be able to do interviews, get out from behind the desk, maybe get back on the street?'

'Remember Detective Inspector, slowly slowly catchee monkey.'

H couldn't help himself and smiled broadly.

He was ready to break the good news when Kasia asked him the question he always dreaded most.

'And your son, Detective Inspector, how are you feeling about that situation now?'

Hammer blow. H had been putting this to the back of his mind, almost too scared to let it take centre ground. He wanted it locked away. It was the one thing he couldn't deal with. Kasia noticed the change in his demeanour.

H felt he needed to talk about it, honestly, openly.

'Haven't heard from him for some time. He rejects all my requests to see him. His mother won't talk to me… I've tried putting it to the back of my mind. This week I've managed not to think about it too much. Keeping busy.'

H then spoke at length, yet again, about the pain, the guilt, the nauseating sinking feeling he had when he thought about his boy. He didn't think he could ever come to terms with it, and the question had brought him back to the real world. He was glad, in a way, to have someone to talk to about his deepest feelings.

But it had altered his happy-go-lucky mood. He never gave the big news.

I've lost boy number one...Boy number two she doesn't need to know about.

51

Terry and Julie Marsh - looking very much the part in their Barbour jackets and wellington boots - were having a delightful stroll through the Kent countryside. They did this all the time these days, now that they had to work less and their youngest had finally left for university. A crisp but golden autumn morning was warming with the rising of the sun, and all was right with the world.

'Here boy,' said Terry as Buster, their French Bulldog, came bounding back to them with his little tennis ball sloppy from the dew and his own slobber.

Terry tore the ball from the dog's powerful jaws and launched it back into the woods; Buster bolted after it.

'I love these walks,' said Julie, 'it's so peaceful and calm. England's so beautiful on a day like this. Let's head a little deeper into the woods.'

They turned right, past a swathe of stinging nettles and on towards the heart of the woods. The temperature dropped a little, the canopy of the enveloping trees shielding the area from the sun. The couple held hands as Terry gave a loud whistle to alert their canine friend to the change of direction. Buster came bouncing from out of the undergrowth with the all the unbridled energy and love of life of a three-year-old dog, and presented the ball to Julie.

She bent down, stroked his head and teased the ball gently from his grip. She threw it in a new direction and Buster once again flew after it in chase, tail wagging, tongue flapping, as Terry checked the map, held it up to Julie and discussed their next move.

Buster returned eager to continue his fun, circled them and leapt up like a gazelle, insisting they pay attention to his needs. They tried to ignore him but he was not an easy dog to give the cold shoulder to, and he won the battle of wills.

Terry bent down, took the ball from Buster and launched it with all his might. They savoured the silence while the dog gave chase.

A few minutes later Buster came tearing back into view. The tennis ball was nowhere to be seen but he was jumping up and barking, even more animated and excited than usual. He sprinted back in the direction he'd come from, then back to Terry and Julie. The process repeated itself. Again. And again.

Julie said, 'I think he wants us to follow him.'

Buster led them down into a ravine and then bolted up the other side of it, still doing multiple to-and-fro sprints. They climbed the other side of the ravine to see Buster in a small clearing, manically scratching and digging as if his life depended on it. Terry reached the spot of Buster's frenzy.

'What's the matter boy? What is it?'

The digging continued. The dog's energy was frenetic, wild, ceaseless. Finally the source of Buster's excitement was revealed - and it made the hairs on the back of Terry's neck stand to attention and his stomach heave. He reeled back in horror, winded by surprise and gasping for breath.

Julie was alarmed. What the hell had he seen? 'What is it darling, what is it?'

The answer would return to haunt her dreams for the rest of her life.

'It's two heads. Two human heads - and their eyes are staring right back at me.'

52

PCs Margaret Hodgson and Peter Dennison - or 'Little and Large' as their colleagues called them - where parked up in their patrol car. It was almost lunchtime and both would soon be off duty.

Peter said 'Pauline's doing a full roast today. A nice joint of beef, home-made Yorkshire pudding, roast potatoes, the lot. I can smell the gravy already.'

Peter, at six foot two and a stout 16 stones 7 pounds, was a large man, with an appetite to match. He spent half his time eating and the other half thinking about his next meal. He'd had a full English including fried bread for breakfast but his stomach was already rumbling, and the hole at its centre needed to be filled.

'Food, food, food. Is it all you ever think about?'

Margaret, by contrast, was a health conscious gym bunny. At 5ft 6in she weighed just a little short of 9 stone. Gym every day, grapefruit juice for breakfast and salad for lunch. It was only the protein shakes after her workouts that maintained her body weight.

Peter was disappointed when a call came in so close to knocking off time.

'There's a report of bodies in the ground in the woods at the north west side of Bedgebury. Can you go and have a look? My guess is it's another crank call; we've had a few lately but get up there as soon as you can and see what's happening. Call came in from one Terry Marsh. Says he's at the scene now with his wife and he'll be waiting on the side road that runs around the back of the woods.'

When the Police Constables arrived they found Terry and Julie sitting on a log. Julie was hugging a French bulldog next to her as if her life depended on it. Both the humans appeared to be in shock. Both PCs realised immediately that this was no hoax.

Peter said 'Two bodies, was it?'

Terry said, 'No, more than two. Buster started digging around. There's more than two.'

'How many more?'

'I don't know.'

'Ok. Show us the way.'

Terry and Julie led the way. Margaret kept pace with them. Peter lagged behind a bit; it was a fair old slog, quite a long way in… He clambered out of what he hoped was a final ravine and descended, bent double, into a clearing. Struggling for breath, he pulled himself up to his full height and focused in on the scene.

Buster had really put a shift in; his manic digging had revealed two more carcasses before Julie had regained the wherewithal to bring him under control. That made four. Peter was staring at the heads and limbs of four corpses. The blood drained from his face. He tried to swallow, but his throat was dry. He didn't know what to make of it. The bodies and upturned soil made a confused mass of impressions on his mind.

He no longer fancied his roast with all the trimmings.

'Better call this in,' he said.

*

'We've got our hands full here. It's no crank call, I can tell you that much…there's more than two bodies in the ground here.'

'How many more?'

'Four at least, maybe more.'

'Fucking hell,' said the voice on the other end of the radio.

Peter wasn't sure how long it took, but it didn't take long. The Emergency Services use at least six types of siren sounds in the UK, and can vary them according to whether they are in a built-up area and how much of a rush they're in. 'Nee-nahs' and 'woo-woos' and all the rest of them were firing off across the county of Kent like the county of Kent had never heard before.

Three local cars of plod were first to arrive; the tape was got out; the crime scene was sealed. Behind the scenes the first hours were a little chaotic. As more information filtered its way across the police hierarchy Detectives and Chief Inspectors and Commissioners were called whether they were on duty or not. Was it two bodies or four bodies...or ten bodies? E-mails and texts and calls made their way across the land, to those the police must answer to. Firstly, to lesser politicians, then to senior ones, then to The Home Secretary, who spoke to the Prime Minister.

All that activity and information couldn't stay under wraps for long. A leak here, a word there to a friend. The media got hold of it and descended en masse. More PCs were called in on their day off. Dozens of them surrounded the death pit. The woods were sealed off. A place was found - the car park of the Boar and Badger, not far off - to herd the media into. The news went global.

The Kent commissioner of Police put together a press conference. He didn't give much away. A crime scene, with several bodies, had been found. It was under investigation.

The journalist screamed their questions: 'How many bodies? How long have they been there?'

The usual platitudes were forthcoming: the scene was still being investigated and further information would be made available shortly. The media circus bayed for more. It was starting to look like one of the most horrendous crimes in modern British history had been committed.

Peter had called in at 12:00. The crime scene was sealed by 12:30. Detectives had arrived shortly afterwards and forensics a little later. By 5pm, the time of the first press conference, they had uncovered 11 bodies. The Kent Commissioner of Police was in regular conference with the Home Secretary, who demanded hourly updates thereafter.

The calls went on through the night. At next morning's 7am call the Kent Commissioner told the Home Secretary that the count was 17 but that things were messy and the forensic people were taking their time. They were collecting evidence as they went.

'Think "archaeological dig" Home Secretary, like you've seen on the television.'

Peter and Margaret had stayed for several hours after the call, helping to secure the crime scene, answering questions and receiving the recognition for being first on the scene. When Peter got home he was exhausted. He answered a few questions for his wife and then fell into bed.

He awoke at 9am the next morning. His wife asked him what he wanted for breakfast.

'Just coffee, please love,' he said as he switched on the radio. The Home Secretary was providing an update. In truth, the facts were still fuzzy; the final body count hadn't come through, the when and why were still to be investigated.

'What we do know,' the Home Secretary said 'is that some of the victims were shot, others appear to have suffocated, and that we are faced with one of the most heinous atrocities ever committed within the confines of this island.'

53

The ambulance was keeping to the speed limit. Two injured prisoners were on their way to the University Hospital of North Durham; one of them was in very bad shape. The prison they had just left did not have the facilities to deal with his injuries. Ronnie Hawkins needed scans to see if the terrible beating he had taken had damaged his internal organs. The prison had x-ray facilities so they knew he was nursing a broken leg, two broken ribs and a shattered nose as well as various contusions liberally scattered across his body. Dragusha, on the other hand, was sporting a few bumps and bruises but was wide awake and double-alert. A quiet word with the prison doctor, advising him it would be best for his long term health, had ensured Dragusha went along for the ride.

Ronnie was heavily sedated, not fully aware of his surroundings. Dragusha, handcuffed to the metal bars of the prison ambulance was, as always, plotting his next move, getting himself ahead of everyone else in the vehicle.

One driver, one paramedic, two screws. One driver, one screw up front. One paramedic, one screw in the back. The two screws were like peas in a pod. Pot-bellied, early fifties, their best years in the service long behind them. No problem.

Bob Woolmer, the driver, was weaving and bobbing through narrow country lanes. He had done the trip plenty of times before and wasn't expecting any trouble. He tuned the radio into his favourite easy listening station and was humming along happily to some light, old school country music. Could have been Dolly Parton, or Tammy Wynette, or someone like that. He wasn't sure but he knew the tune; it put him in a good mood.

'Doing anything tonight Tom?' he said to the prison officer who was half-dozing to his left, enjoying a daydream of his football team, Newcastle United, lifting the league title. He knew for sure it would never happen in his lifetime; he didn't know this would be the last daydream of his lifetime.

The black Volkswagen Golf seemed to come out of nowhere and pulled out of a minor country road, just yards ahead of the ambulance. Inside it were men wearing ski masks. Bob Woolmer instinctively swerved to avoid it and careered into the verge. A tree removed the passenger side wing mirror. He sensed staying motionless was not a good idea. This was no accident. He was in danger, extreme danger. He banged the ambulance down a gear and pressed hard on the accelerator. The road ahead was clear and narrow as he hit sixty miles an hour in less than seven seconds - not exactly Lamborghini acceleration but faster than he had ever moved a fully laden ambulance, even in situations of life and death emergency. The life and death in question had never been his own. His quick reactions caught the driver of the black Golf unawares as he shot past it.

He glanced at the rear-view mirror. There were now two Volkswagen Golfs coming up fast behind him. Another two riders, also wearing the masks...four masked men then. He gulped hard, the fear rising, adrenalin heightening his concentration and his mastery of the vehicle. He knew he couldn't outrun them. He sparked up the alarm. The siren flashed blue. He wanted to make as much noise as possible, anything to alert someone, as he kept his foot hard on the gas, the ambulance now moving at seventy-five miles an hour down a narrow country lane. Tom got on the radio, desperately screaming for help, but knowing that help was too far away.

The first of the Volkswagens was now right behind the ambulance, trying to get abreast of it. A man leaned out of its front passenger window, pistol in hand. The plan had been to get one car in front of the ambulance and another behind. But they'd fucked up. Best bet now was to blow one of the rear tyres. He took aim and squeezed the trigger. The first shot came out of the barrel just as Bob Woolmer broke hard to navigate a tight bend. The bullet embedded itself in a tree. The second flew aimlessly past its target before gravity brought it down to earth. But when the third bullet hit, somewhere behind him, Bob the driver experienced the impact of a blown tyre on an ambulance travelling at seventy-five miles an hour on a winding country lane. He felt the vehicle lurch violently to the left as he broke, and re-accelerated to keep control. He tried to keep the thing on the road as it veered one way then the other, but his efforts were not enough. The ambulance crashed headlong into a massive oak tree. It was a collision in which the ambulance came off second best. Tom's side had taken the brunt of the impact. He was dead, as dead as his dreams of Newcastle United lifting the league title.

The four masked men were all business; they jumped out of their cars and headed to the rear doors of the ambulance. As they did so the doors flew open and they saw a prison officer and paramedic coming at them. The lead attacker gave them two in the head each to slow them down. He then vaulted over their slumped bodies and into the back of the vehicle, where he found a handcuffed Dragusha bent over Ronnie Hawkins, trying to wrestle him off a gurney. He took a keyring from the fallen prison officer, released Dragusha and carried the younger man out of the back door of the ambulance, setting him down on the ground.

Dragusha assessed the situation as the masked men gathered around him.

'You,' he said, pointing at one of his liberators, 'finish driver. Now we move. Me, Ujku and a driver in one car. Everybody else go different direction in other car.'

The shooter whipped off his mask. His face glowed with youth and exaltation 'I drive with you boss,' he said.

'What is your name?'

'My name is Zef Fejzullah.'

'You are son of Besian Fejzullah?'

'No, nephew of Besian; I am son of Konstandin.'

Dragusha held out his hand; Zef shook it, meeting Dragusha's penetrating stare. He was being assessed, evaluated in an instant by the authority figure who stood before him, deciding whether he was up to the job. This was no half-witted Fatos, in a state of constant uncertainty about his next move. This man had an aura; personal power emanated from him like a tangible force. Zef's skin prickled.

'You have guns for us?'

'Yes, here.'

Dragusha packed a gun inside Ronnie's belt, trousered his own and lifted the ailing Ronnie onto his shoulder.

'OK,' he said, 'no time to waste. We go now.'

54

'In a pub, H? Does it have to be in a pub? Can't you meet him somewhere else? You've been doing so well,' Olivia had said over breakfast, when H told her his plans for the morning. He wouldn't be confined to the house any more, slumped in front of the telly; he'd be out and about, seeing people, getting things done.

'It'll be alright. Trust me. I'm back in the game now, babes. Pubs are part of the game, that's all. Orange juice all the way.'

H was on top of the world as he swaggered along a bright and sunny Tooley Street towards the Dog and Gatepost. He'd had a call late the previous evening from Peter O'Reilly, an old lag he'd known for years and had sometimes used as a grass. O'Reilly said he had some urgent news to pass on, but not over the phone. Could they meet somewhere near London Bridge?

They certainly could. H was back in the saddle, it was a pleasant day, and he was going to be a dad again.

H was back, and chomping at the bit.

O'Reilly was already in situ when H surged into the pub, tucked up in a little booth with a pint of porter, studying the racing form.

'Peter. Long time. How are you son?'

'Not too bad Mr Hawkins, not too bad. How's yourself?'

'I'm well. Another pint?'

'I never say no to another pint, Mr Hawkins. You know me.'

H hit the bar and returned with a pint of bitter, an orange juice and two packets of nuts.

'Alright son, fire away. I haven't got all day - I have to meet the missus in a bit. She's in the pudding club - at my age, can you believe it? Says we've got to start picking out bits and pieces for the nursery.'

'Well…now there's a surprise! Congratulations Mr Hawkins. And a coincidence…it's your boy Ronnie I've come to see you about.'

H got the sinking feeling. How good was this news going to be? A man like O'Reilly going out of his way to mark his card about something to do with Ronnie? Not good.

'Well, an old friend of mine has just come out of Durham, Mr Hawkins… Did you hear about what happened to Jack Butcher?'

'No, I've been busy with other things. Why, what's happened to that horrible bastard?'

O'Reilly shifted uneasily in his chair.

'I see they really have been keeping this one under wraps. Well, someone got to him, in his cell, and…'

'And what Peter, spit it out.'

'It was a terrible thing. A terrible, terrible thing. He was killed, and…'

'And?'

'They cut his head off, Mr Hawkins. They cut his fucking head off.'

What?...What? Beheadings in the nick now?

'Jesus. What are you saying …all the way off?'

'Yep. They found the body, but no head. They still haven't found it - as far as I've heard.'

'Well…do we know anything? Who's in the frame?'

'The chap I mentioned, who's just come out of there - he's as good as gold, rarely wrong about anything - says it was that little firm up there, run by the fellow you put away last year…what was his name, Dragusha?'

This stopped H in his tracks. His mind conjured up an image he'd already seen plenty of times before, of Dragusha's eyes, behind a balaclava, silently taunting him as the Albanians pulled away from their attack, the year before, on the Russian firm in Soho, which had left dozens of people in bits. Literally.

Dragusha. Basim Dragusha.

'Fuck me, Peter, are you sure about all this. I…'

'There's more, Mr Hawkins…much more.'

H knew something bad, something very bad, was coming.

'I don't know how to tell you this. But you have to know…you…'

'Get on with it Peter.'

'My man says…Dragusha has taken complete control of your boy. He's become a trusted lieutenant of his firm. It's like he is a different person. People say Dragusha is more than his protector, he's almost like a new father. Ronnie tells everyone there who knows you that he hates you and will kill you when he gets out. And,' the Irishman took a deep gulp, 'it was Ronnie who killed Butcher…it was Ronnie who hacked off his head.'

*

H sat slumped in his chair, his head down, and said nothing.

O'Reilly let a minute pass, and said 'Mr Hawkins, I…'

'You're alright Peter, don't worry about it. Thanks for telling me. I'll see you later.'

O'Reilly left the pub, clutching a crisp fifty-pound note.

H sat alone for a minute or two, rose slowly from his chair, went to the bar and ordered a large scotch, no ice.

Part 3

55

'Same again son, when you're ready,' H called from his chair.

'Are you sure about that, sir? Not had enough yet?' said the young barman.

These fucking pub chains and their fucking jobsworths behind the bar...can't even have a proper drink any more.

H gave the barman the look. 'Same again*…please.'*

There was no arguing with the look; the barman poured another double scotch and looked on powerlessly as Inspector Harry Hawkins of the Yard fell spectacularly off the wagon.

He'd met O'Reilly at 1pm. It was now 8pm and H was feeling the worse for wear. The more he drank the more his body ached for another shot. It had been months since he'd felt the buzz of a good scotch hit the back of his head, and now the buzz was what he needed.

And yet all the drink in all the world wasn't going to help him come to terms with what O'Reilly had told him. He'd gone from riding high to shock and the depths of despair in a matter of seconds. All the effort of the last months seemed irrelevant, insignificant, when set against what he now knew. Oceans of guilt and misery swept over him, as powerful and irresistible as a tornado tossing a doll into the air.

'Sir.'

The barman was getting edgy. He sensed suppressed rage and instability in the drunk before him, but also great presence; this was not a man to be trifled with. He was in a precarious situation: he didn't want to serve him - that was company policy, now, in this situation - but he didn't want to not serve him either. He swallowed hard, and played over in his mind his training on how to deal with difficult customers.

'Sir,' he said, backed up now by the two most strapping of his colleagues, 'you've had a skinful. I really don't think it's in your best interests for you to carry on.'

The barman felt like he'd awoken a sleeping dragon as H got slowly to his feet. He took a step back, and called over a couple of more friends from the other side of the bar for a little moral support.

'Look son, I've got no problem with you, nor do I want one. Just give me one more little drop of gold watch and I'll be on my way.'

'Sorry sir, I really think you ought to leave.'

The mood in the pub changed; the drinkers were tuning into the emerging confrontation, wondering if and when it would explode into violence. They'd seen plenty of that in this establishment, over the years. A few of the more risk-averse punters shuffled quietly towards the other side of the bar.

H was getting the hump. He ran the scenario through his bleary eyes and reeling mind. If it kicked off now he was confident he could take care of all of them, like eyes are winking, even in his current state. But bashing up innocents wasn't his thing.

'Listen,' said H, 'all of you. Do yourselves a right fucking favour and turn it in, now. I've had a bad day and I just want a little drink. I haven't come here to fight with schoolboys...let me have a large scotch.'

'Sorry sir, I really can't serve you anymore.'

H put his head in his hands. What on earth was going on? Ronnie, his boy Ronnie, had not just turned into a drug dealer - he'd now become a vicious murderer at the beck and call of the most dangerous and merciless killers H had ever come across. What the fuck had happened? It was as close to impossible to process as anything could get. He looked about him - everyone in the pub was staring right at him.

He got up, unsteady on his feet, and nearly fell before grabbing onto the bar. He stood, struggling to right himself, a picture of confused despair, now undergoing public humiliation. He swarmed back to his chair and crashed down into it. He needed to sit for a bit, collect his thoughts.

He raised his eyes to the TV screen and sat for a while, taking in the usual sequence of random images as the barman muted the sound. He'd learned this on his training course - mute the sound, change the dynamic, show you're in charge; be respectful but be firm. He flicked through some channels to emphasise the point: weather maps, football goals, adverts for phones and cars, Basim Dragusha, Ronnie Hawkins...

'What!? What the fuck!? Oi! turn the telly up, turn the fucking telly up, *now*. That's a picture of my son.'

56

H had never sobered up so quickly in his life. He was now bolt upright, focused, his eyes wide open, his pupils dilated as if they'd just opened onto another world, an alternative universe that couldn't possibly be real. The emotion in his tone of voice was so forceful and absolute that the barman obeyed his command without thought, and H heard the tail end of the news story.

'Police have said the two escaped convicts are extremely dangerous and should not be approached by members of the public. If you see them, please call the following number…'

H tuned out as the news moved onto the next story. The pub - the bar staff, the punters, the fixtures and fitting themselves - seemed to hold their collective breath as all attention focused on the frightening drunk who was either delirious or had just realised his boy was the subject of a national manhunt. H headed for the door, shouldered it open and burst out into the evening air as the congregation breathed a sigh of communal relief.

H stood in the wet, dark London night, the wind howling about his head. The world was reeling, and spinning off its axis, and breaking up. Nothing made any sense. What was happening, how was it happening? There'd been light, for a while, at the end of the tunnel - he was going to be a father again, with a woman he loved; he was back at work, fulfilling his life's purpose; and Kasia Kotula had convinced him that not everything had to end in chaos and pain.

But now he was back in it, already back in it. Chaos and pain and endless bloody murders and mass graves and hacked-off heads and his little boy, lost, taken away from him by a gang of evil thugs, and the flaws in his own character.

A pain started up in his chest, spreading across the front of his ribcage and working its way around his back. He collapsed onto his haunches and steadied his bulk on the dirty wet ground with outstretched fingers, waiting for it to pass.

*

H had driven in, in the bright lunchtime sunshine, and parked up in a side road just off Tooley Street. He found his way back there now, slowly, feeling a powerful need to get home and see Olivia. He fumbled for his keys and somehow managed to pour himself into the driver's seat. He sparked up the radio and tuned into the London News Channel:

'Two convicts - named as Basim Dragusha and Ronald Hawkins - have made a dramatic escape from an ambulance on its way from Durham prison to the University Hospital of North Durham. Police sources say that it was a well-planned operation involving at least two cars and several armed men. The two men are extremely dangerous and likely to be armed. Members of the public should not …'

H punched the off button, fired up the ignition and set a course for Eltham. He didn't pay much attention to the colour of the traffic lights or the rest of the cars on the road, and was unaware he'd received several angry car horns and a smattering of wanker hand-signals before he arrived at his home.

Olivia was waiting for him as he got out of his car. They embraced and held each other tight for several moments before Olivia spoke.

'You've had calls from Julie, Amisha and Graham. Julie sounded frantic, she was crying so much I could barely understand her. You need to call her back first, she's in a real state.'

Julie was Ronnie's mother and H's ex-wife, an ex-wife he rarely talked to. He was in no mood to do so now. There wasn't much he could do in his current state so decided the best thing was to sleep it off. He began pulling at his clothes, and slogged his way up the stairs, looking back only to say 'nice cup of tea, please love.'

Olivia joined the big man at his bedside. It was even worse than Olivia had suspected: he was rotten drunk. She had the terrible sinking feeling that always accompanied her deep anxieties about H's well-being. 'How are you feeling H? What are we going to do?'

'Right now we're going to do nothing. I'm as drunk as a lord and no use to anyone. I'm going to bed, doll. See you in the morning.'

H drifted off and began to dream; strangely, given the sort of day he'd had, he would have a night of wonderful dreams. Dreams of Olivia and an unborn baby, dreams of a young child cradled in his arms, dreams of ice cream and fairground rides by the sea, of football matches and playing in the park. The dreams would seem to recollect his past with Ronnie and throw them into the future with Harry.

Olivia tucked him in and walked, numbly, along to the hallway to the bathroom; she got down low, crawled to the toilet and, through a face made wet by an overspill of bitter tears, vomited her guts up.

57

Olivia opened the curtains and the light stabbed into H's eyes like a switchblade. They'd been here before. He tightened his eyelids and fought hard to hold back the nausea. He'd been trying to gather his memories, straighten out dream from reality as he emerged from his slumbers. He was at the stage of fooling himself into believing yesterday had all been a nightmare when Olivia's words smashed their way into the foreground of his consciousness.

'So what are you going to do H, lay there feeling sorry for yourself, or go and do something about the mess your son is in?' A tempest was blowing inside H's head, assembling, breaking up and reassembling the fragments of the previous day. He opened an eye; the puzzle of daily reality had been reassembled.

It had been a long time since H had been hungover. He'd drunk so much over the years he'd become immune but after nine months without a drop his spectacular fall from grace had reacquainted him with the experience. Olivia placed a glass of water on the bedside table; H downed it in one. 'Thanks doll,' he said, 'I'm gonna do the latter. Full English and large mug of tea while I have a shower. And four aspirin, please.'

H started to frame a way forward while he went through his morning ritual. He didn't spend too much time on this as he usually did, and emerged from the bathroom in short order looking smart and ready.

Olivia said, 'Sorry about being a bit hard on you before, but what with the pregnancy and all I …'

'No, you're right babes. Absolutely right. I've got to sort all this out. Ronnie needs me - yesterday was a one-off babes, trust me. It was just the shock of hearing about Ronnie. I'll be staying on the wagon...I won't be losing the plot again, can't afford to. Ronnie needs me. I won't let him down again.'

H was zoning in. He knew he had to resolve the situation with Little Ronnie, whatever it took. He had his second son to think of. Little Harry would need all his time and energy. He wasn't planning on fucking up another time. Whatever Little Ronnie had done it had to be properly straightened out. No time for a four-day bender, no time for self-pity, he had to be on top form. As of now.

'Right,' he announced, 'I'm gonna get on the blower. I'll need Graham and Amisha to help me on this. Any updates on the news? Any developments since last night?'

'Nothing about where they are. All we know is Little Ronnie and Dragusha are on the loose somewhere up north. But there's been a lot of speculation as to why they broke out.'

'What kind of speculation?'

'Well, that there was a murder in the prison, and a feud, and Ronnie and Dragusha were attacked. That Ronnie was badly injured. That Dragusha feared for his safety and got out, and took Ronnie with him.'

'Well that's way off the mark babes, I can tell you that for nothing. People like Dragusha don't fear for their safety - they make other people fear for their safety.'

'You know best H. Otherwise, there's a lot of talk that it's connected to the mass grave they found at Bedgebury. How can that be H, how could Ronnie have had anything to do with that? Or Dragusha, while he was prison? Are his gang responsible for all those killings?'

'Seems likely Liv. If it was Dragusha's firm he would have known about it before we did; probably planned the escape thinking his leadership was needed before it all came on top. Too late now.'

'But,' said Olivia, 'why would he want Ronnie with him?'

H took a deep breath, blew it out slowly and gave Olivia the news he'd received the day before, the news that had sent him running for the scotch after a nine-month moratorium. A truth known only by himself and a handful of insiders.

'That killing in the nick you mentioned, the victim was Jack Butcher, an old school villain. I heard from a very reliable source that Ronnie did it.'

Olivia stood still for a time, as if in a trance. The breakfast plate she'd just picked up fell from her hands and smashed to smithereens on the kitchen floor.

'Oh my God!' she said, 'What the hell is happening to the world? All this madness...and Ronnie caught up in it... No wonder you fancied a scotch.'

'Yeah,' said H, 'but that was yesterday. I don't know what they've done to Ronnie, how they've turned him.'

Olivia sat down, weak, breathless, shaken. She was in the mood for a heart to heart, an evaluation of what this all this meant - for Ronnie, for H, for her and for her unborn child. But H didn't have the time. He was already on the phone, organising a meet with Graham and Amisha. It was 10am. Amisha was already busy and in a meeting with Andrew Glass, but she could catch up with them in the King's Arms in Dacre Street after. H rang off, put his jacket on, scrambled around for his car keys, gave Olivia a peck on the forehead and headed for the door.

Olivia could almost see the gears turning in is head, plans hatching. But it was his eyes that got to her. As H arrived at the door he turned to say goodbye one last time and she saw them narrow. There was no mistaking it; there was murder in them. And retribution and repentance were on his lips.

'I'm going to deal with all this Liv, with Ronnie and Dragusha, if it's the last thing I ever do,' he said.

And then he was gone.

58

Graham, as was his habit, hit the shower after his early-morning run around Clapham Common and settled himself for his breakfast. Amisha, who'd spent the night, had already left for the Yard. He got his coffee going, sparked up the tablet and sat at the breakfast bar for his morning scan of the sites that mattered. First stop, Joey Jupiter; Graham had developed a much thicker skin than he'd had even a year ago, and now sometimes almost enjoyed the torrents of infantile social gossip and anti-establishment sarcasm that spewed from Jupiter's warped imagination. Jupiter was more popular than ever these days, and was clearly striking a chord with a public - or a section of it - that was becoming increasingly angry and irrational. Graham called it the 'Twitter effect.' H had other words for it. This morning, as it happened, the big man himself was once again in the firing line:

BEYOND PARODY

> This blog has long maintained that Detective Inspector Harry Hawkins of the Yard, above all the public figures in the life of our great city, is the gift that keeps on giving. But he is now on a run of form that is extraordinary even by his exalted standards. True, he has not been back at work long and should therefore not be held entirely responsible for the Met's utter lack of progress in the Bazza Wishbone case; nor can he yet be expected to have made much headway on the crimes against humanity committed in Bedgebury Forest - he is, after all, only 'London's Top Copper.'

But surely this lumbering hulk of a sleuth might be expected to keep members of his own family on the side of law and order? News that his son 'Little Ronnie' - a cocaine smuggler, no less - has been sprung from the back of a prison ambulance, and is now wanted by the police for questioning in connection with the horror in the forest, is pure gold for the aficionado of *Hawkins absurdus.*

But the joke isn't funny anymore: these are serious times. Chaotic times. Dangerous times. The fabric of our society is tearing; wanton, senseless violence and mass murder stalk the land, and we are fearful. We are looking to leaders, our experts, our men and women of authority, courage and resilience, to show us the way out of the darkness. And what do we get? A political elite that is worse - much worse - than useless, an utterly toothless official media and, in the very front line in the war against evil itself, men of the calibre of Detective Inspector Harry Hawkins - a burned-out hack who should now quit the force and turn his attention to looking for work as an extra in the next remake of *The Sweeney.*

59

The trio sat down in a quiet corner of the King's Head. H didn't hang about or mince his words.

'My Ronnie killed Jack Butcher,' he said, 'that bastard Dragusha's got him tucked up like a lap dog. God knows what he's done to him.'

A flurry of rapid exchanges of shock and disbelief followed the revelation. When Amisha and Graham had accepted the accuracy of H's news they calmed down a little. H moved the conversation on to next steps. He'd called them here to plot and plan a strategy, not to gossip.

'So,' said Amisha, 'why would they escape? Where do you think they're going?'

'I think they escaped because Dragusha's firm are responsible for the thing in Bedgebury Forest.

'What do you think is behind all that H, in the forest?'' said Amisha.

'Well if I had to put money on it I'd say they've been diversifying, getting involved with people trafficking and suchlike, and something went tits up. We know a lot of that is routed through the Balkans. I'd be surprised if they weren't at it, come to think of it. It's easy money.'

'But Dragusha's in the clear. He could hardly have a better alibi,' said Graham.

'Think it through,' said H. 'The escape obviously had to be planned in advance. If I'm right it means Dragusha knew about the bodies before any of us. Realised things were going wobbly in his firm and decided to do something about it. But by the time he got out the situation was already well and truly out of control.'

'So guv, if you're right why not just give himself up?' asked Amisha.

'Well, for one thing there's the murder of Jack Butcher; Ronnie did it but he's got to be behind it. And his little empire is now going to be torn to shreds by everyone from the CID to MI6. This Bedgebury thing is going to be one of the biggest investigations in criminal history, God only knows what they'll dig up. It's all going to be too strong for him to handle. And he is who he is - he's going to try to get out of the country, to fight another day.'

'And is he likely to take Ronnie with him, as a hostage?'

H winced at the prospect. 'Maybe,' he said, 'but from what I hear he's done a proper job brainwashing the boy. Probably a Stockholm Syndrome type of turnout up there in the cell. Ronnie wouldn't have had much choice. We have to assume he's going willingly, that he's part of it all. We need to find them. Quickly.'

'Well, how far can they get?' said Graham. 'This is one of the biggest manhunt ever staged in this country. The world and his wife are on the lookout for them.'

'No, Dragusha won't walk into anything, he's too sharp. He'll find a way. No good relying on the authorities; if they get too close this bastard will kill my boy as sure as he's brainwashed him. I'll find them, and then I'll sort it.'

Graham had heard enough. He shot Amisha a look that said 'We've got to help him.'

Amisha unexpectedly felt a cold chill slide across her bones. She remembered the last time she teamed up with the big man for a spot of off-piste vigilantism. It had ended in her kidnap, torture and rape. She wasn't convinced.

'Amisha, you on board?'

'Er, yes. Of course I'm on board.'

'OK H…this is too much for you to do on your own. You're going to need backup. We'll all do it. The three of us.'

'Well…' started H.

It was Graham's turn - he hadn't done this in a while - to cut H short.

'No ifs, ands, or buts H. Your son needs help and we don't want you going completely rogue - look what happened last time. If we all stick together on this there's no need for you to go off half-cocked and do this on your own.'

'Agreed, Amisha?'

'Yep.'

Amisha was thinking of Olivia and Little Harry, how they were going to need H in the years to come. Maybe, she thought but daren't mention, it was time to let Little Ronnie go.

God help us. I only pray we can keep the big man from going on a rampage with Graham in tow.

'OK,' said Graham. 'Amisha, I'll work on this with H from now on. Cover for us as best you can. Keep Hilary in the dark for as long as possible. If you find a way to get us access to the online case files on the Bedgebury case we can keep up to date with all the latest developments. Do your magic, yes?'

Amisha shrugged her shoulders as if to say it'd be easier than taking candy from a baby. Which, for her, it was. She'd transgressed the Met's security protocols so many times since she'd met H that she had literally lost count. Dragusha might be a cunning bastard but she was at genius level when it came to circumnavigating IT systems, and far brighter than the people the Metropolitan Police employed to check that security protocols were not being transgressed.

'No problem,' she said.

'You'll have to stay on the Wishbone investigation,' continued Graham. 'Keep me and H updated and we'll try and feed into it as best we can.'

H sat back, impressed with and moved by the way Graham had shaped up. He thought back to the year before. Then Graham had been someone who H had truly loathed, or thought he did. Not much more than a boy, really, who'd read all the books on criminology but knew little about crime. Someone who couldn't handle himself when confronted with a real situation. New to the force with all the latest buzzword bollocks pouring out of him like water from a tap. Filled with a mission to reduce the murder rate in underprivileged areas by 2.4 per cent per year going forward, and stamp out a string of 'phobias' H didn't really understand.

And look at him now: scared of nothing, solid as a rock…ready to stick his neck out when it really matters - loyal. He's learned about loyalty.

Real-world, sharp-end experience alongside H had changed the person Graham was, or perhaps revealed it. H wasn't sure. All he knew was that people could become something they should never have been, in a gentler world. He thought of his son; if only things had been different.

'Guv, you ok?' said Graham. 'We need to get moving. We need to think through the next steps.'

'Right you are son,' said H, 'good plan. Amisha, try and bring us up to speed on the Bedgebury investigation as quick as you can. For me and Graham, Wishbone is on the back burner as of now - just make sure you keep feeding Hilary enough morsels to keep her at bay. It's all about Dragusha and Ronnie now. Graham, you and me are off to Bermondsey to see my old mate John. Follow me in your car. He knows what this firm are about better than anyone else we know.'

60

Andrew had been doing what Andrew did best: the gadget-driven investigative donkey work. When Amisha appeared in the office after her meeting with H and Graham he made a beeline for her, eager to fill her in on his latest findings.

His face was bright and lively and his eagerness had become infectious since H had allowed him to shine in the regular debriefs. H certainly knew, Amisha reflected, how to get the best out of people. Despite all his ups and downs H still had a warmth and sincerity that shone through, that people picked up on and repaid with loyalty. She responded to Andrew's enthusiasm with a warm smile.

'Go for it Andrew, I'm all ears.'

'Well, firstly, de Montfort is in an outrageous amount of debt. Seriously, he's going to need to buddy up with Richard Branson or George Soros to get out of this. He owns a massive old 16th century pile in Somerset that's haemorrhaging money and he can't afford to maintain it. Nowhere near. He's had it up for sale for over a year but the estate agent says his asking price is too high so he's had no offers. Apparently the place needs millions spent on it just to make it habitable.

'Well, well; so things are not quite as fragrant in the de Montfort garden as we've been led to believe. Go on.'

'It's more like a cesspit than an English country garden. And there's more: he's also taken out a huge loan to redevelop his townhouse. I'm not sure of the exact amount, but one source I've spoken to says it's more than two million, and that he's used his ancestral estate as collateral.

The parties he holds cost a fortune and he seems to be in debt to everyone. He's started to miss payments to caterers, florists and the like and many of his suppliers are thinking about stopping his line of credit. This may well include his drug connections. Basically, he's living a lifestyle way beyond his means.'

'Outstanding work Andrew,' said Amisha, 'any thoughts on what might connect any of this to Bazza's murder?'

Andrew was waiting for this one. 'Well,' he said, 'I managed to get to talk to one or two people who are regulars at de Montfort's parties. For a while I was getting nowhere. It seems like these celebrities are as thick as thieves when it comes to talking about each other's business, and just shut the shop up whenever outsiders start asking questions. But I eventually tracked down a friend of Jacynta's, Jennifer Goodchild. Have you heard of her?'

'Yes,' said Amisha, 'she's some kind of celebrity lifestyle guru. I think I've seen her on the telly once or twice talking about yoga and meditation and, as Detective Inspector Hawkins would no doubt say, other such bollocks.' Once again Amisha had found herself getting into the mind of the big man. 'And didn't she write a book about how to adopt a vegan lifestyle?'

'That's the one,' enthused Andrew. 'It's called "The Allure of Pure: The Vegan Life and the Path to Self-Fulfilment".'

'Ah yes, not a favourite of H's, so he tells me. He found that one somewhat heavy going I think. Was the sage herself able to cast any light on Jacynta, Bazza, de Montfort?'

'Well she says, on the basis of some conversations she had with Jacyanta, that Bazza and de Montfort were closer than we thought.'

Amisha, who was still pre-occupied with H's Little Ronnie-Dragusha crisis, and worried about where the decisions they'd just taken in the pub were going to lead, now gave Andrew her full attention.

'Go on.'

'Well, the details are still a bit murky but she says that Bazza was not only trying to get himself out of his contract with Blandish but that de Montfort had befriended him, had become his confidant.'

'Snakes like that don't befriend people without a motive, we'll need to find out more about this, put some flesh on it. I think we need to talk to Ms Goodchild at greater length.'

'Already on it,' said Andrew, 'she's coming in today.'

'What?'

Andrew was now looking a little sheepish, given he had invited what could be a major witness to the Yard without letting the heads of the investigation know. He explained himself:

'Well, Detective Sergeant Bhanushali, I only managed to contact her today, she seemed eager to talk and she more or less invited herself. I tried to give you and Detective Inspector Miller-Marchant a call but you were both on voicemail.'

'No problem Andrew, that's really good work. When is she coming in?'

'This afternoon,' said Andrew.

61

The lifts were out of order. Graham held his breath in a vain effort to block out the stench of urine as he and H bounded up the final flight of stairs to Confident John Viney's flat. H balled his hand into a fist and pounded it like a hammer three times on the flimsy excuse for a door; it appeared to be not much more than a makeshift repair job.

The last one, H knew, had been kicked in three months earlier in a robbery that had shaken Confident John's confidence. He'd been in bed at the time, heard the intruders make their entry and decided it was best to leave them to it. He'd pushed the wardrobe to barricade his bedroom door and let them take whatever they'd come for, which had turned out to be his TV. He still hadn't replaced it; but he had his laptop, and his premium membership of *Mature Cum Slurpers*. John was getting by, and there wasn't much else worth nicking anyway. He rarely got up before midday - the racing didn't start until the afternoon - and the hammering at the door startled him awake. He sat up faster than Ronnie Wood ironing out a line of cocaine, his heart beating like a steam hammer.

Who the fuck is knocking me up this time of day?

Have those fucking mongrels come back for round two?

No, he decided - if they'd come to rob him there would be no knocking, just kicking, or they'd have a pop at a window. But whoever it was bashing away at his door was in no mood to be kept waiting. These days he slept with the door to his bedroom pre-barricaded. He'd just about decided to stay put and ride it out when he heard H's growling voice.

'John, it's me, H. Open the fucking door mate.' John felt all the tension drain from his body and a smile of pleasure and relief appear on his face. He jumped up, moved the wardrobe from in front of his bedroom door and went to let the big man in.

'Hello H,' he said through a big shit-eating grin, 'how's it going? Am I glad to see you.'

John saw quickly that this was not a social visit; H surged into the flat, introduced Graham and got straight to business.

'Tell me everything you know about what the firm on the Island has been up to.'

The speed of the entrance and H's line of questioning left John struggling to understand what was going on. H saw it.

'You haven't heard?'

'Heard what?'

'Fucking hell John what planet are you on? It's been all over the news for the last few days.'

'What are you talking about? I've been keeping me head down for a bit. And my telly got nicked.'

'Jesus, John,' said H, exasperated. He looked around the flat and saw what an absolute mess it was in, even by John's standards.

'How can you live in a shithole like this? Where's your fucking self-respect?'

John felt admonished and even slightly embarrassed - given Graham's presence - by the rebuke; but H did not give him time to protest.

'Right John, sit down and fucking listen,' he said before giving an overview of the full story of Ronnie's deeds in prison, the escape from Durham nick, the likely Albanian involvement in the mass murder that everyone in the country except John was talking about and fretting over.

Confident John Viney had lived a sketchy life, and had thought he'd seen it all, thought himself un-shockable. But he was shocked now, almost to the point of disbelief.

'So what do you wanna know H?' he said.

62

'The firm on the Island - have you stayed in touch with them since the dealings you had with them last year, when me and Ronnie Ruddock were going after Tara's killer? I need to know who's who and what they're up to.'

'Well, you've come to the right place mate. The whole thing last year was a proper icebreaker. They're OK if you don't get on the wrong side of 'em. I've been buying my weed off 'em for a while now. Remember that fat doughnut Fatos, the one we had dealings with? I think he's still holding the fort while your mate Dragusha's away. I don't know everything they're into but below him there are a couple of older lumps who seem to be always around him. They don't say much, I call them Thing One and Thing Two - you know, out of the Dr Seuss books - because you can hardly tell them apart. I don't know their real names but I reckon they're the core men after him.'

'And?' said H, grinding his teeth like a speed freak at the end of a long night.

'Well, things changed a bit recently. I've been dealing with some of the youngsters. There's a little mob of them, fresh out of the old country. They're different from the others…they talk a lot more - they're really mouthy, when they're on it - and I've seen them having a beer, mixing in a few of the boozers. They've usually got some right sorts round them.'

'Names?'said H.

'Dunno mate...it's all a bit double-dutch, you know what I mean? The main one, the lairy one, is called something like Zif, I think. Or Zaf. Or Zef. Something like that. He'll be a proper handful when he grows up.'

'So they're a bit more talkative than the older blokes on the firm. Good to know. Anything else?'

'Well, they seem to be breaking out on their own, bit of a law unto themselves. They've been getting into this and that. If you ask me I'd say they're not all that keen on the old chain-of-command stuff. It wouldn't surprise me if they try to make a bit of a name for themselves, without Dragusha around to steady the ship.'

'So, as far as you're concerned this Fatos is the daddy now? The one most likely to know what's going on?'

'Absolutely.'

'Any idea where we're likely to find him? Or someone who might have a clue where he is? Assuming he's not waiting for us to come and find him in his caravan?'

'Well, there's a boozer, the Dog and Duck, just off Tower Bridge Road. A lot of the Albanians have developed a taste for our pubs, and a few of them get in there. They might not work for him but they'll know of him. They won't talk to you though.'

'I've heard that one before mate. They'll talk alright.'

'If you say so mate.'

'I do. You can bet your fucking life on it. Anyway, what are you holding? And I don't want to hear about any of your fucking cowboy guns.'

Graham, who'd been sitting as a more or less mute observer, could not believe what he was hearing.

Jesus, what have I got myself into here?

'Alright Graham?' said H, sensing his unease, 'I haven't got to talk you though all this, have I son? You are on board with me - correct?'

Graham breathed deeply, exhaled, nodded in the affirmative and said 'You know I am H, you know I am. Just don't give me something that's going to blow up in my hand. These are the best armed villains in London. Fire needs to be met with fire.'

‘I’ve got just what you’re looking for boys,’ said John, ‘just give me a second.’ He left the room and went into the toilet, where he seemed to be rooting around for something.

While he was gone Amisha called Graham with an update. Graham put her on speaker.

‘I’ve just been talking to a contact on the Bedgebury case. It’s not been released yet but they have some clear dabs on a bottle of rakia found at the scene. They belong to Fatos Gazjet. They’ll be releasing a photo to the press pronto.’

‘I knew it, I fucking knew it,’ said H.

63

Jennifer Goodchild was waiting in the interview room when Amisha and Andrew walked in. A tiny, elfin-like figure, she was not quite the glowing new age goddess they'd expected. She was wafer-thin, gaunt and pale, with a face like a bag of wet cement. She put Amisha in mind of a shrewish old-school primary teacher who would brook no dissent in class - very prim and proper. Big-world, positive energy she did not exude. It was impossible to say how old she was.

Maybe someone slipped a bit of bacon into her avocado salad this morning. A double portion of pie and mash in Arments or Manzes would do her a power of good.

Amisha extended her hand: 'Hello Jennifer, I'm Amisha. Thanks for coming in.'

'Hi Amisha.'

Andrew then introduced himself and Amisha let him kick things off: he'd hauled this guru in under his own steam, and she wanted to see how he dealt with interviews.

'So moving on from what we said on the phone, can you tell us more about the relationship between Wishbone and de Montfort, and how you know what you know?'

A very open question, thought Amisha, which seemed to work as Jennifer launched into a highly detailed, hundred-word-a-minute account of her relationship with Jacynta Packington, how she had confided in her about everything going on in her, and Bazza's, life.

According to Jennifer, Bazza was at loggerheads with Blandish and had been trying, unsuccessfully, to see how he could get out of his contract. Tarquin had befriended Bazza and coached him in his efforts, and had even met with Blandish on Bazza's behalf - he'd received very short shrift in an ill-tempered meeting. Blandish's goons had literally thrown him out of his office.

'Not exactly something you see on Wimpole Street every day,' said the sage, a hint of a smile appearing on her face for the first time.

'How do you know this?' asked Andrew.

'He has a PA my dear, in my line of work it pays to buy lunch for the PAs now and again.'

'What do you think de Montfort's motivation would have been, in trying to help Bazza?'

'Financial, I would have thought. I understand that he's absolutely broke - as poor as a church mouse. He's useless with money, doesn't understand it, like a lot of them. My guess would be he believed he could help Bazza out of his contract and then take over the management of his career. He couldn't, of course, he'd be about as much use as a chocolate teapot, but he's conceited enough to believe he could do it.'

'How well do you know Blandish?' asked Amisha.

'I've met him once or twice over the years. He's not the kind of guy who would be interested in my services but I've provided dietary advice to some of the stars on his books, so I've heard plenty of inside stories about him. And I've got to know his PA, Emily Green, very well.'

'Do you think he'd be capable of having someone killed?'

Jennifer responded immediately:

'Oh, I should think he's capable of anything, anything at all,' she said. 'Money and ego, they're what drive him. From what I know of him I'd describe him as obsessive and ruthless in pursuit of his goals.'

'OK,' said Amisha, 'one more question. Do you know anything about who supplies de Montfort with his drugs and such? For his parties?'

'Sorry, no idea. Never touch any stimulants myself; it's meditation and yoga all the way for me. I'm the last person Tarquin would invite to one of those things.'

*

After they'd said their thankyous and goodbyes Amisha asked Andrew to grab a couple of coffees for a debrief at her desk.

'Thanks Andrew,' she said, gulping back the coffee, 'so what do you think?'

'I think we need to go deeper into de Montfort's struggle with Blandish.'

'Next steps?'

'We need to get a judge to give us access to de Montfort's bank accounts and put together a team of lawyers to study the detail of the Bazza contract with Blandish.'

Amisha smiled at the young man indulgently, like H had at her when she was an eager beaver full of good intentions but little idea of how to dig for truth.

You've got to put it on them, Ames, see what they're made of. People will feed you bollocks all day long if you let them.

'I see you're a person who likes to pay attention to detail Andrew, that's excellent. Yes, we need to do those things and I'm sure you're the man to get them done. But we also need, I think, to go and talk to Jacynta again. She's clearly been economical with the truth. We need to find out why. And further visits to Blandish and de Montfort are in order. Tweedledum and Tweedledee have messed us about for long enough.'

64

'Come off motorway. We need chemist.'

Whether Dragusha's concern for Ujku was altruistic or because he thought he might be useful Zef did not know. Either way he already knew Dragusha well enough to understand that when he gave a command you obeyed.

He slowed down and pulled off the M6 at Junction 34.

'Follow signs to Lancaster,' said Dragusha.

In the back of the car Ronnie had taken a turn for the worse. They knew he had a few cracked ribs and that, along with the broken leg he'd suffered at the hands of the avenging Butcher firm, had left him more or less incapacitated. But there was more going on than that. He was running a high fever, had severe abdominal pains - his stomach was as swollen as a toad's - and he was dipping in and out of consciousness.

'Internal bleeding,' said their leader. It was something he knew plenty about.

The organs inside Ronnie's body had been torn and crushed by the force of the blows that had rained down on him. Internal bleeding was damaging the body both from the loss of blood and from the pressure the misplaced blood was putting on other organs and tissues. There was no way of knowing the extent of bleeding, nor which organs had been damaged; not without a CAT scan. Treatment, Dragusha knew from experience, was either observation or surgery, depending on the results of the scan. If surgery was required it had to happen quickly.

Zef snaked the car towards a suburb on the outskirts of Lancaster. The place had a back-end-of-nowhere kind of feel to it but it did have a pharmacy. Dragusha guided Zef in, one eye on a Google map.

'Stop here.'

Dragusha looked at Zef as he slowed the car and pulled up. He saw something of his young self in the youth sitting beside him; the kid was arrogant, full of bravado, sharp and quick to act. Something of a liability, if not managed properly. Maybe Fatos was not up to the job of controlling such a livewire, he thought. Dragusha considered sending him into the pharmacy, but figured that with a kid this wired it could only end one way - with a dead pharmacist and the wrong supplies.

'Wait,' he said. 'Two minutes.'

He entered the shop. He was after splints, bandages, a crutch if there was one, the strongest painkillers on offer and some Warfarin or similar to thin Ronnie's blood and help prevent clotting. Best he could do, under the circumstances. Three people were in the shop: two staff behind the counter and a shopper. He browsed until the shopper left. He called the two staff over to an impromptu meeting, jabbering a fake question that neither of them understood, grabbed both of them around the neck and applied pressure until they were unconscious. He smashed open the till, pocketed some of the cash, knocked out the surveillance camera and calmly collected his supplies, making sure only to take what he needed and not to spill or knock anything over. He pulled down the door blind, jammed the lock on his way out and walked slowly to the car. He established himself and his supplies in the back seat and instructed Zef to drive on.

Time to deal with his patient: he administered a mass of painkillers and the Warfarin before feeling around Ronnie's shin. Satisfied that he understood the basic contours of the break, he applied the necessary pressure and did not flinch when Ronnie screamed like thunder. He applied the splint and the bandages and clambered back to the front of the car while it was still in motion.

'Now let God decide if he live or die,' he said to Zef.

65

'You've got to be fucking joking mate,' said H, 'what did I say about the cowboy guns? We're going up against some of the most ruthless, well-armed villains in Europe, who've got nothing to lose now. And you're showing me these?'

John had triumphantly produced, from behind the cistern in the toilet, a brace of IOF.32 pistols. He'd bought them from Zif, or Zaf or Zef, after the burglary.

'He tells me that these are just about the most powerful hand guns in circulation,' John said with pride. 'Got enough punch in 'em to stop any mongrel who wants to come in here and chore my gear dead in his tracks.'

'Not a lot of use taped to the back of the cistern though, are they John?'

'Well, I…'

'Listen mate, if you're going to barricade yourself into your bedroom to keep the bad boys at bay, don't you think you should have your weapons in there with you?'

'Yes but H, it's a seven stretch now if I get caught with a gun in here. I thought tucking them away properly would…'

'Alright John, listen. I know you're helping us, but we can't use these little Indian pop guns mate. The Singapore police use these; do you know why? *Because they haven't got any fucking villains there.* We're going to need something a lot tastier than these.'

'Sorry H, I…'

'Nah, you're alright, I'm sorry mate.'

H sat down and took a deep breath. He looked exhausted,

'It's just, I'm starting to lose it. These bastards have got my boy. They've fucked his head up and made him do terrible things.'

They've taken him to where the wild things are.

‘My sweet little boy…I let him down…he was lost…he needed his dad. All he needed was his dad.’

I’ll always love you dad.

‘I’m going to save him, John. I’m going to save him, and I’m going to put some severe pain on the people who’ve done this to him. I don’t care who I have to go through to do it. Whoever’s fucking with my boy is going to pay.’

The room fell silent. John stared out of the window. Graham reflected, with some unease, on H’s promise to deal with everyone who might get in his way. H sat quietly, his regret suppressing rage.

‘Thing is, John,’ H said at last, ‘we’re going to need some proper hardware. Have you got anyone you can go to right now, to get something on tick?’

‘Yes mate,’ said John. ‘Give me an hour.’

*

John was back, breathless and harassed-looking, forty-five minutes later. He had produced the goods: a Glock 33, with three blocks of .357 Sig rounds, and a Super Redhawk Ruger revolver with a box of .480 Ruger rounds; enough to put a stop to anything or anyone they were likely to come up against. And then some.

H took the Glock; the sheer number of bullets swung it for him.

Now they were in the game.

H and Graham checked their weapons, tucked them into their waistbands and rose to leave. H gave John, for the first time in all the years they’d known one another, a great big man hug. Graham shook his hand.

H stood, pulled on his coat and said to John ‘Wish us luck son.’

He then turned to Graham, and said 'Right then, Detective Inspector Miller-Marchant, time for a pint at the old Dog and Duck.'

66

H and Graham hailed a cab and made their way, though dull skies and drizzle, from Silwood Street towards Tower Bridge Road. Gentrification in this part of London was well under way - even the shabbiest parts of the city were getting this treatment now. They passed gleaming new flats with seven figure price tags, and the old, dull housing estates and tenement buildings; the people who lived in these failed, utterly, to understand how anyone would pay prices like that in their part of town.

Amid the high-end Indian restaurants and estate agents were shops that still catered to the needs of the poorer citizens, who'd just come through a credit crunch and economic crisis that nobody knew the reasons for. They passed second-hand clothes shops, a place with filthy windows and a bright sign that said 'Payday Loans - Best Rates' and a large - supermarket large - pawn shop buzzing with activity.

They alighted in Tower Bridge Road, by a shop proudly proclaiming that everything inside could be purchased for one pound. Nearby was another, undercutting it, called '99p Shopper's Paradise.' Here you could buy any amount of tat for 99p; here in wealthy London utter crap was available, utter crap which had been made in sweatshops in the far-flung corners of the globe.

H caught the whiff of fish and chips as they passed a place he had often frequented as a boy. It was now more of a general fast food outlet that also did pizzas and kebabs and giant buckets of greasy chicken for ravenous dopers. H said 'I'm hungry,' and entered the 'restaurant.' 'Eat when you can, sleep when you can' they used to say in the Paras. H knew he'd be needing plenty of energy if he was going to track down his boy and whoever had him.

The smell of fat permeated the air and H breathed deeply through his nose to fully appreciate the scent. He was used to this smell. He found it intoxicating. The odour triggered the firing of a million and one neurons in his brain that told him he was more than hungry, that he was starving and that the comfort of fat and carbs was there for the taking.

'Hmm,' he said to the young Polish girl behind the counter, 'cod and chips and a tea to take away please love. Strong. Two sugars. Graham?'

'Nothing for me, thanks.'

'Good. You can hold my tea.'

H lovingly lavished his chips with salt and vinegar and stuffed a few into his mouth. He turned to Graham, who was looking around the shop with something approaching disgust, and just managed to prevent himself snigger-spitting his chips onto Graham's jacket as the two men stepped back into the night.

The sun had given up its attempt to penetrate the drizzle and had vanished below the horizon. By the time they reached the Dog and Duck it was dark and the trickles of rain had turned to a full-on shower.

67

'Two orange juices please fella,' H said to the Slovakian barman, disturbing him from petting a hyped-up pitbull terrier. He took their drinks and moved closer to a group of six young men sitting at a corner table. Most were drinking rakia and vodka, but a few had developed a taste for English Ale. That's real progress, H thought, as he listened to some of their conversation.

H was no linguist, but to be a copper in London these days you had to develop some sort of ear. He listened in: not English, or Polish, or Russian. Maybe Romanian, or Bosnian, or Albanian. Not criminals. They wouldn't be sitting here putting the world to rights if that was the case, not with all hell breaking loose and the country on high alert. He looked at their rough, calloused hands. They looked like they were used to doing a regular day's labouring, no doubt on one of the hundreds building sites that covered the capital these days.

Right, better get amongst this lot.

H moved swiftly and took even Graham by surprise. Before anyone had time to realise what was happening he was sitting smack bang middle of the group.

'Alright boys,' he said with a large smile, and flashed his warrant card.

The men looked very uncomfortable indeed. They knew why he was here. The whole world knew. They all felt like they had targets on their backs these days.

'We not talk to police,' a self-appointed spokesman said, attempting bravado.

'Yeah, I know. I get that. I really do. You're the kind of boys who work hard, plenty of cash-in-hand, keep your heads down. No problem, good luck to you.'

'Fuck off,' repeated Mr Bravado.

H took a deep breath.

'Alright boys…it's like this. Forget the script, I don't have time to play any games. I'm going to ask some questions, and you're going to stay calm, be polite, and answer them. Then I'll go and you can get back to your drinks. Any of you who might be tempted to fuck me about should know that there's detainment in a police cell and serious beatings in your immediate future.'

These men were no babes in the wood; they were all familiar with the sharp end of things. They were six, and the men who had come to interrupt them were two. Should be no contest. But H was giving them the strong impression that cooperation was their best option. By far. The big man looked them in the eye one by one, glowering silently.

Bite it off boys, bite it off by all means. But be sure you can fucking swallow it.

The pub fell silent, all action suspended, while they considered their options.

Graham moved around the table with his phone, taking mug shots of the happy band. The silence went on for long enough for H to know he'd gained the upper hand.

'Right then, my beauties, do any of you know an Albanian gentleman by the name of Fatos Gazjet?'

H surveyed each face with lightning speed as he mentioned the name. He read their body language, sensed their speeding heart rates, noted their involuntary movements and scratchings. Every one of the men at the table either knew or knew of Fatos, knew he was the most wanted man in Britain and, although they didn't know the man sitting in front of them, felt increasingly uneasy.

'We not know where he is,' said the spokesman.

'I know that. That's not what I'm asking.'

'Then what you want?'

'Fatos and his firm. When they're not on the Island, when they want a little bit of peace and quiet, where might they go?'

'Don't know.'

H sensed the heart rates of all six men accelerate, their mouths dry up and their muscles tighten in unison as he reached inside his pocket and produced the Glock. He showed it to them for a second and moved his hand under the table, holding the weapon at crotch-height to his seated companions.

'Then you better start thinking, quick. I'm not here on police business. This is a personal matter. The boy on the run with Basim Dragusha is my son and I need to find him, now. Talk to me boys…or a few of you will find yourselves heading for Guy's hospital in the back of an ambulance, with your cock and balls, what's left of them, back here on the carpet for the dog to lap up.'

From the far end of the table a second voice piped up. 'They could be many places. How would we know?'

'I'll take anything you got. Any scrap or rumour. Anything about Fatos and his firm; their businesses, their operations or their whereabouts. Just between us. No comebacks. I just want my son.'

The gun, and the threat to their manhood, had done the trick All six men now spoke up, offering possibilities, rumours they'd heard, ad hoc theories. But nothing concrete, nothing certain. Mostly speculation, hot air and bollocks.

'OK boys, been nice meeting you,' said H. 'Thank you all for your cooperation. Enjoy your evening.'

68

'Now what?' said Graham out on the street, 'Not much to go on there was there?'

'Well, we've had a good trample about in the long grass; the snakes should start crawling out before long. Let's have a little mooch about.'

They walked the windswept streets for a bit. Graham, being unfamiliar with this part of the world, was surprised at how quickly glistening towers and glitzy apartments could give way to bleaker, darker, more menacing vistas straight out of Dickens.

'What next?' he said

'Back to the main road.'

*

They wandered into a pawn store. The sour-looking old Turk behind the plexiglass was watching a game of football on his phone and seemed indifferent to two potential customers. H engineered an argument with him about nothing in particular and strolled out of the shop with threats about burning the place to the ground.

Next they entered a shop that sold sweets, groceries, fags and newspapers. H bit on an apple and tossed it back in amongst the others, making sure he was seen. He picked up a copy of the South London Press and, without paying, strolled outside

They plotted up under the shop canopy and H opened his paper. Bazza Wishbone was still making headlines and there was an article by some smart arsed local comedian about how celebrities in the public eye were always in danger. The comedian went on to say that the very act of performing in front of a live audience was in and of itself an act of courage akin to going into battle, putting your life on the line. H was giggling savagely through his nose and trying to process this puerile imbecility when they appeared.

Black BMW. 3 series. Tinted windows. It pulled up slowly on the other side of the street.

Why do these idiots always behave like they're in the fucking movies?

He folded up his paper and signalled to Graham to stay where he was while he crossed to the other side of the street. There was no time to play cat and mouse, to wait for them to make the first move. No time for all that. He walked as if he intended to go past the car and then suddenly switched direction. He pulled out the Glock, forced it through the half-open window and had it pushed hard into the cheek of the driver before he or the overweight growler riding shotgun could react.

H beckoned Graham over and they both got in the back of the car. He gave instructions to the driver and two minutes later they were parked up in a quiet little side street by the Bricklayer's Arms flyover.

'Out, sharpish!' The command had something definitive about it, a tone that could not be disobeyed. The two men clambered out of the front of the car looking decidedly sheepish and embarrassed at how easily they'd been outwitted. H was out before them, gun in hand. Graham followed briskly - knowing the extent to which H was prepared to go in this mood he feared for the lives of their captives. It seemed to Graham that these two were not even close to being on the top table of the Albanian firm. Slow, clumsy, amateurish. With half the Met running around looking for Fatos and his close cronies all the top boys were keeping themselves under wraps.

H asked, 'Who sent you?'

Captive One was a thin moustachioed type of about forty-five. Just a gofer, H decided. A genial enough little peasant who ran errands and drove people about and did what he was told. The thin man thought he was out of his depth when he got the call. Just go and have a look and report back, he was told. So he went to collect his cousin, Captive Two, who was no use at all given that he was even drunker than Captive One.

Neither of them were geared-up for a confrontation with a Glock-wielding lump of a man barely in control of himself. Captive One began to shrug his shoulders. This was a bad move - H saw the body language which meant 'I know nothing,' which everybody does when they know something, so before the shrug was even half way complete, before a word of deceit had time to emerge into the air, H's gun smashed into the man's cheekbone and broke it. H's other hand smashed full-power into his solar plexus for the old one-two, and the thin man crumpled to the floor.

Graham bent down to check him.

'H, I don't think he's breathing. I think his heart's stopped. He needs mouth to mouth.'

'My first aid certificate's expired,' said H, as he turned his attention to Captive Two.

'Who sent you?'

Captive Two was not stupid; he knew a shrug was not going to cut the mustard, not by a long stretch.

'He my cousin he pick me up fifteen minutes ago.'

'Lovely, happy fucking families all round, but that's not what I asked. Last chance: who sent you?'

'Fatos Gazjet,' said Captive Two, struggling to mouth the words as if he was being force-fed a shit sandwich.

'Where is he?'

'I don't know. He hiding.'

'OK, I believe you don't know. So guess.'

Graham's prognosis had been premature. Captive One started coughing and spluttering and twitching on the ground. H raised his foot and stamped hard down on his ankle; Captive Two winced with disgust and fear as he heard it crack.

H said nothing for a moment, only glowered.

Think it through, sunshine... Do you really want some of what your mate's having?

'Time's up. Give me your best guess. Three, two..'

'Car breakers yard, Belvedere or Dartford, somewhere there. They own some yards there. I heard they hiding in one of them. This all I know.'

Captive Two stood perfectly still, holding his breath, like he'd just looked the Medusa in the eye and had been turned to stone. He had no further information to offer; he would have given it up if he had.

H knew this and knew the time for violence had passed. Violence was a useful instrument if it furthered his cause, but he was not a believer in gratuitous acts of savagery for their own sake.

'Graham, get these two in the boot and make sure they have no phones on them. I know a spot on the way back to our cars, we'll keep 'em out of harm's way for a few days until we find Ronnie.'

'OK. What's next?'

'We're heading down to Belvedere. Our friend here's right - there's a few breakers yards in the area. We'll just have to visit them one by one. I know someone down there who'll loan us a few boys to help with the search.'

H took out his phone, found the number for Terry Treacher and hit the call button. Voicemail.

'Fuck it,' said H, 'we'll call him on the way.'

69

Terry 'two fingers' Treacher was called two-fingers because he had two fingers on his right hand. He was also right handed, which didn't really help. And the two fingers he had were the little one and the one next to the little one, which also didn't help. Whenever anyone first heard his nickname they assumed that he'd received the attentions of some gangland enforcer and undergone a night of horrendous torture with a pair of pliers and a little electrical box, and yet lived to tell the tale. He hadn't; he'd been born that way.

Terry was sixty-five years of age and had been raised in an era before sensitivity to disability had become a social norm. At school he'd been subjected to the kind of vile abuse only children are capable of giving, at a time when children were not told to pull all their punches and horrid words were just a part of everyday life. Adolescent jokes about how he managed to massage his penis were the usual points of attack.

'How do you manage to wank then, cripple,' was a question frequently on the lips of one of his main tormentors, Peter Thompson.

It was the kind of disability and abuse that could have destroyed a young boy, if a young boy had let it. Terry hadn't let it. At the tender age of twelve he practiced his cricket-bat swing with his left hand for several weeks until he'd perfected it, before advancing on Paul Thompson and crashing it with all the force he could muster into the young man's skull. Master Thompson survived, just, but with a few little physical impairments and tics of his own. It was the last time he, or any other schoolkid for that matter, gave Treacher any grief about his disability.

After leaving school he went into business with his father and built up a sizeable empire crushing cars. He was never fully legal, especially with his tax returns, and he'd had to agree to crush and dispose of a body now and again, to keep on the right side of people you had to keep on the right side of, if you were managing a car breaking business in the south east London borderlands in the 1960s and 70s.

In his early years on the force H had done a stint in Dartford and he and Terry had had a few minor run-ins. By the time H was moved on they'd had a few beers together, like Old Bill and villains used to, and stayed in touch thereafter, albeit infrequently. He was good company and H liked him. It had been some years since they'd talked, but H had always kept his number. He punched it into his phone again as he and Graham sped through New Cross.

'Fingers,' - those who knew him well had shorted his nickname - 'it's Harry Hawkins.'

'H? Well, fuck me, how's it going? Do you know what time it is?'

H didn't, but it was half-past midnight. He didn't beat about the bush. He quickly gave Fingers the bullet-point version of the story, or as much of it as he needed to know, so far.

'I'll put the feelers out. If they're hiding somewhere around here we'll find them, I shouldn't think it'll take long.'

'Alright Tezza, thanks. I'm not far off - be at yours in half an hour.'

*

When H screeched the car to a halt Fingers was already waiting for him at the front door of his house in Bexleyheath, phone in pocket connected to an earpiece, co-coordinating a search that was going to prove far more effective than that being undertaken by the combined police forces of England and Wales.

H gave the left hand a shake in greeting, introduced Graham who did likewise and the three men went inside. It was a modest home, a three-bedroom terraced house that had been bought and paid for years before. Fingers lived simply with his West Indian wife, Judith, who refused to let anyone spend any time in her home unless they ate; no matter what the circumstances or time of day food was always ready and on offer.

H wasn't hungry, until the smell of jerk chicken drifted across his nostrils. He understood the form - refusal was not an option. He accepted a piece of chicken, ate it with relish and washed it down with a cup of builder's tea - strong, two sugars. Graham did the same, with some effort and without the two sugars, for politeness' sake.

Fingers spread out a map of the local area.

'I've just woke up everyone I know and marked their cards. Not a lot of love for mass murderers in these parts mate. If they're hiding out around here in a breakers yard there are only three possibilities left. Here, in Belvedere; here, in Erith, and here, in Dartford, just inside the M25.'

They went through the options on the map.

H said 'Graham, get these places up on your mobile with that street view thing you do. Need a better look at the setup on these locations.'

Graham did as he'd been told and H surveyed the layouts with sharp intensity.

He discounted the first - too open, low fencing, no-one would hide out there - but the second and third were possibilities. Both had high fences, both had cabins large enough to keep a small firm out of sight and both, according to Fingers, who always kept an eye on his competitors, had recently been sold to person or persons unknown.

'Sweet,' said H as he gave Fingers a body hug whilst simultaneously reaching for another piece of jerk chicken. 'Fingers, get your mates to have a good look at the site in

Erith, will you? Graham - to the batmobiles. I fancy Dartford is the favourite.'

70

Andrew had been busy on the phone immediately after his debrief with Amisha and set up next day meetings with Jacynta Packington, Nigel Blandish and Simon de Montfort. He'd expected a lot of resistance but they all fell in line pretty quickly; either they'd all become good citizens and wanted to help or, more likely, they wanted to ensure they kept on the inside track of the investigation. Andrew didn't sleep well that night; he was too excited about getting out and meeting some bigwigs.

Amisha had also had a long night and slept lightly. She was worried. Not about the Wishbone case; she knew they'd solve that, sooner or later. She was worried about Graham going off-piste. The more she thought about it the more she wished they'd tried to persuade H to keep it straight.

They were dealing with dangerous people and without proper backup were in danger of being exposed. But H wouldn't have it. She knew he'd find a way to locate his son faster than anyone. And when he found him, and Basim Dragusha, there would be a reckoning. And Graham would most likely be there, and it would be dangerous, extremely dangerous…

They were having an unusual relationship, her and Graham, fused together in the heat of the most intense days of their lives and cemented by the subsequent tissue of lies they'd told to protect their guvnor. A legacy of their initiation into H's world, into H's way of doing things.

At first it seemed to her that lies and pain were all they had in common and that, long term, the relationship could never last. But lately she'd been adjusting to the idea of Graham as her long term man. He was caring, decent, charming. She had come to love him; and now she was having sleepless nights about him.

She was relieved when her alarm went off; she could get up and get on with her day. Put the doubt and the loneliness of the witching hours behind her. She wanted to get an early start - lots of appointments to get through.

*

Jacynta was on a photo shoot at Glyndeborne near Lewes, a cult opera house set in the heart of the Sussex Downs. She had agreed to an early meeting between shots.

Glyndeborne, an hour's drive from London, was unique in the world of opera, the privately owned opera house itself standing next to an ornate manor house. Jacynta considered it an ideal place for her first shoot since the Bazza murder, encapsulating as it did just the right amount of pathos and solemnity. It was an internationally recognised high-quality brand, and she needed to convey an image that represented the exact opposite of the world she dwelt in.

It was early morning. The night's rain had moved on and Amisha and Andrew were met with a breezy sunny day when they got out of their police issue blue Mondeo, one of a job lot the police had bought in bulk - something to do with efficiency savings. It was one of those days that looked pleasant and warm from the confines of a car but was a lot cooler once you'd stepped outside. As they walked across the sumptuous green lawn towards the main house Amisha was feeling distinctly cold towards her interviewee.

A well dressed and well-mannered security guard approached.

Amisha said, 'Hi, we're here to see Jacynta Packington.'

'She's right in the middle of a shoot; do you have an appointment?'

Amisha flashed her warrant card and said, 'Yes, I have an appointment. Please go and get her.'

'I think she's going to be about half an hour do you…'

'Yes, I do mind waiting.'

Amisha was no longer the slightly naïve, sweetness-and-light young woman fresh from Cambridge; she'd been forged, even more than Graham, into something harder and more formidable by bitter experience and H's guidance. She could growl with the best of them now, if necessary. And she was angry now, with Jacynta, for withholding so much information in their previous meeting. She marched past security directly to where the shoot was taking place and straight into the line of the camera.

The photographer said 'Who are you? Can't you see we have a shoot in session? How did you get in here…security…what on earth is going on?'

Jacynta stopped posing and stared at Amisha. The approachable friendly face she'd seen at their earlier meeting had gone, replaced by something more akin to a seething ancient goddess ready to unleash a thunder bolt. She could see Amisha had not come to play nice.

Jacynta said 'Sorry Paul. It's for me, it's important, about Bazza's murder. We'll have to take a break.'

Andrew, Amisha and Jacynta walked to the lawn, away from prying ears and eyes. The sun shone hot and the wind blew cold, animating the trees at the edge of the garden.

'So, you didn't think it important to tell me that Bazza was trying to get out of his contract with Blandish? You, for some reason, didn't think that was relevant to the case?'

'Well, I wasn't really thinking clearly. It didn't seem relevant.'

'And it wasn't relevant that de Montfort had been helping Bazza; it wasn't relevant that he and Blandish have been at loggerheads; it wasn't relevant that two ruthless, greedy men have been feuding over the spoils of a huge fortune? What have you got to hide?'

'Nothing. I don't know anything about the murderer. I was just there. Blandish and de Montfort are not involved. It's not something either would get involved in.'

'I'll be the judge of that. What else have you neglected to mention?'

'I'm sorry. I just wasn't thinking clearly. I ...'

'Who are you protecting?'

'Nobody.'

'You're lying.'

The wind blew Amisha's long dark hair across her face. She swept it back as Jacynta raised her head and met her gaze. Amisha felt let down, betrayed almost, after showing trust to this famous, fragile girl. Was anyone in this world capable of being straight? She stared at Jacynta with eyes that were burning with rage.

'If there's anything else you haven't told me you'd better tell me now.'

Jacynta gave a potted history of the feud. How Bazza had come to realise Blandish had total control over him, forever. How much they hated each other. How Bazza had gone to de Montfort for advice, given he really had no idea what he was doing and didn't know anyone else who could help him. Instead of simply proffering advice de Montfort had seen it as an opportunity to get close to Bazza and take over the management of his career, something way beyond his abilities.

'But Bazza let him go see Blandish and negotiate on his behalf. It was all a bit of a disaster and the two no longer speak, not that they were ever exactly bosom pals. Old Tarquin just made matters worse. At the party last Saturday Bazza told him to get lost, he didn't want him interfering anymore.'

'The party you and Bazza had been to on the night of the murder?'

'No, sorry, the previous week. I was on a shoot in the south of France so I wasn't there. But apparently, there was a major bust up and Bazza swore at de Montfort like a trooper, in front of everyone, and told him to get out of his life.'

Although the account matched what she'd heard from Jennifer Goodchild, Amisha was not placated. She bristled. Jacynta folded her arms, as if the act itself could protect her from further probing, and said the wrong thing:

'I'm sorry, I didn't think it was relevant to the murder, it was personal between the two of them.'

'You didn't think it was relevant! You didn't think it was relevant? Do you know why Bazza was killed? Do you know who killed him?'

'No. I have no idea. How could I? The dispute with Blandish has nothing to do with the murder. I'm sure of it. I would have known.'

'I'm not sure about that, given your judgement. Tell me more about this argument, at the party, what caused it?'

'I wasn't there. But afterwards Bazza went back to Margate with his sister, and stayed there for a few days without accepting calls. Didn't come back until mid-week, and he didn't want to talk about it. Said he just wanted to forget about it. He did his concerts in London Friday and Saturday, and after the Saturday concert we went to another Tarquin party, but Bazza wasn't in a party mood so we left early and went back to the Ritz.'

'So, you didn't tell me about the feud. You didn't tell me about the split with de Montfort. You didn't tell me Bazza went back to Margate with his sister. All this one week before he's killed. Either you're stupid or you're hiding something. I'd say the latter. What are you hiding?'

Jacynta went quiet for some time and dropped her head, and at length 'It's ...Tarquin, I'm close to him. We were once...'

'Jesus wept! I assumed he was gay.'

'He swings both ways. We used to have a thing, we're still friends. I'm certain he would never do anything to hurt Bazza. Absolutely certain.'

Jacynta looked sheepish. Amisha groaned. Andrew, who had been taking everything in from the side-lines, said 'Who supplies Tarquin with his party requisites?'

'That old chestnut. I'm shocked you don't know. A few weeks ago de Montfort was picked up and questioned by the drugs squad, after an anonymous tip-off that he assumed came from Blandish. He's kept it out of the papers. He's not been charged yet, but he's under investigation. I don't know the names of his suppliers. Not the sort of thing I *would* know.'

Amisha looked at Andrew.

'How could we not know that one of our suspects is under investigation by the drugs squad?'

'I… don't know. I…'

'Stop talking Andrew. Get in the car. It's Blandish time.'

71

Amisha asked Andrew to drive so she could do some thinking, prepare herself for the next meetings. But she couldn't get Graham off her mind, so she rang the boys. Graham answered from a location outside a breakers yard in Dartford.

'Hi Graham,' said Amisha 'how's it going?'

'Good. We've had a fruitful few hours. We're watching this place near Dartford…seems there's a fairly good chance that Gazjet and his pals - or some of them - might have tucked themselves away here. H certainly seems to think so. He's with me in my car at the moment, I'll put us on speaker. What have you been up to?'

'Just been talking to our supermodel friend with Andrew, he's in the car with me now. She confirmed that Blandish and de Montfort have been feuding over control of the boy wonder and his contract. Bazza told them both where to get off, so they both have motive. And get this corker: de Montfort has been under investigation by the drugs squad.'

'Jesus, Ames' said H, 'How the fuck didn't we know that?'

Andrew looked sheepishly at Amisha and started to mumble excuses, as if it was all down to him, which it wasn't.

'Alright Andrew, as you were son,' said H, 'We've all had our plates full lately. I'll find out what's what and call you back.'

'Ok,' said Amisha. H ended the call.

'Where are they?' asked Andrew, in a vain attempt to breach the inner sanctum. It seemed to him he was being managed by H, Amisha and Graham on a strictly need-to-know basis.

'In the wilds of outer south east London somewhere. On the trail of a killer.'

'That'd be a good name for a movie.'

Amisha was not amused.

They were driving north on the M23, the motorway that serves the Sussex Downs, and also the main trunk road to Gatwick Airport. It was now mid-morning and the traffic was busy but moving. Not a bad motorway, as motorways go. They were well south-west of London and Blandish's offices were in the West End. Not an easy trip, the route not an easy choice.

Andrew said, 'London orbital and then cut in further west, or straight through town?'

Neither route was particularly appealing to Amisha. It was going to be a slog but she wanted to get there pronto.

'Fire up the siren and head through town.'

Andrew's face lit up and then the siren lit up and soon they were in the middle of Croydon, that monument to architectural hubris. For reasons no one's ever understood they put a flyover through the middle of the town in the 1970s, or was it the 1960s? - nobody cared anymore - and then built a never-ending series of grey concrete blocks masquerading as buildings. Some of the uglier buildings had been knocked down but the scars of those decisions still haunted its main thoroughfare. Andrew had never been there before and was just contemplating how lucky he'd been when the boys called back. Andrew killed the siren and slowed down.

H's voice came over the line: 'The drugs squad received an anonymous tip-off regarding de Montfort's drug dealings some weeks back. Let's assume Blandish was behind it. They've had de Montfort under occasional surveillance but were not planning on doing much. They're more interested in his main supplier, John Tanner, a middle man who caters to the great and the good. He's got plenty of contacts at both ends - the dealers who bring it in and the high value buyers who like stuffing the shit up their conks. Graham will text you his address. Find him, Ames. Put it on him.'

'Did the drugs squad give us the OK H?'

'Fuck 'em. Just go and find him, I'll deal with them if it comes on top. Let's cross our bridges as we come to them.'

She knew H was about to end the call without another word. No time for small talk in these circumstances. But she hadn't finished.

'Graham,' she said, 'be careful.'

'Don't worry babes, I'll be fine.'

H noticed that this wasn't a H kind of 'babes' - *cup of tea please babes, two sugars.* It was a heartfelt 'babes' and he'd never heard Graham use it before. He motioned to Graham to cut the call.

72

The text came in. Beckenham.

'Andrew,' said Amisha, 'John Tanner lives in Beckenham. Fifteen minutes away - let's get over there.'

They drove through Croydon and Shirley and were soon in Beckenham. Beckenham was a prosperous place, part of the London commuter belt, and John Tanner lived in one of the most prosperous parts of it. They entered the Parklangley estate, which comprised of 700 acres of substantial houses built in the first two decades of the 20th century. Front gardens were adorned with trees and shrubberies, and expensive late-model vehicles sat proudly on all the driveways, pristine and flashing bright in the glow of the late morning sun.

'Here,' said Amisha, 'just here, on the left.'

John Tanner's house didn't just have the fifty-foot front garden and the Merc and the BMW on the driveway; it also had an imposing iron gate to keep out the plebs and the police. They got out of the car on the street and Amisha buzzed the intercom.

'He's not in,' said Mrs Tanner, sounding bored. Amisha and Andrew were not the first champions of law and order to have come in search of her husband.

'Do you know where we might find him?'

'Playing tennis, in the club just down the road. He's always there, when he's nowhere else.'

They followed Mrs Tanner's directions and found themselves navigating a small driveway that opened out into a large tennis club at the side of the estate. It had sixteen tennis courts, squash courts and a gym - the people who lived in these parts were not ones to flop around all day watching daytime TV.

The first person they stopped knew Tanner and pointed him out. He was playing doubles but stopped when he spotted them lurking courtside. He knew a pair of coppers when he saw them. The members of the club had no real idea what John did - something in the city, derivatives, he always told them - and he as sure as hell didn't want them finding out now. He made a beeline for Amisha.

His tennis match hadn't been that taxing but he could now feel the sweat on the back of his collar and on his hands. Amisha sensed his unease at their presence. Given she wanted information quickly, and given the circumstances, she thought the best way was to close down his options as quickly as possible, and make him a straight offer he knew would make sense.

'Hi.' she said before he could speak. 'Listen, we're not from the drugs squad. We're working with Harry Hawkins on the Bazza Wishbone murder. We've no interest in you or what you've done or are ever likely to do. Can we talk now, straight, off the record, no notes or comebacks? Detective Inspector Hawkins would be most appreciative.'

'Go on then,' Tanner said.

'Tell me everything you know about what happened at Tarquin de Montfort's party two Saturday's ago; who was there and what you saw before Bazza Wishbone started ranting and raving. And give me some idea of who your main wholesale suppliers are. Then walk away. This meeting never happened.'

Tanner sighed heavily and nodded. He didn't much like the sound of it, but he took it - the drugs squad he could handle, but the last thing he needed was Harry Hawkins coming after him.

'Ok.' He turned to his tennis chums and asked to be excused, and the three of them took it to the car park.

'So what happened?' asked Amisha.

'Well, I was at the party already when Bazza turned up, doing my thing. He seemed in a good mood, surrounded by his entourage, including his sister. As the night went on he got distracted by a couple of ladies and disappeared for a while. That's when Romeo Ferrera made a move on his sister.'

'And you saw this?'

'Yes, I'm a watcher of people, not a party animal. These parties are my place of work. I watch people very closely.'

'Go on'

'I buy drugs from all sorts of people, and sell them to wealthy celebrities and people like de Montfort. I've cornered the market with his people. I buy from all over, from Russians, Albanians mostly - they bring the good gear in through Holland. Sometimes South Americans working out of Spain. I've got good relationships with these people. But lately I've been having a bit of trouble with a few Albanians.'

'What sort of trouble?'

A few of them turned up on my doorstep a while ago. They knew about my uptown clients, and de Montfort's parties. They wanted in - to a party, not the business.'

'Why did they want a party invite?'

'It was some new boys, three young kids. At first I thought they were taking liberties with their chain of command and wanted to cut me out, but I think it's really that they have a taste for the highlife and want to party with some supermodels. And they made me an offer I couldn't refuse - they were armed to the fucking teeth, if you'll excuse my French. So I took them to de Montfort's.

'And de Montfort let them in?'

'Well, he was livid when I first rocked up with them... but they're difficult to say no to. So yes, he suffered them.'

'He hasn't mentioned them. They weren't on his list of attendees.'

'He wouldn't. Even now only a few people know they were there. He'll do anything to keep it quiet - doesn't want the tone lowered.'

'Go on.'

'So, as I was saying, Romeo got hold of Bazza's sister, in one of those little alcoves in the basement. She's sexy, gorgeous...proper jailbait. And not exactly backwards in coming forwards when it comes to male attention. Bazza was out of the picture for a while, as I said, and when he reappeared he couldn't find her. But then he did - find her, I mean.'

Tanner paused for a second.

'I'm all ears John,' said Amisha.

'Well, I didn't see everything. He came steaming out of a side room, sister in hand, followed by Romeo, and went absolutely fucking ballistic, if you'll excuse my French - got right up in de Montfort's face. He was partly furious with our host, partly at himself for losing track of the girl. He seemed to blame de Montfort and just went apeshit about him inviting perverts and lowlifes to his parties.'

'How did her ladyship respond to that?'

'He never batted an eyelid.'

'Nothing?'

'Not a sausage. He just gave a little smirk, and walked away. Anyway, to me it seemed like one law for Bazza, another for his sister. But there was bad blood between Bazza and Romeo… you know Romeo and Jacynta had a thing, before Bazza turned up? Maybe the thing with his sister was Romeo getting back at Bazza for stealing Jacynta from him.'

So Jacynta and Romeo did have a thing. I knew it!

'Did the people at the party generally know that Bazza's sister is only fifteen?' said Amisha.

'As if a guy like Romeo would worry about that! Jealousy's a terrible thing…and anyway, he's an absolute dog where the ladies are concerned. He's famous for it.'

'John, do you think Romeo Ferrera has it in him to have killed Bazza? What's your judgement, as a seasoned people watcher?'

'I daresay a few of the ladies might have felt the back of his hand during one of his fits, but cold-blooded murder? I doubt it.'

'And your new Albanian friends?'

'Don't know. They just slipped away. Didn't see them leave and haven't seen them since.'

73

Even with the siren wailing and the light flashing the traffic had been an absolute bastard, and the ride from Beckenham to Wimpole Street had taken forever. That plus the Tanner detour meant Amisha and Andrew arrived at the offices of Blandish Global Media an hour and a half late. Blandish himself was in his office conducting a meeting. Amisha brushed off his PA and barrelled through the office door H-style, without knocking.

'Detective Sergeant Bhanushali, this is all rather abrupt...if you give me five minutes...'

'Good day Mr Blandish. I wanted to talk about your anonymous tip-off to the drugs squad. You are aware that there is an offence called 'wasting police time' - and that it's imprisonable? You can get up to six months under lock and key for it. Whenever you're ready, Mr. Blandish.'

Blandish dismissed his underlings with a royal wave of the hand. Amisha and Andrew took their places on the two chairs. The picture of Bazza still loomed large, dominating the office - like a ghostly presence hanging around until it saw justice done. Andrew felt intimated in the presence of one of the most successful and well known men in Britain, a man he'd seen countless times on the television.

Amisha didn't. She'd been through too much and had H's advice for comfort: 'Never show exaggerated respect for wealth and fame. They're just people, at the end of the day, like the rest of us.'

She went for the jugular.

'Did you have Bazza Wishbone murdered?'

'Do calm down, Detective Sergeant. Why are you throwing accusations around like confetti at a wedding? We haven't even had coffee yet.'

'You had motive. He wanted out and we know all about your feud with de Montfort. What do you have to say about that?'

'Not a lot. It's just business, a struggle over a contract - par for the course. I've been through it plenty of times before. If you care to check my record, you'll see that none of my prior business struggles has resulted in me being charged with murder.'

His smugness was insufferable, unbearable, but she knew she had to calm down; Blandish had the upper hand. She hadn't thought her approach through. All the way back from Beckenham she'd mostly been thinking about Graham and H, how they were putting themselves in danger. The worry of what H would get Graham into was eating away at her.

'Tell me about the feud.'

Blandish gave the full story. It matched, mostly, what she'd heard from Jacynta, Jennifer Goodchild and John Tanner. He even went, with some relish, through de Montfort's visit to and forced ejection from the Blandish office.

'But Detective Sergeant you must realise that none of this is out of the ordinary in my world. Just another day at the office. You really think it's enough for me to have a man killed?'

Amisha dodged the question by asking another one.

'And the anonymous tip off, to the drugs squad. Was that you?'

'I couldn't possibly comment, Detective Sergeant.'

'How many of de Montfort's parties have you been to?'

'A few. Not many…not really my cup of tea. I've never liked the guy truth be told, even before all this business with Bazza. And he does have some rather unsavoury hangers-on.'

That's rich: One unsavoury character not going to parties to avoid other unsavoury characters.

'Such as?'

'Low life types. Don't ask me who, I don't know them. If you want my advice there are a few characters you should be looking into in that murky little world he inhabits.'

God give me strength.

'Were you at the one two Saturdays ago?'

'No.'

'What did you hear about it?'

'I heard that Bazza went nuts. I heard that four letter words were flying about like it was a Celtic v Rangers game and that he told de Montfort to get out of his life and leave him alone.'

'When did you last see him?'

'Earlier that same day, the day of his bust-up with de Montfort. He came to the office. We didn't speak about our difficulties, just some stuff about his schedule. He seemed calm.'

'So what do you think happened, to turn him from calm to furious?'

'I don't know. I heard he stormed out. But I don't why, I don't know what sparked it. How could I?'

74

Amisha returned to the present when she became aware that the engine was silent. Andrew had navigated with his customary quiet efficiency and parked up outside de Montfort's before she'd considered the best way to approach the interview.

Andrew said, 'How are we going to play it guv?'

'By ear.'

Gaston answered the door, led them in and showed them through, past the grand entrance with the fine décor and the prying eyes of de Montfort's forbears, into the grand drawing room. At places such as this, thought Andrew - near mesmerised by the grandeur - one might once have expected to find *The Telegraph* or *The Financial Times*, or at least *Country Life*; but as they entered the drawing room de Montfort was busy ploughing through the latest copy of *Celebrity Mash Up*.

'Ah, Detective Sergeant Bhanushali. How lovely to see you. Thank you so much for not bringing that other brute with you - what was his name, Gary Merchant? I like this one *much* better, I can see we shall all get along famously - will you not introduce me to your young friend?

'I'm accompanied today by Detective Constable Andrew Glass.'

'Lovely. And how is the investigation going?'

'Well,' said Amisha, 'we've come across a few things we'd like to talk to you about.'

They went through the whole thing again. Bazza, the naïve wannabe who thought he'd made it only to discover he was being royally fucked. His teaming up with de Montfort, the fruitless attempts to start negotiations with Blandish. It all seemed to tally.

'Why didn't you tell us that you had been interviewed by the drugs squad last time we spoke?'

This triggered a performance of mini-operatic proportions, with de Montfort flapping about, apologising profusely and making all kinds of excuses about it not being relevant.

'And what about your supplier, John Tanner; how long have you known him? How close are you?'

'Several years, on and off. Not close, it's just a business relationship.'

'Why do you let him come to your parties? I would have thought you wanted the two worlds to be kept separate.'

The performance continued: de Montfort raised his hand to his throat, gulped and loosened his cravat.

'I never really invited him as such… He made it a condition of our cooperation, said it was a necessary part of his work - "know your punters", that sort of thing. And my guests like him, you know, that olde-worlde cockney charm of his.'

'What made Bazza go berserk, what led up to that?'

'Well things were going on as usual. I didn't speak to Tanner or Bazza much. I assumed Bazza had found a woman - or a gaggle of them - and slinked off somewhere, he usually does…did. Almost before I knew what was happening he was storming out with his sister in tow.'

'His sister is fifteen. Can you explain to us what on earth she was doing here?'

'Bazza brought her along. She wanted to meet a few celebrities. I understood her to be seventeen.'

'Did you see her with Romeo Ferrera?'

'No, not personally. I've heard the rumours.'

'I want a full list. Everyone who was at that party. Not the edited one you sent to Detective Inspector Miller-Marchant - a real one. I want it now, before we leave.'

Tarquin was feeling sheepish. Behind the bluster and the façade of a well-bred scion of a grand old family was a docile man who'd always used his name and background to get by.

Part of the reason he'd gravitated towards the celebrity world was because the worlds of business or politics were beyond him. He found celebrities lightweight, pointless and easy to charm, rather like himself.

He prepared the list and passed it to Amisha and Andrew for review. Many names they would have expected; the usual 'B' list actors, models and wannabe models, mouthy talent show finalists.

'I'm not seeing the names of John Tanner's friends here Tarquin,' said Amisha.

'Who?'

'The one's he brought with him. We know about them, that you let them in. What are you hiding?'

'Oh. I don't know their names, darling. I doubt he does, or could pronounce them if he did.'

Andrew continued double-checking and cross referencing stories.

Amisha pressed on: 'Tell me more about the relationship between Romeo and Jacynta.'

'Well, I know the footballer - slimy little oik that he is, *so* beneath her - had had a thing with Jacynta before Bazza crashed in. He found it difficult to accept and had, so I heard, followed her on occasion and made something of a nuisance of himself. But it had never got ugly, as far as I know. More like a little bit of stalking, that type thing - that would be his style.'

Amisha crossed-referenced him again, asking him if he had ever liked Jacynta, and he confessed to their brief liaison. Everything he said seemed to check with what she'd been told throughout the course of the day's interviews.

Amisha concluded that de Montfort was, essentially, a victim of his own ambition. He wanted more from life than his meagre abilities allowed for and this led him into all types of compromises and mistakes. H had taught her to listen to her intuition and it told her de Montfort was no killer, not because he was moral or right-thinking or good in any way but because, in H's parlance, he didn't 'have the arsehole' for it.

Andrew, who was something of a history buff, recognised a few of the high and mighty who looked down on them from the great hallway as they made their way out. These were people who had usually done what it took, who had fought and killed to get to the top, and stay there. He couldn't help wonder if de Montfort was really of the same lineage or whether his mother had had a quickie with a travelling circus clown.

'What's your assessment, Andrew?' Amisha asked in the car.

'I think we need to speak to Bazza's sister, and Romeo again. Confirm what set Bazza off on his rant. If Romeo was really going at it with his sister and Bazza walked in and humiliated him it might've tipped Romeo over the edge; these celebrity footballers are used to people fawning over them, not abusing them in public. And they have brittle egos. So that, and the jealousy over Jacynta he already had, would give a double motive. I'd say he's our number one suspect.'

'Hmmm.' said Amisha, 'Let's get back to the Yard. Find out where he is now. I need to find a few things out for H and Graham.'

'Where are they - surely if it's a lead on the case I should know?'

'Sorry Andrew, this stuff's on a need-to-know to basis. What you don't know can't hurt you.'

75

H and Graham had been on sentry all night and through the day. It was now mid-afternoon. The yard at Erith had been properly looked at and they were now completely focused on the Dartford site, like beady eyed hawks hovering from a distance, ready to strike at the moment their prey revealed itself. The place was like God's waiting room for cars, which were piled high in several locations, looking rusty and forlorn in their final resting place, in the shadow of the QE2 Bridge - the 'Dartford Crossing' from Kent into Essex.

The traffic on the nearby M25 roared like thunder, hampering full concentration. But they'd figured out what they were looking at: the corrugated iron fence surrounding the site was twelve feet high. H fancied he could scale it, with a leg up from Graham, but the place was chock-a-block with CCTV cameras. A light had been on in the central cabin all night and an occasional silhouette had appeared at the window. There was definitely someone in there, the question was who. Graham had managed to contain H's desire to just crash through the heavily padlocked gate and see what happened. Given there were likely several people with automatic weapons inside, it would be suicide. But H was getting itchy. He'd be going in soon; there was no way round it.

At 15:30 Amisha called: 'Just an update on two things. I've just checked with one of the inspectors running the Bedgebury investigation. The lorry driver gave himself up earlier today and has been very forthcoming. Apparently he's terrified and has been hiding out with his family in a motel just outside Birmingham.'

Graham found this perplexing. 'Why did he split from the others?'

'Says he was just a driver. Had no idea what was happening until our friend Fatos turned up with a bunch of tooled-up nutters. He'd broken down on the hard shoulder of the M2.'

H said 'That's odd; why didn't he get one in the nut as well?'

'Maybe they meant to. He says the whole thing in the forest got out of hand very quickly and he slipped his collar in the mayhem. Seems Fatos and his boys panicked and it just turned into a helter-skelter bloodbath - sounds like a scene from a Heironymous Bosch painting.'

'Well, if this poor bastard is going to play ball with us he'll need witness protection, a new identity, the lot. How many does he say were on the firm?' said H.

'Six, including Fatos. He says he doesn't know any of them, apart from Fatos. Two old hands and three younger guys. I don't think we have a file on the new boys.'

'OK, let's move on. What's the second thing?'

'I spoke to John Tanner. Apparently our friends from the Island are among his suppliers. Some new guys have been badgering him. They showed up at his house and invited themselves along to de Montfort's with him. Made him an offer he couldn't refuse. This would be two Saturdays ago, the week before Bazza copped it.'

'Would these new guys be three young men, by any chance?' said H. He was beginning to twitch.

No such thing as coincidence.

'Maybe. Tanner said they looked a handful but mostly just wanted to meet the girls and get a taste of the highlife.'

'What else, about the party?'

'According to Tanner the reason Bazza went potty was he found Romeo Ferrera messing around with his sister. Dragged her out of the place, screaming at de Montfort and his "low life" friends.'

Graham saw an image in his mind, of a dolled-up kid opening her legs to give him a look.

I shouldn't think Romeo had to twist her arm too hard.

'And Tanner's interlopers?' said H, 'Where were they while all this was going on?'

'He said they had either left or left soon afterwards. He didn't see them go and hasn't seen them since.'

H's intuition was working overtime. The gangsters he was stalking were in some way connected with Bazza - if only because they'd been at the same party. Co-incidence?

No such fucking thing

'So,' said H, 'three new faces from the Island spotted in Bedgebury and not seen since the bodies were found; and three new faces skulking about at one of Tarquin's little fuckfests. Interesting… we've got a couple of things to get our teeth into here kids: three gangsters in Belgravia and the footballer who was at it with Wishbone's underage sister. Where's Romeo now, Ames?'

'Just got information he's at his club's training ground.'

'Yeah I know it. It's not far from here. About ten minutes.'

Better get over there quick, before they all head for the golf course.

'Graham, you stay here and get on the blower at the first sign of human life - or subhuman life, as the case may be. Amisha, send a car for Gina, get her in sharpish, no fannying about with the little darling - if she wants to act like a big girl, we'll treat her like one. I'm off to pay a quick visit to our ponce of a footballer. He'll give it to me straight now, even if I have to strangle it out of him.'

The big man sprang out of Graham's car, sprinted back to his own - a blue Mondeo, standard issue H had managed to nab on his first day back - and, blowing a little hard but otherwise full of intent, slid into the driver's seat, hit the ignition and screeched away.

H had seen Romeo in the interview room, through one-way glass, and was not impressed by what he saw. The footballer himself had never had the pleasure of meeting Detective Inspector Harry Hawkins of the Yard. Within thirty minutes he would be praying it was a pleasure he would never have to endure again.

76

H entered reception, flashed his badge and gave the name of his victim. No hellos, no pleasantries. Just a name.

'Training, on pitch one. Over there. You'll have to wait until the session's over.'

H barrelled towards pitch one, surprised to find footballers still working so late in the afternoon. Big Tony Dawkins, the team manager, was in session. H and Big Tone had met before, at a police charity event. After a few pints H had cornered him and enlightened him on some of the finer points of football tactics, and given him the full benefit of his views on the club he worked for.

Dawkins gave a wave.

'Hello Inspector,' he said, 'to what do we owe the pleasure?'

Big Tone always read the papers. He already knew what the visit must be about.

'Alright Tone, something urgent has come up. I need to talk to your boy Romeo about the Wishbone case. It'll only take a minute. It's urgent.'

Dawkins beckoned his player. Romeo sauntered over, pouting and acting like a spoilt brat about to be admonished by his father.

'I'm not talking to the police without my lawyer,' said Romeo when he finally arrived.

'Romeo, this is Detective Inspector Hawkins, he's a friend of mine. Do me a favour, give him ten minutes. It's important.'

Romeo felt the pressure of the two men bear down on him. He pulled his arrogant face for show, but agreed to the meeting.

'In private, son,' said H, 'I've something to show you.'

They made their way to the changing room. It was empty and smelled like all male football changing rooms the world over, of dirty boots and sweaty jockstraps and bad deodorant. Romeo was lolling about and showboating, as if he were the senior partner in the interaction.

Enjoy it while it lasts…you'll be straightened out soon enough.

'So what do you want to show me?' Romeo asked.

'Nothing, nothing at all. Not a fucking thing,' said H. 'Tell me what happened between you and Wishbone's little sister at de Montfort's party two Saturdays ago.'

'Inspector, I've already given my statement to the police, I have nothing further to add.'

'Except you didn't tell the truth. I'm here to give you a second chance. Take it, while you can.'

'I have nothing further to add.'

Under normal circumstances H would think twice about giving this Premiership footballer a pasting at his own training ground. Under normal circumstances he'd bring him back in for questioning, put it on him, get him to talk. But circumstances were not normal. H was no longer sure he had any idea at all what normal meant. Almost before he'd realised what he'd done his left hand was around the footballer's throat and his right hand had formed a fist that was pressing hard into his cheek.

'Listen, I'm pushed for time. My son's life is in danger. And you won't be far behind him if you don't answer my questions.'

H relaxed his grip and his fist. Romeo started talking.

'Bazza's sister came onto me. She told me she was eighteen. I …'

'Listen son, I don't give a single flying fuck who came onto who, or whether you wanted to get back at Wishbone for stealing your supermodel girlfriend, or any other fucking thing. Just tell me what happened. Just the facts. You were in a side room with her when Wishbone came in. Take it from there.'

'It wasn't just me.'

'What?'

'When I arrived there were some rough guys there, not the type you usually find at the parties. How can we say, "lower down the food chain" I think is the expression? They came to talk to me about football, wanted my autograph. Normally I like that but they were intimidating, scary.'

'How many guys?'

'Three.'

'Go on.'

'Well, Bazza's sister approached us. She was drunk, and up for a good time. We took her into a little room - one of Tarquin's little secret rooms.'

'All four of you?'

'Yes, all four of us. She was naked on the bed with two of the guys when Bazza came in. He flipped out, screamed at her to get dressed and tried to get her out of the room. But one of the guys, the really cocky, arrogant one…'

Fuck me, this Albanian must be a beauty if he seems arrogant to this fucker.

'…he stood in Bazza's path.'

'And?'

'And Bazza told him to get out of his fucking way or he'd hit him. I thought Bazza would get smashed to bits on the spot. The arrogant one took out a gun. Gina begged him not to do anything, to let her and her brother go. Then he just started laughing, he just laughed out loud like a crazy man. And then he spat on Bazza and let him leave. That's when the rest of the guests saw Bazza go crazy at Tarquin.'

Strange. Why did they leave it? These nutters have started 100-year vendettas for less.

'And where did your new mates go after that?'

'Out the back door. Please, don't get me involved in this, they are not my mates. They are bad men, Inspector. They don't care, they're not afraid of anything.'

'They'll be afraid to leave the fucking house by the time I've finished with them. Go back to your game.'

77

H got back on the blower as soon as he'd jumped into his car. He got Amisha to setup a three-way conference call using the police phone system - he didn't know how to do it himself, and never would. Amisha worked her magic, and he brought her and Graham up to speed.

'So here's what we've got,' said H, when he'd finished with the known facts. 'It seems like Fatos was in charge of the disposal of the migrants, fucked it up - which is consistent with what we know of him - and is in hiding with the firm who helped carry out the murders, which probably includes our three young bucks, who we also have to put in the frame as potential suspects for the Wishbone murder, if for no other reason than they were at one of de Montfort's parties and kicked off with him. And if we've got the location right they're all now waiting in Dartford for the cavalry to arrive and get them out of the country.'

Amisha had further information.

'Guv, just before you called I heard from a friend on the team investigating the murders. A pharmacist in Lancaster was raided not long after Ronnie and Dragusha were busted out of the ambulance. No one's seen the CCTV but the description the pharmacist gave fits Dragusha, and another eye witness has him getting into a Volkswagen Golf. There was a driver and another man in the back.'

'What did he take, from the pharmacist's?'

'Cash, bandages, splints, a crutch and some blood-thinning tablets. It fits with the medical report I pulled from the prison. Your son has a broken leg, possible fractured ribs and…'

'And possible internal bleeding,' finished H. 'And Dragusha is trying to make sure he stays alive.'

H already hated Dragusha more than anyone he'd ever met - and he was just getting started. The thought of this man taking care of Ronnie, fixing his leg, going out of his way to find medication didn't change that one bit. It had the opposite effect: he was magnifying H's own failures and flaws - H hated him even more now.

The cunt thinks he can take care of my son.

'This is more serious than I thought Ames. I should have thought about checking the medical records earlier. If internal bleeding is suspected Ronnie needs immediate attention. I thought the race was to stop him getting out the country, but it's just become a race to keep him alive.'

'Graham,' Amisha heard H say 'that's it - we're going in. Check your weapon. No need for hello's. I'm going to smash straight through the gate. I'll pull up, sideways, fifty feet out. Follow me in. We'll get out driver's side, use our cars for cover.'

'And then what, H?' A reasonable question, Graham thought.

'And then we'll get this fucking sorted, Detective Inspector Miller-Merchant. Are you having it with me or not, college boy?'

This was exactly what Amisha had been afraid of. She'd even considered not telling H about the break in at the chemist. Graham had told her they each had a handgun - two handguns versus a mob of cold blooded killers. She feared for their lives.

'Guv, let me call it in. The net's closing around Dragusha and Ronnie. We have the rest of the firm in our sights, we can find out what they know.'

'Not going to happen Ames. Our firm will surround the place, negotiate with them for four days and then they'll either go out in a blaze of glory or give themselves up in front of an army of TV cameras and a million fucking lawyers lining up to protect them. I reckon, if we're lucky, we have a day before Dragusha's out of the country. My Ronnie may have even less than that.' The words that followed stuck in Hs throat: 'If he's still alive.'

He fell silent for a moment, his eyes stinging, his breath short, his soul crying out in despair.

Amisha, too, was in turmoil. She couldn't get over there to help. Too far. H was right: if she called it in Ronnie was lost, one way or another. But the chances of Graham and H coming out alive were not good. She knew H would go in, and she knew Graham would follow him. There was no plan, nothing she could come up with to slow them down. H would go in and all she could do was close her eyes and offer up a prayer to Krishna.

'Good luck Graham... I love you... good luck H. I love you too.'

'Good to know, but luck's got fuck all to do with this one Ames. This is all about speed, surprise and good shooting.'

The plan, or lack of it, was in place. H was about to hit the end call button when Graham piped up.

'Guv, hold it. There's some activity. They're coming out.'

Krishna will hear your prayer.

Graham described the action. The residents of the small cabin in the middle of the yard were moving towards their cars. They'd split into three groups.

'Looks like we've just got that bit of luck. There's five of them and they've split into three cars.'

Amisha said, through tears of relief, 'Only five? We were expecting six.'

'Definitely five,' said Graham, 'two young men are together, two older guys in another car and Fatos is saddling up on his own.'

Krishna responds to everyone according to their desires.

'Now this is what I do call a stroke of fucking luck,' said H. 'Get the number plates and call them in - but not Fatos. He's mine. Just the cars and their directions, keep them tracked. Have them lifted when convenient. Don't go into detail about the breakers yard just yet, we're going to need it.'

Two cars, one containing two young men and one containing two older men exited the compound first. They turned left. Graham made a note of the numbers and called them out for Amisha to write down. Fatos decided to take a different route and turned right. Graham passed on the information and pulled out to follow Fatos.

'I'm one minute away,' said H.

*

Fatos trundled on for a minute or two, doing what he could to draw no attention to himself. H, guided in by Graham, arrived on the plot and got a visual. Before Fatos Gazjet knew what was happening a blue police issue Mondeo careered out of a side street and smashed into his passenger side with the power and precision of the avenging hammer of Thor.

H didn't look much like a Norse God when he jumped from his car, pulled his victim out of the wreck, punched him hard in the head to ensure he remained in an unconscious state and deposited him in the back of his own car.

Three minutes later H, Graham and Fatos were back in the cabin.

78

'Sit him down there Graham, and tie him to the chair.'

H had been here before. He recalled the Russian he had taken and tortured, Vladimir Agapov, in his desperate search for Amisha's kidnappers some nine months earlier. He remembered the vicious beating he'd dished out and recollected returning to the lock up, the scene of his crime, after the events of those days had settled down. He'd expected to find a dead body. But Vladimir was nowhere to be seen, and hadn't been seen or heard of since. Now H was here again, not to save the life of his partner but that of his son - and he was prepared to do whatever it took.

Graham, however, had never been here before - he'd never prepared a prisoner for torture. A large part of him still felt uneasy with H's methods, and thought the best thing to do was to take Fatos to the local police station and turn him in. But another part of him didn't think that anymore. They had to get information that could lead to the salvation of Ronnie and they had to get it now.

H didn't much care that Fatos was a vicious people trafficker, responsible for one of the worst crimes in British history. These were details now. All H cared about was finding his boy. The clock was ticking. Graham secured the prisoner with duct tape and turned to H, wondering how the scene was going to play out. Wondering what H had in store for the hapless lump stiff with fear in the chair.

'Right my old son, easy way or hard way. Think and think quickly because I'm in a bit of a rush. Where's my son?'

'You police officer. I want lawyer.'

Fatos was shocked at the speed and power of the blow that smashed into his teeth, breaking three of them and filling his mouth with blood. He screamed in pain. Despite the realisation that he was in deep trouble and that these police officers were not part of a community outreach department, he had to protect his people, and abide by his code. He had sworn an oath. He spat his blood onto the floor in an act of defiance and followed it up with a 'fuck you.'

H stared at Fatos with pitiless eyes; a deep stare that went inside the man, revealed the flaws in his character. H knew Fatos would give up the information he needed with a few more clumps, but they were clumps he might not be able to withstand. He was no Vladimir Agapov. H's car smash routine method had taken a fair bit out of him, and he'd been bleeding from the ears and nose before H laid a finger on him. The last thing H needed on his hands now was a shattered thug in a persistent vegetative state. He scanned quickly through his fevered mind for the method most likely to get results.

'Give me your pistol Graham.'

'H, I...'

'Give me the fucking pistol son, now!'

Graham held out his hand. H took the gun, opened the cylinder and let five rounds tumble to the floor.

'One bullet left, Mr Gazjet,' he said. 'As you know, that gives you a one-in-six chance. Are you ready to rumble?'

The erstwhile Balkan warrior began to shake, and to weep quietly.

H turned to Graham, who was giving him an anxious shake of the head.

'H, no, you can't just kill him. I'm onside, I'm with you on this, you know I am. But we can get the information with a beating. We can get him to talk. I don't want more blood on my hands.'

H wasn't listening. He turned his back to Graham, spun the cylinder and held the gun to Fatos's head. The countdown began.

'Five, four, three, two, one.'

He pulled the trigger. The hammer moved back, forward again and vibrated against Fatos' temple. Nothing.

Graham's heart was racing. Fatos was weeping, wailing, thrashing around for a few moments like an epileptic, begging for mercy. His bladder gave way. His breathing became short, sharp and sporadic, as if he'd just been plunged into a bath of ice.

H stood silent for a few moments until his victim calmed down a little;

'Your chances just went down to one in five, old son,' said H, as restarted the count, 'Five, four, …'

Fatos lost control of his bowels.

'Three, two...'

'Mother of God! Don't shoot...I tell you everything...everything I know.'

79

A boat had been sent to pick them up at Harwich. Dragusha was already there, or would be soon, waiting in a warehouse just on the edge of the water, for which Fatos gave the name and precise location. There were three of them, Dragusha, Ronnie and Zef Fejzullah. Fatos and the other four were to join them. The boat was to sail at 8:30pm. It was now 5:30pm.

While Fatos spilled the beans Graham took up and reloaded his revolver. He picked up the bullets and loaded them into the cylinder chambers. But the final chamber was empty. He stared at H; the big man took a bullet from his pocket and passed it to Graham with a wink.

'Well, I thought it would be more realistic if you thought it was for real. And I wasn't going to kill him without getting what we needed to know, was I?'

Graham shook his head in disbelief, but said nothing. Fatos started up again with the weeping and the wailing and the gnashing of teeth.

'No need to worry about the other four. Amisha will take care of them,' said H.

Graham said 'I'll check google maps, see how long it takes to drive to Harwich.'

But H had already done the calculation. About 70 miles: through the tunnel, up into Essex on the M25 for a bit and then onto the A12: Chelmsford-Colchester-Harwich. Bish-bash-bosh.

'Normal daytime traffic about one and a half hours, maybe two this time of day,' H said. 'I'll get there. I have to. No need for you to come Graham. Let's get this fat piece of shit into your motor and you can take him in. Give me time to get there first before you spill the location.'

‘H, we know where Ronnie and Dragusha are: let’s call it in now. Let the local boys deal with it.’

‘What? The country yokels up there? They’ll just crash in en masse without a clue what they’re doing. Dragusha and his mate will sacrifice Ronnie, without any shadow of a doubt. Someone has to go in quick, hard, unseen, no fucking about with negotiations and all that. It’s Ronnie’s only chance.’

H might be right on that, Graham thought, but he wasn’t altogether sure it was H’s prime motivation. H could no longer listen to reason. He was past that now. Love and vengeance, twin pillars that wove their path through the history of human motivation, had him in their clutches like the grip of a vice. With a man like H once the need for vengeance was out of the bag it was out of the bag, and nothing could put it back until things had run their course. This much Graham now understood, and acknowledged.

But he thought that H was onto a hiding to nothing with this one, and made one last attempt:

‘Are you sure H? What if we send the Met’s tactical boys up there? H, are you listening? What are you going to do?’

‘Do? What am I going to do? I’m going to kill him, Graham… I’m going to kill Basim Dragusha. Stone fucking dead.’

80

H hauled Fatos Gazjet to Graham's car, cuffed him and threw him into the back seat with a degree of force not usually recommended at Hendon College. Fatos cut a pathetic figure as he lay physically and emotionally broken in the back seat. He'd been caught between two powerful forces, and he really wasn't sure which of them scared him the most.

In some ways he was pleased he'd now find the sanctuary of a British jail; but if Dragusha or other associates ever found out that this policeman broke him - and broke him in a flash - he'd be slaughtered, cut up into pieces and strewn across the prison garden before lights out on his first day. He'd heard H's words and thought Dragusha's death might be the best outcome, for him at least.

H turned to Graham.

'Ok Graham, I'm off. Get this sack of shit down to Dartford station. Let them process him. Then go and find Amisha...she'll be pleased to see you in one piece.'

H unexpectedly found himself with tears welling up in his eyes and put his arms around Graham's shoulders, giving him a big hug. Maybe all those sessions with his shrink had softened him; maybe he was just getting soft in his old age. Or maybe, just maybe, some part of H understood that he was mortal, and that he was now in mortal danger. Maybe he was saying adieu to a real friend.

No further words were exchanged; H burst over to his car, fired up the engine and set off on his fateful journey to the east coast. And then there would be death. His, Dragusha's, Ronnie's? No way of knowing, no way of dodging it. It was time. As the world, alarmed and confused, raged around him he felt OK now; consumed by hate for sure, but also calm, knowing what he had to do. Live or die, he knew what he had to do.

He was so completely focused on the endgame that he hadn't noticed the black Jaguar that pulled out behind him as he left the yard and headed for the Dartford crossing. Inside the Jaguar, a heavy-looking man in late middle age brooded. He was bald, with a thick-set neck and two heavily pouched dark brown eyes of serious intent. His entire being was concentrated and absorbed by the car in front of him. The inside of his own was like a rubbish tip, the packaging and remnants of nasty burgers mingled with other fast food takeaway scraps, empty cigarette packets, and crushed fizzy drink cans. He leaned across to the front passenger seat and caressed his weapon - a double-barrelled sawn-off - as if looking for comfort and reassurance, reassurance that he was up to what it was he was about to do.

Graham pulled out with a blubbering Fatos Gazjet in the back seat and looked at him in his rear-view mirror. Was this really the man responsible for one of the worst mass murders in modern British history? He seemed so mild, passive and compliant. He was no more than a foot soldier who'd found himself in the wrong place at the wrong time. Graham set his satnav for Dartford Police Station and pulled out in the opposite direction to H. He thought about firing up his siren but didn't want the attention. Just drop him off, he thought, nice and easy, then go and back up the big man. There was no way he was allowing H to go it alone. So as Graham pulled out he was focused on Fatos and thoughts of getting on H's tail asap. He didn't notice the grey Toyota Avensis fall in behind him. Inside sat a middle-aged man in a white t-shirt and blue jeans whose brooding concentration mirrored almost exactly that of the man in the black Jaguar. On the inside of his left arm a black swirling tattoo with the words 'Know Thyself' had been burnt into his arm, when he was a much, much younger man. He felt for and found the shotgun beneath his seat. He hadn't used it for a while - was he still up to it, he wondered. He didn't know himself well enough anymore to know. But he'd find out soon.

His mobile went off; he accepted the call and cradled the phone to his left ear as he drove.

'Which way you headed?' said the caller.

'South, towards the centre of Dartford. You?'

'North-east, towards the motorway.'

'OK. Stay sharp. We're going to sort this out once and for all.'

81

Zef Fejzullah, under strict instructions, kept to the speed limit as he drove the pack leader and the injured wolf-boy south. They'd driven nearly 300 miles, mostly on obscure A roads, but were now on the outskirts of Harwich and would soon be arriving at the dockside warehouse. Dragusha was checking the news channels on his burner.

He knew the game was up - the magnitude of the crime overseen by Fatos was so huge there was no going back to the way things were. They had to get out of the country today, or they were never getting out. His, Ronnie's and Fatos' mugshots were now flashing on a regular basis across every TV screen and website in the country. *Britain's most wanted*; representations of pure evil, growing ever larger in the public imagination. The country could not even begin to return to normal until they'd been hunted down and dealt with.

There was no going back to the life he had been living, to the plans he'd been making. His dreams would not be realised now. And who knew what kind of welcome might be waiting for him back in the old country? He had been the top man in the UK, and the destruction of the Albanian interest there would be on him. He'd made the big call. So he'd been thinking hard about his next move. He would need to take care of Fatos after the boat departed; he would be getting a good strong dose of what the migrants had received in Bedgebury Forest. If the bosses could see he had dispensed justice, he might have a chance of living himself.

He looked hard at Zef.

'Why did job to dig grave get so fucked up? You were there, correct? Fatos has told me what happened. Tell me your version.'

Zef's blood froze. He needed to keep the spotlight off himself, shift the blame.

'Fatos lost nerve. Started panicking. Wanted to leave quickly so dug graves too low. He not good leader.'

Zef kept his eyes on the road. His peripheral vision told him that Dragusha was staring at him, hard, trying to get into his head. He had no intention of meeting those piercing, malevolent dark eyes.

'What created panic?'

'Just Fatos. He not a commander, if I can say.'

Zef knew he was in danger. The sense of menace emanating from Dragusha was palpable; the young man felt like an elk being stalked by a hungry leopard. He swallowed hard. Dragusha was alive to his discomfort, and to his obvious attempt to change the subject.

'How is patient?' he said.

Dragusha turned to have another look at his Ujku. Ronnie was drifting in and out of consciousness, dribbling and drooling, making low groaning sounds and twitching involuntarily. Dragusha placed his hand on his head and felt his pulse; Ronnie was burning and his heart rate was slowing. Dragusha was in no doubt that there was significant internal bleeding and that his protégé was in urgent need of an operation.

'He dying,' he said.

Zef said, 'How long to live?'

'Maybe some hours, maybe tonight, one day at most.'

'Why not kill him now? Dump body. He no use to us.'

Dragusha did not answer immediately. Maybe Zef was right; the chances of saving the boy were slim, but he'd been strong and loyal to the cause...and Dragusha now had some strong feeling for him, a feeling he couldn't name. And they may need him - you never know what's around the corner. And he may need Zef, in the short term. He decided to let them both live, for now.

'No, we keep him alive as long as we can. He one of us. And will be useful if he survives.'

Zef shrugged his shoulders and, still trying to avoid more questioning about the debacle in Bedgebury Forest, hit the radio button. He was met with a discussion on what the mass grave meant for British society, migration, 'social cohesion' and the future of Western civilisation.

'Well,' opined a well-meaning commentator, 'what we all need to do is keep a sense of perspective, realise this is a one-off and not part of a new pattern of criminal behaviour.'

'Perspective? Perspective?!' As the second voice interrupted the first Zef realised he'd better get off this station quickly; he tuned to another channel. It was still not a week since the pretty boy's murder and the pop channels were wall-to-wall Bazza.

His latest single, rushed out by Nigel Blandish the day after his death, was already Bazza's biggest ever hit, with millions of the world's youth downloading it in a global wave of sympathy. It was not the sympathy reserved for a pop icon with a world of success behind them; an Elvis or a Jacko or a Bowie. It was a sympathy for youth, for life in full flow, cut down too soon and never lived. Barry O'Doherty was on course to become the icon of his age. "Rocking you in Ibiza" was now number one in 42 countries, a worldwide phenomenon with its jaunty, upbeat message of youthful excess and low-down loving. Zef wiggled his hips as he drove and sang along with gusto:

'Girl, I'm gonna rock you in Ibiza, gonna rock you in Ibiza.'

A sardonic smile spread across his face. It was the smile of someone who knew a secret, and thought this might be a good time to share it. Despite his current situation his natural exuberance and arrogance were irrepressible.

'Concentrate on road. You think is good time to have fun and sing pop song?' said Dragusha.

'Ha ha, yes boss. Is good tune…Bazza like the ladies. Well no more ladies for him. His days of shagging over. I take care of him. I put gun to his face and blow it away.'

Part 4

82

Amisha had wasted no time contacting the local Margate plod and Gina arrived on the dot with her mother in tow. She'd put a big effort into looking her best for her appearance at the Yard and was dolled up to the eyeballs. She had so much makeup on she looked like an android from a science fiction movie. The deep blue and silver eyeshadow made her eyes look fathomless and mysterious. The Met's finest stared in admiration as she made her way to meet Amisha. The three of them went into the interview room. As Andrew joined them it occurred to him that Romeo Ferrera would have gone after Gina like a rat up a drainpipe regardless of any need he might have had to settle any scores with her brother.

Amisha did the preliminaries and registered the condition of Maureen O'Doherty, who clearly remained trapped in a whole world of pain. Her face was thin and gaunt and stretched into lines of grief that seemed to widen as she made the effort to smile and say hello. Amisha imagined all the strife and the struggles Maureen must have gone through to raise her children; all those kids with multiple missing fathers. The sacrifices, the commitment. Then just at the point one of them gets a break and actually makes something of himself she learns that he's been inexplicably slaughtered in the dead of a London night. Amisha felt a surge of empathy for the shattered woman sitting opposite her.

Amisha could also see that Gina, despite being dolled up like the woman she wasn't, was nervous and uneasy. Beneath the makeup and the false smile was a little lost girl who wished the world was a whole lot different than it actually was.

Best take it easy with these two.

Amisha smiled, and said 'So Gina, it's come to our attention that you were at a party two Saturday's ago with your brother; could you tell us about it please?'

This was news to Maureen. Since Bazza's death everyone had slumped about the house, barely communicating. She realised how little she knew about what her children did; or what they thought.

Gina folded her arms, hunched her shoulders and swallowed hard, feeling the penetrating stare of her mother. Amisha realised that, with her mother present, Gina was unlikely to be forthcoming on the events of that night. But as a minor she could not officially question her without her mother present.

'Gina, I need details. Please go through the events in detail.'

'Gina,' interjected her mother, 'listen darling. I've lived long enough to have done and seen my share of monkey business; just be open, don't hide anything. I won't be mad at you. We need to tell the police everything if we're ever going to get to the bottom of all this.'

Gina mumbled something about asking Bazza if she could go to the party and confessed to lying to her mother about being at a friend's house.

'And, who did you talk to there? Did you have a good time?' asked Amisha.

Amisha was met by a blank, listless stare. Mother and daughter turned to face each other. Tears began to run down Gina's face. It was the first time she'd cried since her brother was killed. Her makeup dissolved, making her look like some macabre cabaret artist. Then all the confusion and the grief she'd held in check exploded out of her like a solar eruption, as she began to sob, and shake, and sob some more. The mask of the woman had been removed and the terrified little girl revealed. Mother and daughter held each other tight, and both cried. Amisha and Andrew left the room.

83

It was twenty minutes before Maureen came out of the interview room, wet tissue in hand. This was part of the job Amisha found hardest, dealing with the pain that gets left behind after the murder of a loved one. She walked over to Maureen and put her arms around her and held her tight for several seconds.

'I'm sorry Maureen, I'm so sorry.'

Maureen accepted Amisha's expression of regret.

'She'll speak to you now. She's told me what happened. Let's go back inside.'

Unburdened and a little less tormented after talking openly to her mother for the first time, Gina opened up to Amisha. She was economical on details, and did not reveal she'd been naked on the bed when Bazza came into the bedroom and found her in a compromising situation with Zef and co.; she claimed that she'd just been flirting with them. Amisha didn't push her on this point, she wanted the rest of the story. She wanted the Albanians' reaction to Bazza pulling Gina out of the room, so she moved the story on.

'After he swore at them one of them got his gun out and I thought they were going to kill him. I was terrified, really scared. When the arrogant one let Bazza pass I was surprised. I didn't know them but it didn't seem like they would let Bazza take the piss out of them. They weren't pretend hard men, acting tough like the boys in Margate. They were really scary.'

'As you left the room, what did they say?'

'Well Bazza was in front of me and steaming ahead, pulling me by the hand. I looked back and the arrogant one said to the others "Don't worry. He be dead next week."

'Are you sure?'

'Everything happened so quickly… that's how I remember it.'

'Gina, I can't tell you how important this is,' said Amisha. 'From what you've said they issued a specific death threat. Did you tell your brother what you'd heard, or thought you'd heard?'

I told Bazza but he said don't be stupid. He said if we lie low for a few days the whole thing will blow over.

'So you've been in Margate ever since?'

'Yep. Bazza left on the Thursday. He returned for rehearsals for his gigs Friday and Saturday at the O2. There was an after party at Tarquin's on the Saturday but he said I couldn't go and had to stay at home. He wouldn't let me have tickets for the concerts either.'

'Gina, why didn't you tell us this when we came to see you in Margate?'

'I don't know, I'm sorry. I tried to block the whole thing out.' The sobbing started again but this time Gina gained control quickly. She didn't have much sobbing left in her.

'So you went straight back to Margate that evening, and Bazza stayed until the Thursday. How did he seem?'

'It was wonderful,' said Gina, 'to have him back for a few days. We sat in my room and talked the whole time. It was the closest I'd felt to Bazza ever. It was like he was a real brother.'

'What did you talk about?'

'He told me about his business and how cut throat it is and all the people trying to do him out of his due.'

'Go on.'

'He told me how Blandish had a contract that meant he got hardly any money, except for those two number one songs he wrote himself, and even then Blandish is down as co-writer. He told me the songs he just records he gets nothing for but because he'd written two successful songs Blandish gave him an advance of half a million quid.'

'Did he now? Did he tell you what he did with the money?'

'Well he said I shouldn't tell anyone but I don't suppose it matters now. He said he lent it to that weirdo who runs the parties.'

Andrew and Amisha spoke in unison: 'de Montfort!'

'He told me that once he got the money back and sorted out the contract with Blandish that he'd buy us all a new house and make sure we had everything we wanted, and that we shouldn't worry because he would have more hits and make loads of money anyway.'

'Did he say why he gave the money to de Montfort?'

'For investments, financial things. He was told it would be invested and that he'd get much more money back. In the long run. He was told he could get it back anytime but when he asked de Montfort for some he said he didn't have it.'

After the interview Amisha gathered Andrew for a debrief at the coffee machine.

'Well?' she said.

Andrew slurped some coffee from the cup in his right hand, passed the cup to his left hand and rubbed his chin in deep thought.

'Interesting,' he said.

'To say the least. It seems we need to have another pop at our old friend de Montfort. If he really has got a lump of Bazza's money that big he's got a lot of answering to do. What did you make of the death threat?'

'Well, it does put a different perspective on things. Everything we think we know about these guys suggests they would, at the very least, have given Bazza a good kicking. Or killed him on the spot. So the question is why did he decide that revenge is a dish best served cold?'

'There are only two possibilities,' said Amisha, 'both of which put this Zef in the frame as our number one suspect. Either he was smart enough to know it wasn't the time and place and that he'd be able to plan a murder for another day or…'

Andrew finished the sentence: 'Or the murder had already been planned.'

84

H surged along the M25, switching lanes and ignoring the speed limit when he could. He had over two hours to get to Harwich and find the warehouse. He was totally focused and in control of his wits but there was a ringing sound in his ears, his eyes were stinging, and his skin - all of it, from the crown of his head to the underside of his feet - tingled like it was being stuck by a thousand tiny needles.

Hold on boy, I'm coming…hold on tight.

The Dartford Crossing consists of the QE2 bridge, which runs across the river north to south, and two tunnels running south to north - from Kent into Essex. H bullied his way into the lane he needed - he could handle any motorway police if it came to it - and sped towards the right hand tunnel, knowing it was likely to be the faster of the two. He saw a big electronic sign; it said 'Delays.'

Fuck! Fuck! Fuck! Fuck! Fuck!

The traffic ground to a halt, 200 yards from the tunnel's entrance. H sat motionless, his hands on the wheel; his skin was burning now, and the ringing in his ears had intensified. He found himself rocking back and forth, his eyes closed, his teeth working against one another like angle grinders. Sweat dripped onto the sleeves of his overcoat.

It was building: the adrenalin and the frustration and the anxiety were seething, rising, getting ready to blow.

A wobbler? Another wobbler? Now? Is that all you can do when things get hard - wobble?

Sort yourself out, you fucking melt.

He let his hands drop from the wheel and rest on his thighs. His mind raced back, way back, to a cold waiting room in a Bermondsey doctor's surgery. He was a little boy, struggling to breathe, holding his mother's hand. 'Bronchitis,' said the doctor. 'Breathe slowly son, as slowly as you can: seven seconds in, eight seconds out…slow it all down.'

H sat back, wound down the window, and breathed like his boyhood quack had shown him. His breath became regular. His heartbeat slowed. The traffic began to move, inching forward just far enough to get him 300 yards inside the tunnel. And then another dead stop, with cars backed up in front of him as far as he could see. His hands tightened around the wheel.

His phone rang. The screen showed 'Shrink Kasia.' He answered it.

Kasia Kotula, he guessed, was probably calling to get on his case for some reason, but just hearing her voice soothed him, helped him regain his composure:

'Hello, Detective Inspector. I trust you are well. You know why I am calling?'

'I missed our meeting.'

'Yes, you missed our meeting. You broke our agreement.'

'Listen Kasia, something's come up, something very urgent. I didn't just…I just forgot to phone you. I…'

'What could be more important than getting your career back on track? I thought we understood one another.'

Kasia, after all their sessions together, knew very well now how to push H's buttons; she had conditioned - or re-conditioned - him to believe that emotional honesty was the best policy. She'd started to teach him to speak in a new way.

In the end it came in a flood, and he told it straight and direct.

'Kasia, it's my boy. They've got my boy. He's in a bad way, needs to be in a hospital. He needs me. I've got to find him...they've captured him, and brainwashed him, and made him do terrible things. And they've made him hate me. Says he wishes I was dead. I'm on my way to get him…I've got to sort all this out, once and for all.'

Kasia had heard enough; H's tone told her he was in crisis, whatever the actual facts were.

'H!'

H? Why the fuck is she calling me by my name? She's never done that before.

'H! Enough! Listen to me now. Who has Ronnie? Where is he being kept? Who are you working with?'

The traffic began to inch forward again.

'I can't go into all this now Kasia…I've got to get moving.'

'H, don't hang up yet. Tell me how you're feeling…and what you are intending to do when you find whoever has Ronnie.'

'I'm feeling fine Kasia, don't worry about me. I've got a few funny symptoms, but in my mind I'm as clear as a bell.'

'What sort of symptoms?'

H laid it out for her: the stinging eyes, the burning skin, the sweating, the palpitations he was now having.

'Listen to me H…you are extremely stressed. You are in great danger. These are psychosomatic expressions of your inner turmoil. You must slow down and get yourself in hand.'

There was light at the end of the Dartford tunnel.

'I'm in hand Kasia. I know what I'm doing, and I'm well in hand. Don't worry about me. Got to go now.'

H ended the call and burst out of the tunnel like a man reaching the surface of the sea after diving too deep. The road ahead looked clear as he careered around the M25, towards the A12 exit, at full throttle.

85

John Swan had come up the hard way. All the usual south east London things. He left Walworth Comprehensive school in 1972 at fifteen, did a bit of ducking and diving and larking about and fighting at football matches, and livened himself up in his early twenties when it was time to steady the ship and get hold of some proper money.

By the early 80s his best friend - they went all the way back to primary school - had established himself as a force with one of the top local firms specializing in armed bank robberies. Back then if a bank got the treatment anywhere in England, it was a good bet that the men behind the stocking masks were from within a few square miles of one another in Bermondsey, Rotherhithe, Walworth, Peckham, New Cross and Deptford.

Swan got on board, worked his way up, and disappeared when things got too lively for him in the late 1980s, to the south of Spain, in a car adapted to contain more fifty pound notes than he could carry. The better part of it had come not from the bank jobs but from the wholesale investment he and his friends had made in the narcotics trade when running around with shotguns got to be too much like hard work, and the rewards became less as banks started to hold less and less cash. He lived the dream on the Costa Del Crime for a few years before the call of home got to him and he returned to the old country. The police never acquired anything solid on him, so he managed to stay away from the game and set himself up as a cab driver.

He'd lived quietly for years in Blackfen and rarely saw any of his old friends, until Paul Walsh phoned and asked to meet him. Over a pint or two in the Thrush and Nightingale, Walsh, whose brother was languishing at Her Majesty's pleasure in Durham, had given him the news. It had hit him hard; John Swann and Jack Butcher went back a long, long way.

*

His head was set; his old gun was oiled and ready; his purpose was clear: Little Ronnie Hawkins and his bastard of a father were going to die. Everything was in place. The only trouble with his plan was that keeping tabs on Harry Hawkins was like herding cats. His only chance of finding the son was getting to the father, but his prey drove like a lunatic and exposed him to all sorts of risk in the course of the high speed pursuit along the M25 and the chaos in the tunnel - the last thing he needed was the motorway police giving him a tug for a driving violation and coming across the bonus of a sawn off on the passenger seat.

He emerged from the tunnel just in time to see that Hawkins had stepped up the pace, and was accelerating in and out of lanes like a man possessed. Swann phoned Walsh to put him in the picture, steeled himself, and hit the accelerator pedal as hard as he could; he would have to match Hawkins' speed and recklessness to have any chance of catching him.

But he had no choice: he needed the father alive for as long as it took, to get to the son. Before long both were going to feel the full weight of his old blagging gun.

86

Graham was in turmoil as he pulled up outside Dartford Police station with Britain's most wanted mass murderer in the back of his car. The correct thing to do, he knew, was to take his prisoner in and shout out loudly and clearly what the situation was. Get a tactical team setup in Harwich within the next half an hour and hope and pray they'd be able to extricate Ronnie and collar the Albanians. Keep the big man out of it. If things turned out right he'd come around - eventually.

But Graham didn't do the correct thing. Graham did the H thing. He hauled the wounded, blubbering idiot out of the car, bundled him into the police station, flashed his badge and screamed at the officer in charge to lock the man up and call Chief Inspector Hilary Stone of New Scotland Yard. He told him he was in hot pursuit of further parties wanted in connection with the Bedgebury case and couldn't stop. Before the officer in charge had time to understand the implications of what was happening Graham was out the door, back in his car and heading like a man possessed for the tunnel.

Paul Walsh was right behind him. His brother Billy, currently banged up in Durham nick - and who'd been told by Ronnie Hawkins as a prelude to the brawl in the recreation room that he would be parted from his genitals, and that they would be forwarded to his mother - had made it clear to him that Hawkins the younger was responsible for the bloodbath in Jack Butcher's cell. Paul, who was some years younger than his brother, had virtually been raised by Butcher after his own father's early demise. His love for and loyalty to his guvnor knew no bounds.

It had taken him less than a minute to persuade Swann that the copper's son would have to go, painfully, and when they'd heard through the grapevine that Harry Hawkins and another copper were sniffing around a breakers yard in Dartford he'd got on them like a dose of salts.

When Hawkins and his partner went different ways out of the breakers yard Swann gave his instructions.

'Alright Paul,' Swann had told him, 'we'll have to split up. I'll go after Hawkins; you stay on this other cunt. Don't lose sight of him. Update me every ten minutes.'

After Graham had made his deposit Walsh put his phone on speaker and did what the senior man had told him:

'John, I'm on him. He's just dropped some lump off at Dartford nick…looks like he's heading for the tunnel. He's not hanging about; he's really putting some down.'

'Alright son, stay on him. Hawkins has just come out of the tunnel, his motoring like he's chasing Lewis Hamilton around Brands Hatch. I reckon your one must be headed the same way.'

They know where the boy is.

'Get back to me as soon as he exits the M25.'

The copper was bobbing and weaving in and out of the traffic like a lunatic; it took all of Walsh's nerve and skill just to maintain sight of him. By comparison with H they moved quickly through the tunnel; a broken-down car had been cleared and the traffic was now flowing smoothly.

It was 6.30pm when Graham surged out of the Dartford tunnel and back into daylight.

87

H was in the zone. The traffic had cleared and he felt back in control. He'd find his son, he'd bring him back under his wing, make things good like they should have been. Him, Ronnie, Olivia and Little Harry would be a real family; in the future, once this was all sorted out, they'd stick together, make things work out.

He'd make Harwich before Dragusha could escape and take his boy out of the country. Since the snarl-ups in the Dartford Tunnel he'd made reasonable progress, but not quite as much as he would have liked, and this was the final leg of the journey. It was 7:30pm when he reached Colchester and moved onto the A120, around thirty minutes from his destination. It was a stretch of road that had recently had its speed limit reduced to 50mph, to improve safety. But H wasn't concerned with safety, he needed to quicken up. He got his car up to near one hundred miles an hour - at these speeds one mistake and they'd be more than a whiff of the grim reaper.

He was going too fast for the cars in the fast lane. He swerved into the slow lane then back into the fast lane, zig-zagging in between the traffic like a demon. The exasperation and the toots and the flashes of headlamps came thick and fast from the drivers of the cars whose life he was endangering. But they no longer mattered; they weren't there.

He checked his rear-view mirror; and it became obvious that someone was on him - a fair way back, but on him, trying to keep up.

Who the fuck can that be?

John Swann was a first-rate driver but was finding it increasingly hard going. He guessed that the urgency being shown by Hawkins meant that he'd found out where his son was. There was no way Swann was going to let him out of his sight now. He navigated the traffic at speeds most people would never drive at in their lifetimes - using the skills developed over his long experience of street racing and weaving in and out of traffic in his efforts to evade the long arm of the law.

No fucking way am I losing this bastard.

H mused. The car was too far away to make out who was in it but he could tell it wasn't Graham's car - wrong shape. His mind raced through the possibilities but nothing obvious came to mind. This was a new ingredient. H didn't like new ingredients: you had no idea how they would affect the mix, not until they'd been understood and dealt with.

The idea of turning up at Harwich with someone who was not there to deliver friendly fire jumping out behind him did not appeal. As the car sped on H saw a narrow country lane off to his left. He broke hard and positioned the car as far to the right as he dare, so as to increase the size of the near impossible arc he was about to navigate. He released the brake and swung the car as close as he could manage to the left apex of the left turn. As late as possible he gently applied the break for a semblance of control, whilst still allowing maximum traction, reapplied a little throttle and careered over to the right side of the lane. Against the odds he maintained control of the car, it stayed on the road and came to a stop some eighty yards later. H opened his door and rolled out of the passenger side like a stunt man in a Mission Impossible film. He continued his role into the dense bushes that adorned the side of the lane. The impact winded him and the bushes cut into his face. His gun, which he had tucked inside his trousers, fell to the ground. Dazed and muddled, he scrambled about for it.

John Swann had a little more time to execute the manoeuvre and arrived at the spot a little slower than H had, but the veins were still popping out of his head as he screeched to a halt, grabbed his shotgun, slid out of the car and took cover behind it.

His heart was beating faster than Bazza Wishbone's Ibeza hit was being downloaded off the internet. He knew he'd been tumbled when H hit one hundred miles an hour - at those speeds there was no way he would go unnoticed. The plan now had to be to capture Hawkins, force him into telling him where the kid was. He scanned the area around H's car. No one. Nothing. A shotgun blast from this range would likely wound but probably not kill, with a reasonable chance of hitting a man lying low in the bushes. He fired the first round.

He was nervous about firing off a second. Reload time would be against him. He stayed low for several minutes until the tension got too much for him. He stood up with his shotgun raised at waist level, and began investigations into the bushes around H's car. No sign of the big man, but there was a Glock lying on the ground. Swann's spirits lifted as he nonchalantly tossed it aside – he was dealing with an unarmed adversary. The odds were now on his side.

H had been lucky. The buckshot splintered twigs and hit the earth close by but he wasn't hit. He'd forced his way through the dense, wide hedge and got to the clearing on the other side. He scuttled on his stomach, keeping low, the way he'd practiced hundreds of times in his army days, staying close to the hedge for cover. He'd made the most of Swann's timidity and was already fifty yards further on while his assailant was mooching slowly around the hedge with his shotgun. He reached a gate that gave entry to a farm and decided to go for the oldest trick in the book. The stone he threw hit Swann's car and Swann swivelled and fired instinctively.

The contest was now clear. A fifty-yard dash from an overweight copper versus a twitchy villain unloading and re-loading a double-barrelled break action shotgun. Favourite:

the shotgun, probably. H leapt the fence and was ten yards in before Swann got control of his fear and started the reload. Swann fumbled and wasted a few more precious moments before pulling the latch that released the barrel from its lock. Twenty yards. Swann took out the spent shells and threw them to the ground. Another mistake - he only needed the one shell. Thirty yards - H was closing in like a Rhino on a charge and had reached maximum speed. Swann scrambled around in his jacket pocket for two more shells. He loaded them both. Forty yards. Swann brought the barrel back up until he heard the lock click and started to raise the gun. Bang! The buckshot dispersed into mid-air as H smashed shoulder first into Swann with more force than Swann had ever been smashed into before. The force lifted him off the ground and by the time gravity brought him back to earth an angel of death was looking down at him. This angel had its foot firmly entrenched on Swann's throat.

'Swanny…Long time, son. I should've figured it'd be one of you fucking muppets.'

Swann tried to push H's foot away but only took just enough pressure off his throat to allow him to speak. 'H you know what your boy did inside. You must have heard.'

'Yeah, I heard.'

'Your boy's dead H. If not today, then another day. What he did went way beyond the pale. He has to pay H - if it takes me the rest of my life I'll make him pay.'

H said nothing. He saw and retrieved his Glock from where Swann had tossed it. He aimed the gun at Swann's head and pulled the trigger. The bullet glanced his right ear.

'Your ship has sailed you useless piece of shit. All that's left for you is to crawl back under your stone and stay there for the rest of your fucking life.'

H had to make a point. He lifted his right foot and brought it down on Swanny's shin. The tibia snapped immediately. Swann screamed and screamed as H dragged him into the bushes and put the Glock next to his temple.

'Listen. I'll say it once. When the police come to pick you up make up a good story. If I see you again, I'll kill you.'

H tore off a piece of Swann's shirt and stuffed it into the petrol fuel hole of his jag. He pulled out a lighter and set fire to the cloth and jumped back into his own car.

By the time of the explosion he was several hundred feet further down the A120. His enforced diversion had cost him fifteen minutes, but he still had time. Just.

88

Graham was feeling angst as he sped on towards Harwich. Had to catch H – he didn't want him going it alone. He had to be there when it came on top. He had to be. The Dartford Tunnel had been forgotten about and he was making good progress now. He didn't notice a black Jaguar and H's police issue blue Mondeo parked inauspiciously on a side road as he raced past at eighty miles an hour on a fifty mile an hour stretch.

He reached for his hands-free phone and punched H's number in. No reply.

Then Amisha called.

'Graham, what's happening? The whole of The Met is going crazy with speculation. I know you dropped Fatos off at Dartford police station. Where are you now?'

'I've decided to go and back up H. He'll almost be in Harwich by now. I'm a bit behind him.'

Amisha felt sick. She wanted Graham back, safe in her arms. That was all.

'You were meant to be finding Fatos and bringing him back to the Yard. You promised.'

'But he needs me, Ames, I can't let him go into a situation like this alone.'

'Graham, why not? We're always doing things his way. We should have called this in. We still can.'

'No, don't, please. If we do, and it results in Little Ronnie's death, we'll never be able to forgive ourselves.'

'What if it results in H's death, or your death? How will I be able to forgive myself? Turn around Graham. This is wrong. There's no need for you to do this.'

'Sorry babes, this has got to play itself out now. I'm in too deep. We both are.'

'You've become just as stupid and stubborn as he is. For God's sake Graham, think about this. Haven't we already told enough lies and had our lives messed up because we keep falling in behind the way H does things?'

'We made choices.'

'Maybe they were the wrong ones.'

'I don't think so.'

'Maybe you're too enamoured with the glamour of going it alone. Maybe you've become too much like your guvnor.'

'Why are you saying this now? What's changed? We're in this together… we have to stay united.'

They were in it together, yes, but Amisha had come to a different conclusion now. The best way to protect Graham and H was to not let them go it alone.

'I'm calling it in Graham.'

'Amisha, no. For God's sake, don't be a fucking idiot.'

This was the first time Graham had sworn directly at Amisha. It bit deep and produced an equally aggressive response.

'There are only two fucking idiots in this mess and you're both on your way to fucking Harwich.'

Amisha ended the call. She still wasn't certain. She hit her contacts button and found Hilary Stone's number. Her hand hovered above the call button. She was a mess of conflicted possibilities, trying to consider the consequences and potential outcomes of different courses of action.

Graham was shaken by Amisha's tone and change of heart. Was that their first real fight? He tried to put it out of his mind as he motored inexorably towards his destination. He didn't know what Amisha would do but it was now beyond his control. He had to complete the journey, back up the big man, see what happened. He gave him another call. Nothing.

A few hundred yards behind him the driver of a Toyota Avensis broke sharply, swerved lanes and just manged to avoid a Suzuki Jeep, whose driver tooted his horn in anger. The anger of the Jeep driver was only as strong as a summer breeze when compared to the fury raging in the other car. For Paul Walsh this was the day that Ronnie Hawkins and his cunt of a father were going to die. Damn the consequences - the bastards that had taken out Jack Butcher were going to die, and he was one of the executioners. Things were resolving themselves now, and it dawned on Walsh that they were headed for Harwich. He grabbed his phone and called Swann. No answer.

Graham didn't notice he was being followed. His mind was fully occupied with other things. His satnav told him to stay on the current road and that it was eighteen minutes to his destination.

89

The smoke from the burnt-out Jaguar was still visible in H's rear view mirror when his mobile rang. It was Olivia. H decided it was a discussion he needed to have.

'Hello doll, how are you?'

'I'm fine H. Just got back from the hospital after a check-up. Just wanted to let you know that all's good with Little Harry and me, we're both fine.'

A relieved smile made its way across H's face. A daydream, strong but fleeting, pushed its way into his mind. Him, Ronnie and Little Harry were having a kickabout in a park. They were joking, laughing. Little Harry was about five and doing his best to tackle the ball from his much older brother. A simple dream, albeit one unlikely to become reality, given what Ronnie had done. He forced it out of his head - no time for this stuff now.

'I've been worried. You haven't called for a couple of days,' said Olivia.

'I'm doing what I said I'd be doing. I've found out where they are - Ronnie and the bastard that's turned him against me. They're both holed up in Harwich trying to get out of the country.'

Olivia knew this. She'd just had Amisha on the phone begging her to try and talk H out of it. But she knew she couldn't and wasn't even sure she wanted to. She decided not to tell him about Amisha's plea for him to call it in - what was the point, it would only get in the way. She knew H far better than Amisha ever would. The carrots were already cooked.

Back him up, support him, it's all that's left to do.

She'd planned to say all the things she ought to say, like "Be careful" and "Everything's going to be OK" - but she said none of those things. It was possible, maybe even likely, this would be the last time they ever spoke, but it was no time to get emotional, things were far too serious for that.

'How long before you get there?'

'Twenty minutes if I'm lively.'

'Amisha called. She said Graham's followed you - she thinks he's something like fifteen minutes behind you.'

He's probably in fucking front of me now.

'I asked him to keep clear. It was his call.'

'Yes, I know.'

Moments of silence followed. Olivia understood H - and she understood there was nothing left to say.

'Come back to me H.'

'Count on it doll, count on it.'

90

H sped on. Thoughts of John Swann were already far behind him now; he was working hard at making up for lost time and getting himself into the frame of mind - or rather frame of *being* - he would need to get the job done. His phone rang. Amisha. Another of the women in his life, no doubt wanting to reason with him.

It's too late for all that now.

He blanked the call, focusing instead on his steady resolve to eat up the final miles as quickly as possible. The adrenalin surge from his run-in had subsided; his aches and pains were returning. There was no time to stop for tea; he switched the radio on, thinking it might liven him up.

'Here is the news,' he heard. 'Bedgebury Forest.' 'Bazza Wishbone.' 'Migration crisis.' 'Breakdown of law and order.' 'Celebrities in distress.' 'Crimes against humanity.'

He gave it ten minutes and punched the off button.

He was now ten minutes from Harwich. He passed car after lorry after car with ruthless overtaking manoeuvres, taking no prisoners, closing in on his target.

Kill my boy? They want to kill my fucking boy?

H had, not for the first time, moved towards a place where reason could no longer reach him, where animal instinct submerged the lessons of civilization, a lawless place; a state of nature.

His phone rang again. Amisha again. He took the call.

'What? What do you want Ames? I've got a lot on my plate here. I'll be there in ten minutes, if I'm lucky, and that's not going to give me a fuck of a lot of time to spare.'

'Have you spoken to Graham recently H?' She was using a tone he'd never heard from her before; she sounded anxious, fearful, angry.

'Not for a bit, no.'

'Oh, I know where he is H. He was at Dartford nick for about a minute and a half, and then he shot straight off after you.'

'I told him to...'

'It doesn't matter what you told him H, it's what he's doing. He's coming to back you up. He's right behind you, or in front of you, for all I know. Are you satisfied now? Now you've turned him into your mini-H? Obeying orders when it suits him, doing his actual job when it suits him, flying off on tangents when it suits him, putting himself in harm's way for the sake of bloodthirsty revenge when it suits...you?'

'Don't bother me with all this now Ames, I ain't got time for it. Graham's a big boy - he can make his own decisions and look after himself. Where did you say he was?'

'Closing in on Harwich like you, to help you do whatever you think needs doing.'

'Good man. I'll...'

'Fuck you, H! You're going to get him killed. And yourself. Have you given a second's thought to what Olivia - remember her, the woman who loves you - might need?'

H kept his own counsel.

'H? H? ...Not talking now? Terrific. Absolutely terrific. Well, I've had enough, enough of your man's-gotta-do-what-a-man's-gotta-do bullshit. I'm calling it in. Now. I'm putting Hilary in the picture, right now.'

'Do what you fucking like,' said H, as he punched the end call button.

91

Graham pulled up in a side street close to the water's edge in Harwich, in the belief that H was already in the vicinity. He decided not to try him on the mobile again; he might be bang in the middle of something tasty.

He'll probably have it switched off now anyway – he'll be scouting the warehouse.

He jumped out of his car, checked his weapon and made a beeline for the waterfront and the string of warehouses scattered along it. He easily found the warehouse Fatos Gazjet had identified; it was set a couple of hundred feet back from the dockside. It was three stories high, windowless and made of corrugated iron. It had four separate storage areas, which were essentially separate buildings, each connected by a short passageway.

Graham did a quick recce. The front of each storage area had a rollup door for lorries to enter through. At the back there was a small door, in the storage area nearest the docks, that led out to the dockside. Not easy to get inside there without whoever was already there knowing about it.

Mounds of rubble and dirt were scattered outside the front and Graham used one to hide behind and think. It was dark now, and drizzling, and a crescent moon, hazy and indistinct, sat behind a layer of clouds. There were no street lights or nearby buildings to shed light on the isolated structure.

Graham had looked about for signs of H, or his car. Neither were anywhere to be seen. In the distance the cranes were hard at work, picking up and releasing their loads.

It's too quiet. Wonder if they've boarded already - maybe the action is over by the dockside.

Graham was about to make his way to the docks when the rollover door nearest to him started to open. He took out his gun and aimed. The door mechanism strained its way upwards until a figure was revealed. Graham couldn't make him out - it was too dark.

Fucking hell H - where are you?

The figure came out into the open and looked about. Graham couldn't tell who it was but could see that the man was holding a gun. Graham had found the right location, no doubt about it. The figure turned, went back to the door and disappeared inside. He left the door open enough for a car to drive through, as if he was waiting for someone.

Probably expecting Fatos and the boys. Good luck with that.

Graham took a deep breath, leapt from his hiding place and ran for the opening. He made the side of the building and crept along its edges towards the door. He reached it and peered inside.

The place was filled with pallets upon pallets, stacked high with huge cardboard boxes of what could have contained anything. Graham was nervous and his hands were sweating as he got down onto his belly and slithered unobtrusively to a spot behind one of the pallet mountains. He heard people talking and edged towards the sound.

He saw three men. Basim Dragusha was talking quietly to a young man Graham had never seen, giving a few last orders before they made their way to the waiting ship. Ronnie, pale and barely breathing, lay motionless on the floor.

Gotcha. But where's the guvnor?

I'll have to go in alone.

Graham made his move, hoping the element of surprise would give him the upper hand and that he could handle the situation.

'Hands up please, gentlemen. This is as far as you go.'

But Graham had made the biggest mistake of his life. It was based upon two erroneous assumptions. The first was thinking that Little Ronnie was incapacitated. The second was thinking that, even if Ronnie was not incapacitated, when he saw an officer of the law taking charge he'd be thankful someone had found them and would release him from his captors - surely he'd only been playing along with this brainwashing nonsense to protect himself?

But Little Ronnie Hawkins was not incapacitated. Nor was he thankful. For Little Ronnie was no longer a callow boy. Little Ronnie was a now wolf, and a wolf followed the leader of the pack.

92

Dragusha had made the arrangements. He'd been confident that Fatos and the others would soon arrive; even if they were picked up there was no way any of them would speak to the English authorities, at least before he'd made it out of the country. No way whatsoever.

So how had this officer of the law found them?

He stared hard at Graham and held him in his gaze. His eyes were dark, like whirlpools sucking him in; Graham sensed a capacity for limitless evil in them, and remembered with a shudder what H had told him about a bloodbath on a rainy night in Soho.

Dragusha spoke a single word. 'Ujku.'

Ronnie raised his gun from his position on the floor. He did not think nor flinch. He did not stop for a moment to consider he was about to murder a policeman. He fired two shots into Graham's torso. The rounds thumped into Graham's flesh and cracked open his ribcage. Graham felt a strange, dreamlike mixture of incredulous surprise and resigned horror as his gun fell from his hands and he dropped to the floor, trying to keep his internal organs from spilling out.

Dragusha said 'Maybe more coming. We move to boat now.'

He moved fast and heaved his protégé up onto his feet, so that Little Ronnie had one arm around Dragusha's shoulder and one arm to work his crutch with.

'Well done my brother. Once more you prove yourself. Come, I will help you to ship. Soon we will be on way to the old country. You will love it there Ujku. We find you good wife.'

If you live.

Little Ronnie smiled; the approval of the man who had become his mentor and leader, his father, filled him with satisfaction. They made their way slowly to the furthest of the warehouse's chambers, the one with the door that exited out to the dockside.

And then further shots, or blasts, rang out. It had been a while since Paul Walsh had fired a gun in anger, but his aim was good and a shotgun shell blasted straight through Zef Fejzullah's heart, killing him instantly. Walsh's idea had been to take the young man with the gun down first - given that Dragusha was carrying what looked to be a near-dead Ronnie Hawkins and would not be able to respond.

But Walsh then made the same error as Graham Miller-Marchant. He hesitated for a few moments, waiting for a clear shot of Ronnie.

While he waited Ronnie killed for the second time that night. He fired directly into Paul Walsh's heart. Walsh went down with a whimper, his reeling senses letting him know that his time was done, and that Jack Butcher's killer was still on the move.

'Fuck, they coming out of woodwork like cockroach. Who next?'

Dragusha eased Ronnie's arm from around his shoulder.

'Walk Ujku. I must stand ready now. Your father is coming...I smell him.'

'Quickly, Ujku. To ship.'

*

H screeched to a halt, jumped out of his car and heard two gunshots. He rushed towards the warehouse without a thought for his own safety. When he arrived he found Graham, mortally wounded and bleeding out on the ground.

H put his arms around Graham and held him tight.

'You weren't meant to be here Graham. This wasn't meant to happen.'

Graham was barely conscious. Blood was pouring from his wounds and glugging from the side of his mouth. He had barely a breath left in him as he whispered his dying words:

'I had them H. But…it was Ronnie. Ronnie shot me,' he said.

H's body shook as he suppressed the rage inside. He could not fully make himself believe it before. That Ronnie had been completely turned. He'd clung silently to the belief that Ronnie was waiting it out - when the moment came he would know who he was, and do the right thing. Now he knew different.

May God have mercy.

Graham was gone; H kissed him on the forehead and laid him down. There was no time for grief - this would have to wait until another day. H heard more shooting, coming from somewhere else in the building. A shotgun blasts, a short silence and then another shot from a different weapon. H made the sign of the cross over Graham's still-bleeding corpse and sprinted headlong towards the source of the noise.

93

H followed the sounds of barked commands, cries of pain and slow shuffling through the three storage areas, observing the bodies of two dead men as he went; as he approached a fourth chamber he saw two living figures, twenty yards short of a door that led to the dockside. The door was closed but he smelled familiar smells and heard familiar sounds - his father had worked in the Surrey Docks, back in the 1970s, before containerization changed everything: the shouting, the clanging, the massive chains banging against steel. The final containers were being lowered onto the ship, which was scheduled to leave in ten minutes.

So here, at last, they all were. Ronnie up against a wall, breathing heavily, barely aware of his surroundings and holding onto a crutch with one hand and a gun with the other. Dragusha - shark-eyed and composed as ever, H noted - standing in a relaxed, defensive mixed martial arts posture, with his back to the boy.

Facing the father.

'Look Ujku,' he sneered, 'your so-called father has come to wish us *bon voyage*.'

H said nothing. He moved away from the door and further into the dimly lit storage space, until he could properly see his boy's purple, grotesquely swollen face.

He raised himself to his full height, took a deep breath, pulled his overcoat off and threw it to the ground.

Dragusha moved a few feet further towards him. They stood facing one another in silence. H pulled out the Glock, showed it to Dragusha, and cast it aside. Dragusha could not ignore the challenge. He tossed his gun aside, extended his arms outward and rotated his open hands, showing H that they were empty.

Dragusha opened his mouth to speak. 'So, you have come…ugh.' H was on him before he got the sentence out, roaring with rage, head down like a bull going for a matador. Dragusha, with all his long experience of hand-to-hand combat and deep understanding of the need to strike first, had never been met with such rapid effective physical force. H had got the jump on him, and was now driving him back towards the wall with his head pressed hard into his belly and his hands up high, clutching frantically at the Albanian's face, feeling for purchase.

H's momentum gave him the initiative: Dragusha was wheeled backwards and slammed, hard, against the wall, his upper body and head juddering and snapping back, crash test dummy style. Before he could draw breath and compose himself he felt H's fingers scrabbling around his right eye, his thumb probing around the socket for the right spot to punch into. Dragusha raised his hands instinctively in an attempt to remove his attacker's hands from his face, and left himself open. H drove his elbow savagely into Dragusha's solar plexus, winding him and forcing him to the ground.

H turned Dragusha onto his back, braced his own arms against the wall and drove a foot down towards Dragusha's exposed throat, aiming to end things there and then by breaking his windpipe. Dragusha managed to get his left hand in between his throat and the heel of H's shoe with a millisecond to spare; but H kept working his leg and brought his heel down once, twice, three times, breaking the trapezoid and capitate bones in the back of Dragusha's hand.

H, tired and breathless now, straightened himself up and examined his handiwork. Dragusha was down, clutching at his throat, struggling for breath, and bleeding from the ear.

Job done. Almost.

Coming to his senses, he heard Ronnie coughing, spluttering and trying to say something but producing only terrifying gargling sounds.

No time to waste…need to get the boy an ambulance.

H turned, went back to his coat, fished out his phone, hit the number for emergency services, and bent down to pick up the Glock.

94

Dragusha was on him before he got the gun in his hand, exploiting the imbalance in his bending posture with a low rugby tackle at the ankles. H hit the ground like a bag of wet sand, face first into the rough concrete. He felt his nose break and wondered, for a frozen instant in time, how it was possible that Dragusha was back for more after the treatment that had been meted out to him. H had spent a lifetime tangling with seasoned street fighters, enemy soldiers and drug- and alcohol- fuelled nutters. He had gone through the card.

But this was a first: no one had ever come back from the windpipe and fractured skull treatment. *No one.*

Yet here Dragusha was, large as life and twice as ugly, straddling H's back, forcing his weight down onto him, screaming ancient Balkan curses and working frantically to get his fingers into H's face. He succeeded, and H felt something he didn't know the name of somewhere in the vicinity of his shattered nose split and disgorge a fresh torrent of blood onto the ground.

Dragusha moved his hands out from under H's head and hammered at the back of it with the unbroken one while scrambling around for the gun with the other. His shifting weight gave H an opening and he managed, with a mighty heave, to rotate his body, getting onto his side and dislodging Dragusha.

They fell to formless, hand-to-hand grappling, both on their knees, both exhausted and reeling from their injuries. Head-butts and poorly coordinated punches were exchanged as both tried to rise to their feet; they both knew that whoever rose first would be in a position to finish it.

The pace slowed; neither could stand. They clawed at one another in slow motion, each trying to make a solid move, until H roared, lunged forward and sank his teeth into Dragusha's cheek, clamping them together into a hate-powered vice. He felt his mouth fill with blood. The tissue tasted like squid. With another roar H straightened his arms and forced Dragusha back, at the same time snapping his own head back as hard as his neck and shoulder muscles would allow. He came away with a chunk of Dragusha's flesh the size of a large marble in his mouth, steadied himself on his knees and spat it back into his victim's face.

Once again Dragusha's hands rose involuntarily to the wound in his face. Freed from his grip, H, with a superhuman effort, staggered to his feet, moved around behind his man and kicked him, repeatedly, as hard as he could in the back of his head and back, going for the kidneys. Dragusha seemed unable to get himself up and remained motionless, rocking backwards and forwards under the assault. At length his head went down, silently, and he curled himself up into a ball.

H was dead on his feet; it was all he could do to stagger over to Ronnie, whose condition seemed to be worsening. There was nothing H could do for him; it was all about the ambulance now. Father and son stared at one another for a second, through their blood-drenched, ruined faces. Only one of Ronnie's eyes was partially open; H could read no emotion in it.

95

H heard sirens in the far distance, followed by a dragging sound behind him. He turned to face it. Dragusha, he saw in amazement, was crawling back for more.

Unfuckingbelievable...what have I got to do to put this cunt down?

H moved to meet his adversary on unsteady legs, looking around for the Glock as he went. But there was blood in his eyes, and his head was throbbing, and the world was spinning round...

Dragusha reared up onto his knees slowly, like a bull walrus. His breath was still catching in his throat. His broken hand was pressed weakly against the hole in his cheek, trying to stem the flow of blood. H felt like lying down and going to sleep for a long time, but knew that one more push was needed. Dragusha had to die.

H was incapable of tactical reasoning, running now on animal instinct and what was left of his adrenalin. He took as deep a breath as he could, straightened up and ran at - or stumbled towards - Dragusha with the aim of knocking him back over and stomping him into the ground.

But Dragusha had other ideas. With his good hand he raised the Glock, aimed it straight at H's head and fired. Wide. A second shot passed through H's right upper arm. H was onto him before he could get another round off but slipped as he arrived and just collapsed onto Dragusha, knocking the gun away and smothering his adversary's face and upper chest with his torso.

H found that he had Dragusha pinned down through sheer force of body weight, which was better than nothing but made further movement risky. Blood bubbled from H's arm wound like water from an old-fashioned drinking fountain. Dragusha thrashed around and tried to get out from under but was too weak now to push against the big man's mass. H moved his left hand up, with great difficulty, and slid it between his belly and Dragusha's mouth and nose, hoping it would be sufficient to suffocate him with.

Still they fought on, if fighting it could be called. It was now a slow motion, heavy-gravity contest between Dragusha's futile efforts to move H off of him, and H's attempt to sustain enough pressure with his hand to prevent Dragusha from breathing. It had become a surreal, low-action sumo death match.

Dragusha stopped breathing, or seemed to. H rolled himself off, groaning with pain and exhaustion, so that they were lying side-by-side, and put his hand across to Dragusha's neck to feel for a pulse, wanting to be sure. To his great dismay he found a faint one; it occurred to him that the only way to finish this man off would be to find the Glock, force it into his mouth and unload it through the top of his head.

He tried to get himself up onto his knees, but found that he had not an ounce of energy left. He could not move, at all, and collapsed back, on the verge of unconsciousness. They had fought one another to a standstill and now lay together, motionless in mutual victory and defeat.

H had nothing left to give, and was all but unconscious when he heard a cough, a sharp intake of breath and a shouted cry of 'Ujku!, Ujku!...come to me, Ujku!'

*

The sound of the cranes loading the ship and the other dockside hustle and bustle had subsided; the ship was about to set sail. In the quiet of the warehouse the only sounds to be heard were of a man struggling to breathe through a damaged throat and someone staggering along slowly, very slowly, on a crutch. H opened his eyes in time to see Ronnie arrive, in slow motion and wincing in agony, at the scene of the battle. He was still holding a pistol in his free hand. It was impossible to read from his bloated, distorted features and half open eye what he was thinking or feeling.

Oh, son…how did it come to this?

He looks like something from one of the zombie films he used to watch... my little boy. My poor little boy.

Dragusha was the first to speak:

'Look at him Ujku. Look at your "father". The old, useless, drunk man who betray you. A man of no honour. The man who ruin your life…See how he hate you.'

Ronnie stared blankly at his father.

'Now you have chance to make him pay. You are man now Ujku…a true warrior. We take boat now. We do great things together. Finish him, Ujku, finish him!'

Ronnie raised the gun slowly, unsteadily, and aimed it at H.

'Do it now Ujku, do it now! We must get to boat. Kill him!'

Ronnie steadied himself and put his finger on the trigger.

H sighed, raised his head as far as his neck muscles would allow from the cold concrete floor, and said 'I deserve it son. I'm not saying I don't deserve it…I've done you wrong.'

Tears began to trickle from Ronnie's open eye.

'But I love you, boy…my little wild thing…I loved you then, and I love you now, and I'll always love you. Just…do what you've got to do.'

For a moment Ronnie stood silent, saying nothing but with tears cascading down one side of his face. Then he shifted position, steadied himself on his crutch, and fired three shots into the head of Basim Dragusha.

96

Amisha and Andrew pulled up, sat in the car, and made sure everything was in order before going in to make the arrest. Andrew had spent days digging and doing what Andrew did best: delving into private lives, making and cross-checking connections, finding his way through a maze of details. They had a good case now - more than enough for the powers that be to have signed off on the arrest warrant.

The naive young man known as Bazza Wishbone had woven, or had woven around him, a tangled web he had no hope of unravelling. The half a million pounds he had entrusted to de Montfort had been used up on creditors almost immediately. There was no chance de Montfort would ever be able to repay the debt, Andrew concluded, either now nor at any time in the future.

Andrew interviewed the estate agent tasked with selling de Montfort's ancestral home, who had come to the view that he wasn't prepared to sell it at all. Despite advice to lower the price he'd kept it high and refused all reasonable offers out of hand. He was making it appear to the world, thought Andrew, that he'd soon have the money to pay his debts, keep his lines of credit open by fooling his creditors into believing he'd soon have more than enough to spread around.

'Maybe there's more to him than we think,' he'd said to Amisha as he told her about his meeting with de Montfort's man in real estate.

'All those pictures of ancestors bearing down on him. People like that are ruthless, they never give things up. They always find a way…if he was prepared to rip Bazza off for half a million without batting an eyelid, what else might he be capable of?'

*

When they'd found a note on Zef Fejzullah's body with the phone number of Svitlana Kovalenko and a plan of the layout in the Ritz everyone had thought it was an open and shut case. Ruthless and impetuous gangster gets insulted at a party, leaves it for a week and goes nuclear on the offender.

'All the evidence points one way, Andrew. It's done and dusted. We'll be handing over to the Crown Prosecution Service soon,' Amisha had told him.

'But I can't get over the way Gina described Fejzullah's words to his cronies, as if arrangements were already in place.'

'Andrew, they were talking in a foreign language and Gina was unclear about what she heard.'

'Yes, I know. It may be just a language misunderstanding but the more I think about it…'

Andrew had proved to be like the proverbial dog with a bone. He wouldn't let go. 'Copper's intuition,' H had called it.

Trust it son, it's not always right but don't ever let a hunch drop until you've followed it through.

So Andrew had followed it through. He'd tracked down the account into which Bazza's money had been deposited by de Montfort. He went through every transaction, followed them all through. Large payments to John Tanner and several years of back taxes took care of much of it. Then there were the legitimate creditors: high end food and wine suppliers; antiques dealers; art galleries; tailors who catered to people with more money - much more money - than sense. Old Tarquin had gone through Bazza's lump like a hot knife through butter.

But there was one transaction that stood out. Ten thousand pounds to a smaller hidden account, which was then transferred on to another. Andrew followed the money until he discovered that de Montfort had eventually taken it out in cash, a week before Bazza had verballed Zef Fejzullah at the party, two weeks before his face was blown off.

'What's he doing with ten grand in cash?' Andrew asked Amisha.

And then they found out. They got a call from one of the officers leading the Bedgebury Forest investigation, who'd been involved in the forensic search of the caravan site in south Bermondsey. Wedged under the caravan in which Fejzullah lived they'd found an attaché case containing just over nine thousand pounds. Dabs were checked; Tarquin de Montfort's prints were on the case. Thorough searching, proper research. The bread and butter of police work, in the end, had nailed a second guilty party.

*

Amisha and Andrew got out of the car and, flanked by a brace of the Met's finest, walked up to the front door of the Belgravia mansion and hit the buzzer. To their surprise their man, and not Gaston or another of his bizarre underlings, opened the door. Amisha, stone-faced and implacable, gave him the news.

'Tarquin de Montfort, you are hereby charged with conspiracy to murder Mr Barry O'Doherty. You have the right to remain silent…'

The Drama King of Belgravia gasped, hyperventiliated, fanned himself with his hands and hit the deck like a bag of spanners.

'Pick him up boys,' said Amisha, 'we can read him his rights at the Yard.'

97

He became aware, slowly at first, of the quiet humming and purring of machines and a low drip, drip, drip coming from somewhere behind his head. He tried to move, but could not. There was not a place in his body that didn't hurt. He tried to open his eyes but it seemed like the lids were stuck down with superglue. He felt panic rising within him. Was he dead? Had he been buried alive?

He felt a wave of nausea and anxiety sweep across him, across his soul. Where was he? Who was he?...*What* was he? He began to weep, and felt warm, wet tears trickle from his right eye. He worked the muscles repeatedly - tension-release, tension-release - until a flash of light came into his head, making him wince. He continued the process, struggling to get the eye open wide enough to figure out what was around him.

Things came into focus. A bright, white room. A man in uniform in the corner, holding a big gun. A nurse busying herself with something on the other side of the room. He tried to call her, but his voice wouldn't come. He tried again, this time whispering. She heard him, came across to his bed and bent down low, the side of her head inclined towards his mouth, so that she could just about hear him.

'My dad,' he said, 'where's my dad?...I want to see my dad.'

*

H woke up; he had pains and soreness in every part of his body. He felt like Wile E Coyote must have done after the Roadrunner dropped a mountain on him. But there was a pleasant, comforting feeling as well, at the centre of it all;

after a few moments he discovered that his hand was nestled inside Olivia's. He was in a hospital room.

'Where am I?'

Olivia stroked his head. 'You're in Ipswich Hospital, H.'

'Well, it makes a change from Guy's, I suppose. No view of Tower Bridge though…'

Thank God, he's OK

'How long have I been here babes?'

'Four days. They've had you sedated. You were in a lot of pain.'

'Still am. What's the damage?'

'Well, a flesh wound in your arm…they say that's OK, but you lost a lot of blood. Seems like Ronnie tied the arm off for you - otherwise you'd have been in real trouble. Severe concussion. Broken nose and shattered cheekbone and a couple of bruised ribs. Other than that, you're as right as rain. What do you remember?'

'Last thing I remember was Ronnie shooting Dragusha. Where is he now?'

'They won't tell us. In a hospital somewhere, under armed guard. In intensive care, but they say he's going to make it. They're keeping him under wraps. Seems like Dragusha trusted him, let him into a lot of secrets. Amisha thinks they'll probably try to turn him, get him to testify against the rest of them. Make him into a supergrass. It's all about Bedgebury Forest…someone's got to be brought to justice for that, she says, and they'll be trying to use Ronnie. There's a lot of talk about bringing back the death penalty - they're having a big debate about it in parliament next week.'

'And Dragusha. Is he dead?' said H.

'Dead as dead can be. Ronnie put three bullets into his head.'

H tried to think back, put all the pieces together. Suddenly he had a horrible sinking feeling. He remembered that Graham was dead. Another fallen comrade. A sadness swept over him as he recalled who'd killed him. But who knew that for sure, except Ronnie and himself? Best to keep it under his hat, at least for now.

He struggled to get himself upright, but it was all too much. Olivia soothed his brow, careful not to disturb the dressings that took up most of the central part of his face, and eased him back down.

'Graham,' H said.

Olivia sighed. 'Yes, Graham.'

'When's the funeral?'

'Next week. It'll be a big official thing, with all the top brass in attendance…but Amisha says she doesn't want to see you there. She's furious with you H. I've never seen her like this before. She blames you for what happened to him.'

'She'll come round.'

'I doubt it.'

'I'll have a word with her…she'll be alright.'

'Well, you can try. I can get her to come in when you feel up to it - she asked me to let her know when you revived. Said she has something to tell you. Something important.'

'Fair enough…How are you and Little Harry?

'Me and Little Harry are fine H, just fine,' she said, patting her belly. 'Don't worry about us. Get some rest.'

*

Amisha - or someone wearing a mask representing terrible grief and suppressed fury based on her features - appeared the next day at dinner time, while Olivia was spooning semolina into a grateful H's gullet. He was the only person she'd ever met who actually liked hospital food. Especially the puddings.

Olivia rose from the bedside, embraced and kissed Amisha, said 'Alright, I'll leave you to it,' and left the room.

'Alright Ames? It's good to see you,' said H. 'Sit down.'

‘No. I’m not staying long.’

‘Loosen up Ames, sit down. Let’s have a little chat, talk it all through.’

‘I’m not here to talk anything through H. I will never forgive you for what you’ve done.’ She was speaking through gritted teeth, holding her emotions down and just communicating essentials. H knew the signs.

‘So there’s nothing to say. I don’t want you to come to Graham’s funeral, even if you’re able to, and I don’t want to talk to you. I’m just here because I wanted to give you the news in person.’

‘What news?’

‘The news that your career as a copper is over. The official story will be that you’re a national hero for bringing the head of the Bedgebury Forest firm down, and that you are now retiring with honours after thirty years of extraordinary service to the people of London. But they’ve had enough of you now…enough of your going rogue whenever you feel like it, of all the violence, of all the pain and chaos you leave behind you for someone else to tidy up.’

‘Yes, but Ames…’

‘Just keep quiet, will you? For once in your life. It’s too late for all that now. You’ll be getting their request to accept voluntary retirement at the end of the week. Accept the offer, take your medal and go. They won’t take no for an answer this time H, and I can’t say I blame them - you’re off the firm.’

Epilogue

H and Olivia were all newborn baby smiles as Olivia pushed the three-month old boy through the crowds at the Intu shopping centre in Bromley, where south London meets Kent. They didn't come here very often but after being cooped up with a baby for a few months they'd decided a Saturday afternoon shopping trip was just the ticket. Olivia had always liked Bromley; she found it pleasant and friendly, and there were lots of nice cafes to choose from.

'I'll just pop down the escalators here doll,' said H, 'you trot along to that little café just on the left and plot yourself up. I'll get the newspapers, catch up with you and get us both a nice cup of tea. I'll be able to have a quick read of the paper while you feed Harry.'

'Alright H, sounds like a plan.'

Olivia found her spot and made herself comfortable. Little Harry was sleeping soundly in his buggy, so she stretched her legs out and looked forward to drinking her tea in peace. A friendly-seeming man approached her table and struck up a conversation in what she thought was a Russian accent.

'Beautiful baby. How old?'

'Three months.'

'He sleep through night yet?'

'He's not too bad, and getting better. On a good night we get four or five hours sleep.'

The man laughed, remembering his own sleepless nights as a young father many years before in Moscow, although it had been decades since he'd seen either of his two children.

'Here. I have present for him.'

It wasn't much. Just a rattle that made a musical noise when you shook it.

'No, really, there's no need.'

'Oh, it's nothing. Please accept.'

Olivia didn't want to accept presents from people she didn't know and now wanted the stranger to leave her.

'OK, thank you.'

She tried to make her tone final, to give the clear impression she wanted out of the interaction pronto.

'OK. I go now.'

'OK, goodbye.'

'Please say hello to baby's father. He old friend of mine.'

Olivia's slight irritation turned swiftly to anxiety; her pupils dilated and her skin began to crawl.

'What do you mean you know him. Who are you?'

'Please say hello to father, tell him I see him soon,' said the friendly man as he disappeared into the crowd. 'My name Agapov. Vladimir Agapov.'

###

Thank you for reading our book. If you enjoyed it, won't you please take a moment to leave us a review at your favourite online retailer or book review website?

Thanks!

Garry and Roy Robson

Other Titles in this Series

London Large: Blood on the Streets

A corrupt system. A city in meltdown. A rogue cop, bent on revenge.

Who will deliver justice?

Blood on the Streets is the first in the London Large crime thriller series, featuring the exploits of Detective Inspector Harry 'H' Hawkins, an old-school London copper with over thirty years of besting villains under his belt. When a bloody international gang war threatens to rip the metropolis apart, 'London's top copper' finds himself under siege as never before.

Haunted by flashbacks of the horrors he experienced in the Falklands War, held accountable for the unstoppable wave of violent chaos that is turning the streets of his city red with blood, hounded and ridiculed by a media he cannot understand and continually thwarted by an establishment cover up of he knows not what, the big man is bang in trouble.

As the chaos in London reaches boiling point can H, against all the odds, bring the streets under control, see through the fog of a high-level conspiracy and rescue his partner Amisha before she is killed by her ruthless kidnappers? And will he himself be forced to step outside the law to do so?

If you like the hard-boiled, gritty and action packed novels of Martina Cole, Stephen Leather and Andy McNab you'll love Blood on the Streets – let it take you through a thrilling rollercoaster ride through the dark underbelly of criminal London.

###

This title is **FREE** from the following link: https://instafreebie.com/free/AWqTu

BOOK ONE OF THE INSPECTOR HAWKINS STORIES
LONDON LARGE
blood on the streets
WHERE EVIL REIGNS
CAN ONE MAN STAND ALONE?
G & R ROBSON

London Large: Bloody Liberties

Book three of the London Large series will be titled "Bloody Liberties". Details to be announced on the London Large website at http://www.londonlarge.com If you wish to be kept informed of the release date, please subscribe to the website.

London Large: Tipping Point

A father and son standing together. A brutal political conflict. Can they, and their bond, survive?

Tipping Point, set against the backdrop of the dark days of the 1974 three-day-week crisis and wildcat strikes, follows the fifteen-year-old Harry Hawkins through a crucial, formative week in his life. When his father persuades him to get involved in his strike-breaking activities Harry is launched onto a steep learning curve that will test both his ability to hold his own in a violent street-level struggle and his allegiance to his father.

Can, and should, the strike be broken? Will the son live up to the expectations of the father? Will they get out of the conflict in one piece?

Get your **FREE** copy of Tipping Point from the following link: **https://instafreebie.com/free/zLDJ3**

About The Authors

Roy and Garry Robson are, unsurprisingly, brothers from the Elephant and Castle, south east London.

Their father (variously a pig farmer, cab driver, haulage contractor and general ducker and diver) and mother (homemaker, cook and doctor's receptionist with a well timed left hook) raised them and their siblings with some old fashioned south London working class values. These included hard work, respect for their elders and a willingness to duck and dive when required.

One day, whilst enjoying a beer or two, they decided to write a Crime Thriller Series. They awoke the next day and were surprised to discover that they meant it.

Roy lives in Bromley and works as a Service Delivery Manager for an International IT Consultancy. Garry lives in Krakow and is now, of all things, a sociology professor. Both career choices served as a source of confusion and humour to their parents, who were born and raised in the days before computers and sociology professors existed.

Harry 'H' Hawkins, the protagonist of the London Large novels, is not based upon Garry or Roy, neither of whom would survive the first chapter of a Harry Hawkins novel.

Contact Information

Website: www.londonlarge.com
Twitter: https://www.twitter.com/londonlarge
Facebook: https://www.facebook.com/LDNLarge
Email: info@londonlarge.com

Printed in Great Britain
by Amazon

42770656R00196